26/7

GULL

Glenn Patterson was born and lives in Belfast. He is the author of nine previous novels and three works of non-fiction. He also co-wrote the screenplay of the film *Good Vibrations*, based on the Belfast music scene of the 1970s.

GLENN
PATTERSON

GULL

First published in the UK in 2016 by Head of Zeus Ltd

9 7 5 3 1 2 4 6 8

A catalogue record for this book is available from the British Library.

HB ISBN 9781784971762
XTPB ISBN 9781784971847
Ebook ISBN 9781784971762

Typeset by Ben Cracknell Studios, Norwich

Printed and bound in Germany
by GGP Media GmbH, Pössneck

Head of Zeus Ltd
Clerkenwell House
45–47 Clerkenwell Green
London EC1R 0HT

WWW.HEADOFZEUS.COM

For CC – co-conspirator and friend

AUTHOR'S NOTE

I made this all up, apart from the bits you just couldn't.

Whatsoever thy hand findeth to do, do *it* with thy might; for *there is* no work, nor device, nor knowledge, nor wisdom, in the grave, whither thou goest.

Ecclesiastes 9:10

For we wrestle not against flesh and blood, but against principalities, against powers, against the rulers of the darkness of this world, against spiritual wickedness in high *places*.

Ephesians 6:12

1

On the morning of the day it all ended, Randall stumbled out of the elevator on the thirty-fifth floor of 280 Park Avenue to find Carole, DeLorean's secretary, holding the outer-office fort on her own.

She came round from behind her desk as he passed at his best, jet-lagged version of a run.

'You missed him,' she said. 'He left for LA forty minutes ago.'

Randall thought of the delay before take-off on the runway at Shannon, the longer than usual lines at passport control on landing in New York.

Forty minutes.

Another day he and DeLorean would have been standing here laughing at how close they came to missing each other. Instead their cars must have passed somewhere on the Van Wyck Expressway north of JFK.

'Mr Hoffman called first thing to fix a meeting,' Carole said, and Randall's legs went from under him.

* * *

Already in Belfast it was mid-afternoon. Liz sat on her bed listening to the pips for the three o'clock news: one hour until the boys got home, two hours until Robert did, four hours, said the newscaster, until the deadline expired on the DeLorean Motor Company Limited. Either John DeLorean came up with £10 million by seven o'clock this evening or the factory at Dunmurry would cease to exist.

Liz reached under the bed and pulled out a suitcase, dust all over the top.

She set it sideways on the bed, snapped the locks (dust all over the bedspread) and began to pack.

The last hanger she dragged up from her – left – side of the wardrobe had her spare overalls folded over the horizontal bar. She thought a moment then packed them too, DMC crest up. You had to have at least one thing to remind you. She pushed down the lid of the suitcase: snap, snap.

She was out of the room before she remembered she had left the radio on. She didn't go back.

Randall leaned for support on DeLorean's own desk, next to the bust of Lincoln. He had driven through the night to make the flight and had not closed his eyes between the first fasten-seat-belt sign and the last. He took from his inside pocket the envelope Jennings had given him before he left Belfast, dyed pink now from contact with his shirt, his sweat.

Useless.

Here and there about the room, paintings taken down in the move from the forty-third floor were stacked against the walls. Only one had so far been rehung, next to the spade that forty-eight months before had broken ground in a Northern Irish field: a not-quite-life-size photo of DeLorean, kicking through the surf, holding his infant son's hand. A caption ran along the bottom, Joni Mitchell, 'Both Sides Now', *It's life's illusions I recall...*

Commit all this to memory, Randall told himself: Lincoln, the photo, the ground-breaking spade, the stacks of paintings, the brass telescope in the corner, pointed at the ceiling, as though to track the distance already fallen.

He was pretty sure he would never set eyes on any of it again.

2

He had first set eyes on John DeLorean ten years before, at the 1972 Chicago Auto Show: the launch of the '73 Chevrolet Vega. Randall felt an almost sentimental attachment to its predecessor, the '72 being the car on the cover of the copy of *Motor Trend* that he had bought on the way to his interview at the auto pages of the *Daily News* (RIP). Pattie had spotted the ad. Randall until that moment had had no particular interest in cars. He did not even at that stage of his life own a car himself (a bone of contention with Pattie). But he had begun to drift a little, he knew that without Pattie having to tell him, and now there was a baby on the way and the *Daily News* auto pages was the first opening that presented itself, or that was presented to him, on the breakfast table, circled in red.

'Tell them you used to write for your college paper,' Pattie said.

'About track, and even then I didn't understand half of what I was saying.'

'So? It was a paper. You wrote for it. Tell them.'

'Can you tell us,' the chairman of the interview panel asked before Randall had a chance to say a single word, before he was even settled in his seat, 'the name of the current Car of the Year?'

Randall hesitated, wondering if this was not in fact some kind of a joke, if the panel had not – don't ask him how – watched him from the moment he stepped out of the drugstore on Wabash, all the way up here in the elevator, reading his magazine, stuffing it in the wastebasket only when he arrived in the corridor leading to the candidates' waiting room.

'The Chevrolet Vega?' he said.

The chairman looked to the men sitting on either side of him. His left eyebrow curled itself into a graphic surtitle of disdain, for everyone, it seemed, bar Randall himself. 'You would not believe,' he said, 'how many people coming through that door today were unable to tell us even that.'

Randall shook his head: the chairman was right, he could not believe it.

And so there he was, four months on, an Auto Show virgin in the vastness of McCormick Place, beyond Ford and Dodge, their Pintos and their Demons, looking over the shoulders of more seasoned reporters at the dais on which the '73 Vega stood, still under wraps, while before it a comedian who had had a couple of Hot 100 novelty hits in the early sixties tried to wring every last drop of drama out of the moment. (He had already, judging by his patter, given up on the humour.)

'Folks! Folks! I know you are all as impatient as I am to see what is under these covers, but bear with me, bear with me, I guarantee you, you will not be disappointed.'

A flashbulb ignited, perhaps prematurely, but the comedian turned on it anyway his once instantly recognisable slantways smile.

'This is a truly special car,' he said to that particular quarter, 'and a truly special car deserves a truly special person to perform the unveiling. Folks, will you please join me in welcoming out here the head of General Motors' Chevrolet Division, Mr John Z. DeLorean!'

And now the cameras flashed in good and earnest as he strode out, pale grey suit, sky blue shirt, blacker than black hair, frowning, as though burdened by the increased weight of expectation, a very tall young woman – with heels, nearly as tall as him, which was saying something – on each arm.

A reporter in front of Randall took the cigarette from his mouth to bark into his friend's ear beneath the whistles and the cheers. 'What year would you say *they* were, '53, '54?' The friend closed a red-rimmed eye, assessing. 'Fifty-two at the outside.'

The young women stationed themselves on either side of the car while DeLorean raised his hands to still the audience.

'Thank you, Bob,' he said with a backward glance (the slantways smile turned sheepish), then facing forward once more, 'and thank you all.'

The voice was deep, drawly, the mouth from which it emanated a little downturned towards his slab of a jaw.

'A head of division is really only as good as the team he has around him.'

The friend of the reporter in front of Randall cupped

his hands about his own mouth and earned himself a few laughs, hollering, 'Come on, John, don't be getting all modest on us.'

Up went DeLorean's hands again. Up briefly went the corners of his mouth. 'No, no, it's true, I am blessed with a great team at Chevrolet who have all been hard at work with me the past twelve months trying to improve on the '72 Vega. Now, some companies with a Car of the Year on their hands would be content with a tweak here and a tweak there, but at Chevrolet we don't believe in resting on our laurels – I believe that's the polite word for it – we keep looking to the future, and for the brand new Vega my team have come up with – wait for it – three hundred improvements, friends: three, zero, zero.'

All around Randall reporters were scribbling in notebooks, although he had not heard anything yet that could not be carried in the head.

'But what am I talking for?' DeLorean said, hamming it a little now. 'Why don't you have a look for yourselves?' He half turned to the young women. 'Will we show them, ladies?'

As one the two of them bent low, grasping opposite corners of the sheet covering the car, and as one they rose again and with three steps backwards laid it bare. Coupé. A blue so metallic it was practically neon, the body's long, slow slope up from the trunk breaking like a dune at the top of the windshield, falling sharply to the hood, which curved away between raised headlights to the grille.

In style, in other words, not a whole lot different from half a dozen other cars on display elsewhere in the Convention Centre and – bar the finish and perhaps the depth of the bumper beneath the grille – to Lucas's eyes pretty much identical to the photo on the front of the *Motor Trend* he had discarded on his way into the interview at the *Daily News*.

The reporters were writing faster, the photographers pressing closer to the dais. DeLorean was still talking.

'Now I recognise a lot of the faces here at the front – you've been in this business nearly as long as I have. You boys remember what we did with the Pontiac back in the sixties. The Old Lady's Car, isn't that what they used to call it? Well they weren't calling it that by the time we were through with it.' No one ribbed him this time about that modest 'we', although they would have had greater cause to. Sure, there was a team there too, but he, John Z. DeLorean, more than any other person, had remade the Pontiac, and more than any other car the Pontiac had made his name. Even Lucas knew that. 'The Vega' – DeLorean had changed register again, this was the sales pitch – 'is going to be for this decade what the Pontiac was for the last. Take my word for it.'

The audience took it: hung on it.

The young women had opened the car doors and were perched sideways on the front seats, long legs elegantly crossed.

'So,' said DeLorean, 'does anyone have any questions?'

The first one came from so far to the right it was practically in Dodge territory.

'Is it true that you've been promised the presidency of General Motors before your fiftieth birthday?'

'Hey!' DeLorean's eyebrows rose theatrically. 'Let a guy get used to being forty-seven before you start talking to him about fifty.'

'But it's only a matter of time, right?'

'The birthday or the presidency?' The comedian, banished now to the sidelines, could not have bettered it for timing. 'But what about this beauty here behind me, anything you want to ask about that? Yes, at the back there.'

He pointed straight down the room, straight at Randall, who was as surprised as anybody, looking up, to find that his hand was indeed raised. He cleared his throat. 'It's not a question so much as an observation. I hear what you say about looking to the future, but the only thing that looks different to me from last year is the depth of the bumper.' The reporters immediately in front had turned to look at him – to scowl – and the reporters in front of them and in front of them again. Randall faltered. 'I mean, is that the most we can hope for from the future?'

DeLorean held his gaze, jaw set. It was a weapon, that jaw. (Randall later learned that he had had reconstructive surgery on his chin. 'The people who say it was vanity don't know the pain I used to be in.') He kept it trained a moment or two longer then smiled. 'Well, you see, it was a question after all,' he said and when the laughter had died down turned to address the audience at large as though Randall had been a mere plant. 'Like I said, there are three hundred improvements and if you care to come on up here I am sure these two delightful ladies would be only too happy to point them out.'

The words were no sooner out of his mouth than there was a rush towards the dais. Randall, still smarting from the put-down, took advantage of it to lose himself in the Auto Show crowd, or that at least was the idea.

'Hey! Hold on there!'

He looked over his shoulder to see GM's president-in-waiting striding towards him. The stride was something else he had in his armoury. The stride and the height – six four or more to look at him, closing fast – that powered it.

'What's your name?'

'Randall. Edmund Randall.'

'What do your friends call you, Ed? Eddie?'

'Pretty much everyone calls me Randall.'

DeLorean nodded (hair could not grow that black) as though it were a marketing matter they were discussing. 'I prefer Edmund,' he said and before Randall could respond had offered his hand. 'John DeLorean.' Randall's hand in comparison was like a child's. 'You're new to this, aren't you, Edmund?'

'Well, if you mean what I said back there, I didn't mean to offend, but I thought it was my job to ask questions.'

DeLorean rocked back on his heels as though amused at his innocence then snapped forward again, bending at the waist and speaking out the corner of his mouth. 'Your job is to print the lines the manufacturers spin you in return for getting your cock sucked.'

Randall pulled his head back out of range. 'What makes you think I want my cock sucked?'

(A woman passing too close put her hands over her grade-school son's ears.)

'I never met a man yet in this industry who didn't.' DeLorean drew himself up to his full six-foot-four-or-more and glanced back at the Vega stand. The reporters on the dais were paying as much attention to the very tall young women as they were to the car. His eyes slid round on to Randall again. 'Actually, there is a party later, ought to be a blast.'

'Thanks, but I have a review to write.'

The weapon of a jaw shifted to one side then the other. Another nod. 'I should probably be getting along myself. I'm expected back in Detroit for dinner.'

This time it was Randall who called after him. 'What about the party?'

DeLorean barely broke stride to answer. 'Oh, I only like organising them.' He waved above his head, his voice already three strides fainter. 'Be kind!'

'I'll be honest,' Randall shouted, though whether it reached its intended target is anyone's guess. Still, plenty of other people heard him, and after that, well, what else could he be?

'What is this crap?' the auto pages editor asked, handing him back his copy. 'Three hundred improvements and all you can talk about is the bumper?'

Two days later a memo landed on his desk informing him of his transfer, a week Monday, from autos to real estate.

'At least I am staying in the building,' he told Pattie.

'For now you are,' she said.

They were both beginning to realise that they had maybe married in too much haste. The marriage counsellor they had started seeing dwelt a lot on the timing of their meeting, a mere month after Randall's return from his tour of duty. She had seen it before, she said, with vets. Despite all that they had been through over there they missed the heightened emotions... 'They used those exact words?' Randall asked. '"Heightened emotions"?' Maybe not those exact words, but the point was they would do anything, some of them, to make the colour flare again, even for a single (wedding) day.

'Talk about being wise after the event,' said Pattie.

'And what was your excuse?' he asked her.

'Don't,' she said. 'Just don't.'

So when a few years later the phone rang on his desk early on the second Wednesday in June – the middle day of the middle month of the middle year of the decade – Randall was a recently divorced father of a two-and-a-half-year-old daughter, Tamsin, who he had to go through a lawyer to see.

He picked up the receiver on the third ring. 'Apartments and Condos?'

'Edmund?' said the voice. 'So this is where they have you hidden away.'

'Who is this?' he asked, though he already knew the answer: no one had a voice quite like that, and no one, other than his mother, called him Edmund.

'John DeLorean.'

'This is a surprise.'

'Is it? I was thinking we might have lunch.'

'You're in Chicago?'

'Detroit. If you leave in the next forty-five minutes you can make the eleven-thirty flight. There'll be a ticket in your name at the desk. Tell your editor you are comparing prices in Kenilworth and Bloomfield Hills.'

Randall pushed his chair back from the desk. The motion only added to his feeling of light-headedness. 'Sure,' he said. 'Where will I meet you?'

He spent thirty of the forty-five minutes before he left in the microfilm library, figuring that whatever John DeLorean had been doing in the years since he had last seen him it was unlikely to have gone unreported.

He did not have far to look: 1 April 1973, resigned from General Motors, walking away from a $600,000 salary as well as that promised presidency, becoming instead president of the National Alliance of Businessmen in Washington with a pledge to increase the number of young black kids in America's largest corporations ('I started on the same side of the tracks as them'); same month married for the third time, to Cristina Ferrare, a model whom he had fallen for after seeing her photograph in *Vogue*. (The story got cuter: he had torn out the photo spread and carried it in his wallet until he met her in person at a Gucci show where she was modelling the fall range.) Both articles reported his dream of setting up his own motor company. 'One day,' they were quick to add. 'One day.'

Last thing Randall did before walking to the departure

gate was buy a tie, tweed-knit: he was going for lunch with John DeLorean.

There was, besides the ticket at the desk, a man waiting for him at the other side – from that day on there would always be a man waiting for him at the other side – who led him, this first man of many, to a car that drove him the thirty or so miles to Bloomfield Hills. They passed the Country Club, they passed any number of likely and inviting-looking restaurants and hotels. (Randall, for all that he was nervous, was beginning to feel very hungry too.) They stopped finally before a concrete and steel triple-decker of an office building, the name Thomas Kimmerly, Attorney at Law, prominently displayed on the lawn sloping down to the road.

'Is this it?'

The driver, who had not spoken more than half a dozen words in the forty air-conditioned minutes he and Randall had spent confined to the car together, nodded. 'This is where I was told: 100 West Long Lake Road.'

For a fleeting instant Randall imagined some retrospective action for his temerity at the Auto Show.

The driver turned in his seat. 'I have somewhere else I am supposed to be.'

'Sorry.'

He let himself out into midday, mid-year – who knows: mid-decade, maybe – Midwest heat and walked up the winding path to the door where he hesitated again, checked back... but the car was already gone.

The receptionist had been monitoring his stop-start

progress. She had one hand on the phone as he entered.

'I was hoping you could tell me where to find...' Randall began, but got no further.

'Hey, you made it!' DeLorean was leaning over the first-floor stair rail, gone greyer than seemed mathematically or biologically possible, and looking somehow younger for it, dressed in a denim shirt and jeans, finished off with a pair of tooled silver-on-black cowboy boots. The receptionist took her hand from the phone. Randall put his hand to the knot of his tie. 'Come on up!'

By the time Randall had reached the top of the stairs DeLorean was already halfway along the landing and was holding open a door – Suite 206 – for Randall, when he had caught up, to pass through. The only thing about him that did not always seem to be in a hurry was his voice.

'Tom is letting me have the use of a couple of hundred square feet here until we have the prototype ready to show investors.'

Inside, Suite 206 was part office, part workshop, with drawing boards and flipcharts between the desks and file cabinets and a full exhaust up on one table as though for dissection.

So it was true.

'You're really doing it? You're making your own cars?'

'GM and their cronies at Chrysler and Ford will probably do everything they can to stop me, like they stopped Preston Tucker, but, yes, I am, even if I have to go somewhere else to do it.'

He strode through the room, indicating as he passed it a large platter of fruit – 'This is lunch, by the way, help yourself' – stopping finally before a table, just along from the exhaust, on which stood a model – balsa wood, Randall wanted to say – maybe twelve inches long. He picked it up with the fingertips of both hands.

'And this is what they are all afraid of. *This* will change everything. We're calling it the DSV – DeLorean Safety Vehicle, the world's first ethical car. Forget the *minimum* requirements, this car will have, as standard, features no other company has even thought of before, or if they thought of them it was only to say they were too expensive: airbags for a start, on both sides, side impact strips, copper facings on the brake discs for fade resistance, rustproof stainless steel, and an integral monocoque structure – that means the chassis and the body are a single unit – spreads the stress in the event of a collision...' ('Integral monocoque structure,' Randall repeated to himself: there could be a test after this for all he knew.) 'It'll be light too: two thousand pounds. We're using a brand new process, ERM, stands for Elastic Reservoir Moulding.' (Randall's brain had reached the limit of its own elasticity.) 'I've bought exclusive rights in it... Here.'

He held out the model to Randall whose first instinct was to fold his hands behind his back.

'I have to warn you, I come from a long line of klutzes.'

'Take it.'

And how could he refuse a second time? The lines were sleeker than the Safety Vehicle name suggested, sportier. He was conscious as he turned it about of DeLorean's eyes on him.

'It's... It's... Wow,' he said, a different kind of ineptitude.

DeLorean nodded nevertheless, accepting the compliment on the model car's behalf. 'How much do you think a car like that ought to cost?'

There was no getting a question like that right, not that DeLorean was inclined to wait for an answer. 'Twenty, twenty-five thousand, would you say?'

'About that.'

DeLorean smiled. 'Try twelve.'

'Twelve thousand dollars?' Randall didn't have to feign the astonishment.

'Within reach of two-thirds of American households. Cheap to run too.'

'The People's Sports Car,' Randall said and thought as he did that he caught out the corner of his eye a decisive movement in that formidable jaw.

'It stayed with me,' DeLorean said, measuring the words, 'what you said in McCormick Place about wanting more from the future... Oh, don't get me wrong' – the thought had barely had the opportunity to form in Randall's head – 'I had been contemplating something like this for a while, a long, long while. The thing is, I am putting together a team here. I want you to join it.'

The model slipped in Randall's hand. He righted it at the second attempt. 'You know I have no experience in this business? I didn't last six months on the auto pages.'

'You have something better than experience: you have a nose for bullshit. That '73 Vega? You were absolutely right, the only new thing about it *was* the bumper. It's a year on year racket to part people from their money.'

'I spent twelve months running supplies in the An Hoa Basin,' Randall said, out of embarrassment as much as anything. He almost never spoke about that time to anyone who hadn't been there. 'If you didn't have a bullshit detector before you went there you sure as hell had one by the time you left.'

DeLorean seemed to assess him differently. 'Don't tell me, the further up the chain of command you went the worse the smell got?' It sounded like another potential trap of a question, but no. 'I did a couple of years myself: '43 to '45,' DeLorean said. 'Never made it out of the US. I kept telling them ways they could improve their basic training, they kept sending me back to take it again. They hate it when they can't make you exactly the same as them. I guess that's why we're both here.'

Randall looked at the model again, not knowing where else at that moment to look. Suddenly he frowned. 'I hope you don't mind me saying, but there is one slight problem with this.' He gave it back: 'No doors.'

DeLorean's own frown lifted. He ran a finger along the model's undercarriage, pressed something... pressed again, a little more firmly. A portion of each side of the car rose up slowly, coming to rest finally in perfect symmetry, like the wings of a bird riding a current.

'There are your doors,' DeLorean said.

That was it for Randall; that was the moment the flame was lit. It flickered at times; it was all he could do at others to protect it, such were the winds whipped up, not least by DeLorean himself, but it never, ever, until the very end, went out.

On his way back from the airport he had the cab swing by Pattie's place, her parents' place once upon a time. He had shaken her father's hand on this porch: sealing the deal, the old man said. A week later he was dead. Brain haemorrhage. A week after that Pattie and Randall were married. He wasn't the only one who had issues then, or now.

She opened the door to him, a smile on her face from whatever she had been doing in the moments before he knocked, which withered on the instant.

'You're supposed to give me forty-eight hours' notice,' she said from behind the screen door.

The TV was on. He could see over her shoulder the back of Tamsin's head, dark against the scalding oranges and yellows and pinks of her cartoons. Pattie shifted her weight, from left foot to right, closing off the view. That's what they had come to.

'I'm thinking of moving to Detroit,' Randall said. Pattie's eye narrowed. 'With work, I mean.'

She shrugged away any suggestion that it mattered to her what he was going for. 'Well that ought to make things easier for everyone.'

Randall made the same left-right switch in his weight, gaining momentary advantage. Cartoons, Tamsin's head. 'Do you think since I'm here…?'

'I don't think that would be a good idea,' Pattie said.

Word got around pretty quickly that the editor had told him not even to bother working his notice, but to collect his things and go: the last thing this paper needed was someone working there whose heart wasn't in it.

Randall was clearing his desk when Anderson from the business pages wandered over and leaned his not inconsiderable bulk against the partition between Randall's desk and Hal Lewis's, though Hal had, in the time it had taken Anderson to get from one side of the room to the other, made himself scarce. There was another man with him, soberest of sober suits, hair going white at the temples. Anderson did not introduce him but instead lit himself a cigarette and stood for a moment watching, smoking.

'So,' he said at last, 'you're going to work for John Z.'

'That is correct.' Randall pulled open a drawer. Paperclips and thumbtacks. He pushed it shut with his thigh.

'Going to make your fortune.'

'All we talked about was making cars.'

'Cars, of course.' Anderson let that sit a moment then jerked his thumb. 'This is Dan Stevens. Dan started in Chrysler when Walter Chrysler himself was still running the show, 1935. He knows the industry better than any man alive.'

Dan Stevens inspected his fingernails during this brief encomium. He looked up now, blinking against the smoke of Anderson's cigarette. 'I suppose Mr DeLorean was telling you that Bank of America has already pledged eighteen million dollars.'

'It came up in the conversation,' Randall said, 'yes.'

To be precise it had come up as they walked downstairs to the lobby at the end of lunch (an apple, a banana and three lychees), Randall's mind already made up.

'And Johnny Carson, I'm sure... half a million?'

'That came up too.' And Sammy Davis Junior, Randall did not say, and Ira Levin, and Roy Clark. *Hee Haw*!

Anderson smiled, practically licked his lips. 'And did it also come up that John Z was arrested back when he was at college for selling stuff that wasn't his to sell?'

Randall couldn't help it, he froze.

'Advertising space for the Detroit Yellow Pages. An old scam. Lucky not to do time for it.'

Dan Stevens frowned. His entire demeanour suggested that unlike Anderson he took no pleasure in communicating any of this. 'The way I hear it his departure from GM wasn't quite how he has been describing it. The board had his letter of resignation ready and waiting for him to sign when he went in looking for a showdown.'

Anderson took another draw then crushed his cigarette in the ashtray Randall had just that moment emptied. 'The man is a liability. He loves the limelight too much. Nobody in the industry will touch him any more.'

Randall stared at the last of the smoke drifting up from the butt then he tipped it into the wastebasket and shoved basket and ashtray both into Anderson's arms.

'Bullshit,' he said, and with a nod to the other man as he headed for the door, 'A pleasure meeting you, Mr Stevens.'

That was the summer that Liz and Robert bought the orange Morris Marina. Only four years old and less than seventy thousand miles on the clock. They took it a day here and a day there over the July fortnight: Ballywalter, Castlerock, Whitepark Bay, the Ulster American Folk Park, which was as close, Liz had thought, walking around its reconstructed settlers' cabins, as they were ever likely to get to the real thing. They had talked about a package holiday on the continent – Torremolinos, Benidorm – had gone as far as making an appointment with Joe Walsh Tours in Castle Street the first weekend after Easter, but even at their rates, what with the new car and everything... No, it was just too much of a stretch. Maybe next year, they said, just as they had the year before. Instead, the next year Liz buried her brother, Pete, and felt guilty enough those first few months just breathing in and out, never mind lying sunning herself somewhere on the Costa Brava.

Anyway, a day here, a day there... Meant you weren't tied, didn't it?

3

The team that DeLorean was putting together was still under
half a dozen strong when Randall moved into the on-loan
Kimmerly offices. Besides being temporary landlord Tom
Kimmerly himself was acting as the company's attorney and
chief secretary. His was the name entered in the Michigan
State Business Register next to number 190407, the
DeLorean Manufacturing Company. Bill Collins the chief
engineer was another GM refugee – another former Pontiac
man – who had felt the life, and the spirit, being slowly
squeezed out of him by the sheer weight of the behemoth.
Almost the first thing he and DeLorean had done together
on his defection was fly to Europe, to the Turin Auto Show,
searching for a designer they could work with. Actually,
searching for one particular designer, Giorgetto Giugiaro,
whose concept car for Lotus – more space-age architectural
sculpture than automobile – had been shown in Turin the
same year as DeLorean's last ever Vega was being unveiled
in Chicago.

('You can drive yourself nuts in this world comparing

things that bear no direct comparison,' DeLorean told Randall. 'Or you can spur yourself on.')

Giugiaro was intrigued by their vision: a high-concept design in the mass-produced quantities he had recently achieved with the Volkswagen Golf...

The scale model Randall had seen (it was epo-wood, he had since discovered, not balsa) was the first fruit of their three-way collaboration, although by the time DeLorean handed it to him the plans had already been modified. It was clear even without the benefit of a full-size prototype that the Safety Vehicle name was not going to stay the course: too awkward on the tongue – too much drag. They settled instead on DMC-12, the concluding digits a reminder to everyone involved that despite the name change the ambition of delivering a safe – and ethical – car at an affordable price remained undimmed.

Also notionally installed in Long Lake Road was Dick Brown, who had made a name for himself with Mazda, taking it from nowhere to fourth in the American export market in just two years, and whose job it was to build up a network of dealers willing to part with $25000 in advance for the rights to sell the DMC-12 at a profit to them of $4000 a car. His target was a hundred and fifty dealers nationwide in the first twelve months, hence 'notionally installed'.

More rarely sighted still, but of even greater importance to the whole operation, was Roy Nesseth, Big Bad Roy, one of the few people Randall encountered in those circles taller than DeLorean, six-six, with the heft to go with it. Roy had started out as a dealer himself – still had an interest out in the 'field', as Randall quickly learned to call it, Wichita direction, and still had some of the abrasiveness with which members of that trade were traditionally associated, unfairly you might think, unless you had actually met Roy. The more other people complained about his manner – and other people did complain about it, a lot – the more it seemed DeLorean valued him. He it was who coined the nickname, and revelled in using it at every opportunity. 'Most times you run up against a wall you are able to find a way around it. Other times you have no option but to go straight on through. Those are the times you need Big Bad Roy.'

DeLorean talked at times like a football coach (he had a share in the San Diego Chargers) deploying his specialists according to the play. Roy was his gunner, bearing down on the opposition's punt returner, putting the fear of God into him. It wasn't always pretty, but you couldn't argue with the results.

As for Randall he was, to borrow from another code, a classic utility player. Whatever needed doing, he did it. Technically he was in the employ of Tom Kimmerly and the DeLorean Manufacturing Company, which controlled the DeLorean *Motor* Company, but at any given moment of any given day in the years that followed he could be acting for the John Z. DeLorean Corporation, the DeLorean Sports Car Partnership, the DeLorean Research Limited Partnership, or the Composite Technology Corporation, whose function it was to oversee development of the Elastic Reservoir Moulding process for the car's body.

JZDC
DSCP
DRLP
CTC
DMC squared

Almost from the start there were accusations – Randall's old pal Anderson ran one of the first in the *Daily News* – that as much energy and imagination was expended on moving capital from company to company as on designing and developing sports cars. DeLorean invoked Preston Tucker again, and his ill-starred attempt in the post-war years to break the Great Triopoly of Chrysler, GM and Ford. Tucker's problem wasn't so much that he had only one basket: he had only one *egg*. He left himself too get-at-able.

Besides, walk into any boardroom, or barroom, anywhere in the country and what else would you hear but talk of investment opportunities, rates of return, tax-saving options, *making money work*? Some made it work harder, and more effectively, than others, but not to have made it work at all was not just unprofessional, it was close to un-American.

The state of Delaware, anybody? Second smallest in the Union, but holding the registration for *half* of its publicly traded companies, including General Motors and the Ford Motor Company?

Another friend, Herb Siegel, head of Chris-Craft, the powerboat manufacturer, had given DeLorean the use of a suite in his building on Madison Avenue whenever he was in New York, which once the first prototype was ready was more often than not. Before very long Randall was there too with a third-floor walk-up giving him a view over – but alas no key to – Gramercy Park and a salary that made what he had been earning at the *Daily News* look like a pittance.

(As if to further prove the wisdom of his decision the *Daily News* itself – struggling all the time he was there – had, since he left, suffered the greatest ignominy that a newspaper could: it had folded.)

They had the Detroit headquarters, the New York offices, and a queue of people wanting to invest. All that was missing was a factory.

DeLorean had told Randall all along he did not want to commit until he had found the perfect site, although from what Randall could see it was the sites that came to him, trying to convince him of their perfection. Delegations arrived from half a dozen points on the North American compass: Ohio, Pennsylvania, Rhode Island, Louisiana, Alabama, Georgia (so much for no one wanting to touch him); there had been an enquiry from Spain, another from Portugal. One guy turned up at Long Lake Road from Dublin, Ireland. He had been driving from Chicago when he caught an item on the car radio – Detroit itself was preparing a bid for the factory (hear that, Anderson? Detroit) – and decided to detour out to Bloomfield Hills and offer to make representations to the Irish government, for whom he was some kind of unofficial ambassador. It sounded far-fetched – farther fetched for some reason than Portugal or Spain – but DeLorean insisted on following it up.

Limerick was the city mentioned (Randall up to then did not even know there was an actual Limerick city), sitting at the head of the Shannon estuary, giving ready access to the North Atlantic – a three-day crossing in the right conditions – and with an airport half an hour out of town used to handling transatlantic freight.

'The Irish are our kin,' DeLorean said. 'They sent their people here to escape hunger and want. They know what it is to struggle against oppression.'

By a tyrannical neighbour in their case, he meant, by the Big Three in his.

Liz read a report in the *Belfast Telegraph*. Car plant, Limerick, though to be honest it was the photo of the man behind the whole operation that caught her eye: the square jaw, the silver hair, the open-neck shirt and leather jacket, the name that the voice in her head made *Delloreen* of. There was a big man called DeLorean, whose something-something-something obscene. She turned the page. Prison dispute, men in blankets. She turned again. Tonight's television: 1, 2, and UTV. Hopeless, hopeless and worse than hopeless.

The unofficial ambassador arranged a dinner with Irish businessmen and politicians in Pittsburgh. DeLorean was irked that the invitation had not included Cristina, even though she was out of town herself, auditioning for a part in a TV movie with Larry Hagman, acting, as Randall had heard her husband say many times, having always been her first love. He had no sooner left the office for the airport than she rang to wish him luck.

'I'll leave a message at the check-in desk for him to call you,' said Randall to whom she had been redirected. He got the impression his name did not mean a single thing to her.

DeLorean arrived back in the middle of the following morning, morose.

'So?'

'Some people seem to think you should be getting down on your hands and knees to thank them for the privilege of bringing thousands of jobs to their country,' was as much as he would volunteer and Randall did not press him further.

'Did Cristina reach you?' he asked instead.

'She wanted to read me my horoscope. It mentioned Uranus in Capricorn: a good omen, apparently.'

Randall paused. He knew – it too having cropped up more than once – that DeLorean did set some store by these things, or by his own birth date, at any rate – 6 January: Epiphany. How better to account for those moments of revelation to which he had always been prone and on which he had never been afraid to act?

His smile on this occasion, though, was distinctly wry. 'Luckily for Capricorn it's too far away for me to sue, and as for the other one... Let's not go there at all, shall we?'

'There was another call after you left, from an Alejandro Vallecillo... The Puerto Rican Economic Development Agency, Fomento? Said he was calling at the behest of the governor…' Randall turned towards his own desk for the piece of paper on which he had written the name.

'Romero-Barcelo.' DeLorean beat him to it. 'I met him a couple of times when I was in Washington with the DBA.'

He looked at Randall, inviting him to elaborate. Randall blushed. 'And that was all.' All Vallecillo was prepared to divulge to *him* at least: 'The governor had asked him to call.'

DeLorean sat for a time holding a pencil between his thumbs and forefingers. 'The Economic Development Agency,' he said, 'Puerto Rico,' then said them both again as though simple iteration could fill in the blanks. Maybe this all went with the revelations – was a precondition for them: the self-induced trance. Either way, Randall was trying to fight down the impulse to push the phone across the desk to him – 'Ring him, why don't you?' – when a light in the corner of the dial pad began to flash: the Chris-Craft switchboard with an incoming call.

DeLorean took it himself. 'Sure,' he said, 'put him through.' He placed a hand over the mouthpiece. 'It's Dick.'

Randall started to leave, but the same hand now stayed him. He wandered instead to the window. A chopper appeared out of the clouds to his left, long enough for him to notice the pilot's bright red hair, banked, and was lost again among the buildings.

DeLorean replaced the phone on its cradle. 'We're going to LA,' he said.

The dealers' network was not expanding as fast as had been hoped – as fast as was necessary – especially in California, which it had been anticipated would account for 40 per cent of total sales. Twenty-five thousand, Dick had said, was a big buy-in for some of these guys, even with a share option on top of the guaranteed four-grand-a-car mark-up. He had had a promo film shot – very smooth, lots of sunlight through trees and flutes playing under a commentary that emphasised the durability of the design and therefore the reduced likelihood, 'to virtually nil', of obsolete stock – and Roy had been offering to add his weight to the negotiations. Dick, though, thought that this was a wall that needed to be got around. He thought the only person who could do it was DeLorean himself.

DeLorean, as he explained this, was on his feet in the office, the jacket he had taken off barely five minutes before back on.

It wasn't just the stake money the network was to have generated that he had to think about – vital though that was – but the reassurance it provided to other would-be investors: one hundred and fifty dealerships taking one hundred cars a year for two years was thirty thousand sales upfront, three hundred and sixty million dollars' worth of business.

'The Puerto Ricans...' Randall said.

'Can wait for a couple of days.'

In the end they stayed in LA three days – stayed in and strayed from – eating up hundreds and hundreds of miles of Californian highway, as far north as Fresno and as far south as Imperial Beach. Wherever the car stopped dealers greeted DeLorean like an old friend. He seemed genuinely affected, humbled even, by the warmth of his reception. One dealer

– this was in Thousand Oaks – told Randall, as he waited with him by the coffee vendor, how much they had always appreciated DeLorean's solicitousness, going right back to his Pontiac days. 'He never forgot we are on the front line. Some of the executives would come down here from Detroit and expect to be treated like goddamn royalty, wouldn't put their hand in their pocket from the start of the trip to the end, but not John.'

Another dealer, one of the converted, over in Anaheim, did complain ('a lot less than he did to me,' said Dick, 'and in longer words') that he had had customers coming in for the past six months asking when the cars were going to appear and wanting to make a down payment – pay the whole $12000 asking price in advance, some of them. A greedier person could already have made back his $25000 investment four times over.

'And a patient person,' said DeLorean, 'will be making closer to *forty* times over when the cars do appear. From the seventh car you sell it's all profit.'

With which finally there was no arguing.

It was already gone nine o'clock when they got back to the hotel at the end of the first day. Roy was waiting for them, just blown in and blowing out again first thing tomorrow to Wichita. (That damn dealership was more trouble than it was worth.) DeLorean apologised to Randall. He and Roy had a bit of catching up to do, numbers they needed to run.

'It's all right,' Randall said. In truth, although Roy had been nothing but civil to him any time they met, Randall couldn't help feeling surplus around him. Perhaps, there being so much of him, Roy just didn't see that company other than his was ever needed.

DeLorean laid a hand on Randall's shoulder. 'Tomorrow night,' he said, and was as good as his word.

They dined just the two of them the following evening in the grillroom of the hotel. No: they sat the following evening in the grillroom of the hotel at a table with food on it, and a phone. When he was not making or taking calls, DeLorean sipped from a glass of white wine – the same glass of white wine throughout – and addressed his plate with head tilted back and jaw thrown forward, as though each new dish required a recalibration of the apparatus. A forkful or two, a sip of wine, plate pushed away. Done.

Randall found that the appetite he had worked up in the course of his day in the field was suddenly gone.

A little jazz outfit was playing off in one corner of the room, unobtrusive for the most part, but every so often becoming involved in a niggly-sounding argument between piano, drums and guitar, distracting DeLorean even more. He set down his fork at one point and turned in his seat. The maître d' was at once on the alert, but relaxed into watching mode again as DeLorean turned back to face Randall.

'Did you ever play?'

'An instrument? No. There were votes taken to keep me away from them. You?'

'A bit.' DeLorean put the wine glass to his lips, tilted it, and took it away again. 'A lot, actually, once upon a time.

Clarinet. We had a band at Lawrence Tech, I was going to be the next Artie Shaw.'

Randall's face was evidently a blank.

'You don't know Artie Shaw? You don't know "Nightmare"?'

Randall laughed. 'If by knowing you mean actually *know*... no.'

DeLorean's hands, which had been poised momentarily about the ghost of an instrument, fluttered in the air between them. 'I'll start your education when we get back to New York.'

He picked up his fork and moved a small segment of artichoke from the rim of his plate to the centre. Left it there. He laid the fork lengthways across the plate.

'I remember reading that his mother was Austrian.' Artie Shaw's, he meant, or so Randall guessed. 'Same as mine. I kept thinking there had to be a connection, the way my own mother pushed me to take music lessons. I mean those were tough times to be trying to find five bucks a week, there weren't too many people working on the assembly lines with her who were willing to make the sacrifices.'

Randall had spent enough time in his presence over the past couple of years to have become familiar with his parents' assembly-line experiences, although DeLorean had never until now talked to him about them directly like this, facing him across a table, no eager journalist standing by turning the anecdote to screeds of shorthand.

'Back then they could lay you off right across the summer while they got the lines ready for the next year's model.

You can't imagine the strains that put on a family.'

His parents had separated, Randall had already picked that up. There were spells as a child living with relatives of his mother here in California. Or was it his father who had come west? A difficult man, he had gathered that by now too. It wasn't Austria he was from, somewhere else beginning with A... Alsace, that was it: home of Bugatti. That was the first time he had heard DeLorean suggest a regional affinity passed down the family line: the artistry in the manufacturing, the conviction that weight was the arch-enemy of innovative design.

DeLorean was tapping lightly with all eight fingertips on the grillroom tablecloth. 'I remember this one time a piano turning up in the house. Don't ask me where from, some kind of shelter it looked like. There were keys missing, dampers, but we were going to fix it up. My father was good at that sort of thing, as long as he didn't have to talk too much. Anyway, I woke up one night to a lot of crashing and thumping from downstairs – I was eight, nine, something like that – crashing and thumping at any time is unnerving, but in your own home, in the middle of the night... And what it was, Ford was having a crackdown, stolen tools, or tools suspected of being stolen. There were men in our house, to this day I couldn't tell you how they got there, if they knocked the door, or kicked it in, but they were in there, crashing and thumping, when my brothers and I crept down the stairs to see what was going on... And, well, I guess a battered piano looked to them a likely hiding place.'

The band had stopped playing. DeLorean raised his hands to applaud over his shoulder.

'I hope I need hardly add that there were no tools, not there, not anywhere in the house.'

'I can't believe they could get away with something like that,' Randall said.

'It was Detroit. They knew they had the people.' He closed his fist: this tight. 'Where else were they going to go for work?'

They reached the magical one hundred and fifty midway through the third morning and by the end of the day had added another eight dealers to the list. That evening they were driven out to Burbank as special guests at the recording of The Tonight Show. Randall had fielded two calls in the course of the afternoon from the Puerto Ricans, but DeLorean spent the entire journey on the car phone to Cristina, head turned to the window, and from the moment they arrived at the studios they had production assistants and hospitality staff in close attendance and then the show was starting and they were standing – such was their access – out of shot at the side of the stage, with its mess of cables and monitors, its young men and women with stopwatches and clipboards, watching Johnny Carson coax a beauty of a performance out of Peter O'Toole.

'The last time you were on here people thought you were bombed out of your gourd…'

'*I* thought I was bombed out of my gourd.'

'But you were just exhausted, weren't you?'

'Well, it's half your truth and half mine. I had been flying back from Japan and we left there on a Monday and arrived in the States on a Sunday, which alarmed me, and everywhere we stopped along the way it was cocktail hour and one doesn't want to be discourteous...'

Under cover of the applause that greeted its conclusion Randall finally had an opportunity.

'Romero-Barcelo's people have been on the phone again. I really think you should talk to them.'

DeLorean nodded. 'Did Roy Clark call? I'd hoped I might see him here. I know he's been filming a guest slot with the Muppets.'

'No,' said Randall as the studio manager tried to wind up the applause and get Peter O'Toole to vacate his seat, 'he didn't.'

Afterwards, while the set was struck and Johnny was in make-up for his make-down, they went across to the Sheraton Universal Hotel, where, as Randall had observed him do many times before, DeLorean opted to stand in the lobby rather than sit, as though reluctant to commit himself too soon: *Say Johnny doesn't come at all...?*

He attracted plenty of looks of his own, even in that lobby where whichever way you turned you saw someone who looked like someone you had seen on TV. That chestnut-haired woman holding up the shoe with the broken heel? Pure Mary Tyler Moore. The four men at the table over to the right, all open-neck shirts and heavy gold bracelets and furtive glances over the shoulders as they talked? Straight off the set of *The Rockford Files*.

DeLorean had checked his watch two or three times already, had muttered two or three times more about another invitation he had had, which perhaps it would have been polite not to have declined, when the hotel doors revolved and out at quarter-turn intervals stepped Johnny Carson's entourage, the young men and women from the wings, minus stopwatches and clipboards, with, at their centre, Johnny himself. He spotted DeLorean at once. The entourage parted as he did a little shuffle, feinting left and right before throwing his arms wide.

'Hey!'

'Hey!'

They hugged. Johnny and John. Brothers. Back-clapping. Johnny was first out of the clinch.

'So, when can I expect my car?' He turned to the entourage as to a studio audience. 'You know I'm going to do ads for this man? I must be the only schmuck in television history to *pay* half a million bucks to appear in an ad.'

DeLorean took it, as it was given, in good part. Every comedy act needed a stooge and he for the minute was it. 'We just signed up our one-hundred-and-fifty-*eighth* dealer, that's enough to take the first two years' output and then some.'

'You've settled then on where the plant will be?'

'We're' – not a flicker of hesitation – 'very nearly there with that.'

Johnny leaned closer, but his head was angled to ensure that the entourage-cum-audience was privy to his stage whisper. 'Did I hear *Ireland*?'

'Well, I had talks with some people from the government there, but then the governor of Puerto Rico called...'

'Several times,' Randall said. (DeLorean cast him a quick sidelong look.)

Johnny straightened, slapping DeLorean's back again. 'Begorrah, I know the Irish need the jobs even more than the Puerto Ricans do, but I thought that had to be a lot of blarney.'

The Rockford Files guys were doing more than glancing over now, they were turned in their seats openly staring. Randall watched over DeLorean's shoulder as one of them stood and made his way across the lobby, buttoning his sport jacket, with some difficulty, over his stomach. Randall's instinct was to head him off, but as he took a step forward DeLorean himself seemed to sense the presence at his back.

He turned. The man's face broke into a smile. 'John!'

'Well in the name of...' DeLorean's eyebrows went up, but the eyes themselves registered only confusion. He stalled. 'Johnny...' but Johnny had been grabbed for a photograph by the woman with the broken shoe, '*Edmund*, this is...'

'Jim Hoffman.' The man shoved a hand into Randall's and almost at once took it back. There was something of Roy Nesseth about him, his truculence, only concentrated, and even less palatable.

'You haven't been at the ranch in a while,' he said to DeLorean.

'The ranch, no.' Certainty had returned to DeLorean's eyes. 'Jim here's a neighbour in Pauma Valley,' he told Randall, who nodded. He didn't like this guy. The guy's mouth went up at one corner. The feeling was clearly mutual. DeLorean talked on, oblivious. 'What has you in town tonight?'

'Oh, a friend here bought a hangar down in Mojave. You remember Hetrick?' DeLorean smiled, a little uncomfortably, Randall thought: yes, he remembered Hetrick. 'He's thinking of going into the air haulage business.'

'Hauling what?' Randall asked.

'I guess whatever needs hauling.' Hoffman had his hand on DeLorean's sleeve, turning him slightly, making a circle of only two. 'But what about you? What about the car? I hear you're still on the lookout for capital.'

'Oh, we're in pretty good shape.' DeLorean's turn to play the gagman. 'About another seventy-five million, build us a factory, and we'll be ready to go.'

Hoffman gave a laugh (it sounded as though he had the loan of it), clapped his pockets. 'Seventy-five million? A bit out of my league... at least for now.'

'That's the spirit,' said DeLorean. '"For now."'

They shook hands.

'Keep me posted,' Hoffman said. 'And, hey – good luck!'

He unbuttoned his sport jacket as he walked back to his table. Randall watched him all the way. Mary Tyler Broken Shoe had got her photo and an autograph to go with it. Johnny and his entourage were moving on, *in*.

'You coming, John?'

'Be right with you,' DeLorean said then dipped his head level with Randall's ear. 'Get me Romero-Barcelo on the phone first thing in the morning.'

As Randall turned to go he saw Hoffman cock his thumb and squint down the barrel of his squat forefinger at him, taking aim.

The men with him laughed and shook their heads. Hoffman crooked the finger: *bang.*

4

The deal tabled was for half a million square feet of factory, rent free in perpetuity, on the site of a decommissioned army base at Borinquen, not far from Aguadilla, which was itself about a two-hour drive north from the Puerto Rican capital San Juan: half a million square feet *and* exclusive use of the base's former airfield. They would be as good as self-sufficient: a state within a state, or to invoke the language of Puerto Rico's own constitutional position, an unincorporated territory within an unincorporated territory.

Randall got to know the island's precise legal status pretty well in the months of negotiations leading up to the letter of agreement. He got to know Washington too – the road from the airport to Governor Barcelo's offices on 17th Street at any rate – having been dispatched there half a dozen times to work with the governor's chosen people on amendments to the early drafts, early drafts that did not, for instance, include help in fitting out the fifty thousand feet of office space that went with the factory and the airfield. Every last word – every comma, colon and dash – had to be weighed and evaluated and weighed again.

'I want what we begin here to last for generations,' DeLorean said, over and over. 'It is essential that we get the foundations absolutely right.'

To that end too the company had been trying for some time to identify a suitable permanent home in New York, which it found at last on the forty-third floor of 280 Park Avenue, formerly the home of Xerox, which had copied itself across, Randall could only suppose, to somewhere pretty much identical in another part of town.

Two-eighty Park Avenue was in effect two buildings – a mid-rise West joined by a passage to a high-rise East, which in turn was served by a choice of two elevators, the first car servicing all floors, the second, express car taking you straight to the very top and number forty-three.

Within days of the lease being secured the entire suite had been fitted with apricot carpet on the advice of one Maur Dubin, whose floor-length mink coat was such a fixture that Randall came to think of him not so much as a man wearing fur as an overgrown mustelid that had acquired a human – and entirely bald – head.

He busied about the forty-third floor, in and out of offices, as though it was his private domain, supervising the installation of desks one day, the hanging of a piece of art the next, and the day after insisting that the piece of art be taken down, the desks rearranged, removed altogether. Randall never once heard DeLorean gainsay his advice. And with reason. For all his oddness and his affectations Dubin was good, better than good. (The apricot carpet, when the sun shone through the forty-third-floor windows, was out of this world.) *He* would probably have said the best.

There was, even among DeLorean's closest associates, an amount of muttering: who was this guy? And where had he come from? Randall remained aloof from it. Where had he come from himself, after all? He had got on the lucky side of one of those epiphanies, the moment that John DeLorean knew for sure an expanded bumper did not a new car make.

So, paintings went up and paintings came down, desks were tried here and tried there and replaced by other desks till at long last Dubin declared himself as satisfied as he was ever going to be. (Because, really, to get it absolutely right you would want to start from the ground floor up: what lay beneath your feet – and he wasn't talking apricot carpet here – was as important for the harmony of a place as what lay before your eyes.)

At long last too DeLorean pronounced *himself* satisfied with the commas, colons and dashes of the Puerto Rican deal.

Randall arrived on the forty-third floor one morning to find a memo on his desk asking him to book conference rooms in the Crowne Plaza for early the following week and to make 'all other arrangements necessary for an exchange of contracts'.

Randall did not see DeLorean at all that week, had not, come to that, seen him for most of the previous week either. This was not unusual. On the contrary, it was a rare week when he was in New York or any other city for more than a couple of days at a time. He had, on top of everything else that was going on, a baby daughter at home, her arrival in this world a source of genuine – almost mystical – wonder to both parents. (His son, the only child from his two previous marriages, was adopted.)

A source of wonder and, Randall didn't doubt, the cause of more than one night's lost sleep.

Alejandro Vallecillo from the Puerto Rican Economic Development Agency – reconciled in the months since his initial phone call to dealing with Randall as an equal – moved into the Plaza several days in advance of the signing and Randall spent the larger part of that week shuttling between there and the company's lawyers up on E 42nd Street. He looked in on the conference rooms first thing every morning and again before he left for home at night. The Plaza's management was installing extra telephone lines in the main room and bringing sofas and armchairs into the rooms opening off it.

(Maur Dubin, to the best of Randall's knowledge, was in Miami, recuperating, otherwise he might have wanted a say in it too.)

The night before the ceremony he worked so late he did not even bother with the cab home, but took the room the hotel offered, going to bed with the curtains open as an added precaution against oversleeping.

He need not have worried. He was up and dressed at five-thirty, standing by the window, watching the mist on the East River slowly recede to offer up, like something long buried in desert sand, the monument that was the Long Island Ferry

Terminal. By seven he was down in the conference rooms for the flowers being delivered direct from the market: orchids and amaryllises and royal poincianas, deep, deep red with here and there a white and yellow throat.

The baskets of fruit were brought up from the cold store an hour later to give them time to achieve room temperature. An icebox arrived, already stocked with juices and sodas. (The champagne, he had decided, should remain in the care of the sommelier until the moment that the pen nibs were unsheathed.) The DeLorean legal team arrived and set up base in the side room nearest the door.

At nine o'clock to the second the Puerto Rican delegation came into the room, headed by Vallecillo. Bringing up the rear was a small, barrel-chested man with white hair swept back from a high forehead, the governor, Romero-Barcelo himself. Without being asked or directed he took a seat at the head of the conference table, the window at his back. The seat facing him – and the strengthening sun, unless the blinds were tilted to repel (Randall would make damn sure that they were) – was, for the time being, empty.

'Perhaps,' Randall said, once he had made sure that everyone had the necessary papers in front of them, 'you would like some coffee?'

Coffee, the governor indicated with a dip of his head, would be most welcome. It came, it went. Pages were turned, cross-referenced with earlier drafts. The room turned blue with smoke then grey. The chair at the far end of the table remained empty at ten. It remained empty at eleven. Half past.

Romero-Barcelo beckoned to Vallecillo, seated nearest to him on the right, who listened stony-faced for several moments before coming down the room and taking Randall by the upper arm into one of the side rooms.

'What the hell is going on here?'

'I'm sure there is a very good explanation,' Randall said.

'There had better be.'

They left the room together. Vallecillo returned to the governor's right hand. A quarter of an hour passed. The governor shaped as though to push back his seat.

'What about lunch?' Randall said and before anyone could react had crossed the room and picked up a phone. 'I'll ring down.'

'Mr Randall,' said the woman on the other end of the line. 'This is a coincidence. I just had a call come in for you, long distance. It is a very poor line. One moment while I try to connect you.'

There was a sound as of the phone being immersed in a tub of suds, which cleared then to leave a voice, *that* voice. 'Edmund, is that you?'

Randall was conscious that the governor was watching him. The entire room was watching him. He faced away, endeavouring to keep his voice low and steady.

'Where are you?'

'Ireland.'

'*Ireland?*' It came out strangulated. 'But Ireland's off, you told me: "Ireland's off".'

'Not the south, the north.' There was a warble on the

47

line – something moving on the Atlantic seabed perhaps – swallowing what he said next. He repeated it, louder. 'I'm in Belfast.'

It was as though someone had tossed a grenade into the room. Randall instinctively hunched his shoulders, pulling the phone closer to his chest, trying to absorb the impact.

'John,' he managed at length, 'I have the governor here.'

'And I have the British secretary of state for North Ireland here. He has already put a proposal before the cabinet in London. We are going to make an announcement tomorrow. We're building the factory here.'

Randall could nearly not take it all in. 'We're building it in Borinquen.' But even as he was saying it he knew it was no longer true.

'I'm sorry I didn't say anything before now,' DeLorean went on, 'but I couldn't risk a single word of it leaking out for fear of the whole deal collapsing.'

'But what do you want me to do?'

'I want you to get on the first flight you can over here.'

'I meant' – Randall's voice now was scarcely more than a whisper – 'about the Puerto Ricans.'

'Tell them they just didn't move fast enough. This is the deal we need,' DeLorean said and with another deep-sea warble was gone.

Randall replaced the receiver carefully then turned back to face the room again. Everyone around the table appeared to have lit a fresh cigarette. From the looks of the smoke billowing out, possibly two or three apiece.

The governor for the first time addressed him directly. 'Well?'

'If you could excuse me a minute,' Randall said and let himself out into the corridor. The elevators were directly facing; the doors of the one farthest left opened the instant he pressed the call button. He rode all the way down to zero then walked quickly across the lobby and out, down the steps, on to the sidewalk. Breathe, breathe, breathe. He spotted the bar on the opposite corner of the street. He didn't even bother with the walk sign but stepped on to the road, taking his chances with the buses and the cabs and the cars.

Once inside (because even if he had willed it nothing that day would have hit him) he set a ten-dollar bill on the counter and pointed to the Polish vodka, that being more or less the first thing that caught his eye.

'Double,' he said, and when that was gone pointed a second time: same again.

Then he walked back out on to the street, through the traffic, up the steps and across the hotel lobby to the elevator, reached out his finger to press up. Missed.

He got on a flight that same evening and, the following morning, having slept off in the intervening hours the effects of the previous day's vodkas (of which there had been several more after his extended dressing down by Romero-Barcelo), picked up another flight on a plane a quarter the size from a corner of Heathrow so remote and dismal it seemed to belong not just to a different airport but a different decade entirely.

An hour and a half later that plane came in to land on a runway bordered on one side by fields and on the other by a military base of a kind he had hoped never to see again when he flew out of Tan Son Nhat for the last time.

DeLorean had told him that a member of the secretary of state's team would be in the arrivals hall to meet him and sure enough when he came through from the baggage claim a large sad-looking man, in an even larger, sadder-looking suit, stood holding a piece of paper with Randall's name written on it in blue.

Randall stopped before him and held out his hand. 'Jennings?'

'McAuley, Mr Jennings is out in the car.' The man bypassed Randall's hand and reached down instead for his bag, affording Randall a glimpse of his gun, an old-fashioned pistol, holstered beneath his left arm.

'I can manage that myself,' Randall said, but McAuley had already hoisted the bag up behind his shoulder and started walking. Randall followed, a couple of steps off the bigger man's pace, trying not to fall further behind, but trying too to take in his surroundings, which on first impressions appeared more closely aligned with that remote corner of Heathrow he had taken off from than the cosmopolitan airport he had had to walk through to get there.

A newspaper on the sole newsstand carried a photo on the front cover of a bearded man – haggard – draped in a blanket against the backdrop of a wall smeared with... well Randall had no idea what exactly, although the accompanying headline – *Cardinal: Prison 'Unfit for Humans'* – made him fear the worst. He lifted a copy and set a note on the counter, which the young woman standing on the other side heaved a sigh at.

'Is that the smallest you've got?'

McAuley and his bag were disappearing under the exit sign.

'It's all right,' Randall said to the woman. 'I don't need the change.'

'No!' She scowled, not at the money now, he thought, but at the suggestion that she had been on the make. 'Here...' She dragged the coins – big ungainly things – one at a time from their compartments in her cash drawer and counted them into his hand. 'There.' She smiled, tightly, triumphantly: *you've nothing on me now.*

He stuffed the coins into his pants' pocket and ran.

A cool breeze hit him as he reached the end of a corridor walled with yellowing Plexiglas, having made up all but a couple of yards on McAuley. Smell of new-mown grass cutting through the aircraft exhaust fumes.

The car, a large Ford (he recognised the emblem but not the model), was easy to spot: it was the only one parked within a hundred-yard radius of the terminal. Two cops stood by, sub-machine guns clutched to their bulletproof vests, the glossy peaks of their caps pulled so low they had to tilt their heads to see past them.

One of them said something out the corner of his mouth to McAuley as he passed, don't ask Randall what, though

McAuley smiled, a surprisingly pleasant smile, which Randall took to be a good sign.

With his free hand McAuley pulled open the rear nearside door. A man in his late fifties, at a guess, with the most precise side parting in his hair Randall had ever seen sat over against the other door, a stack of papers resting on a buff folder on his lap. He crossed a t or dotted an i and replaced the lid of his fountain pen before turning his attention to Randall, taking him in from the newspaper up.

'Welcome to Bilfast.' A softer accent than McAuley and the girl at the newsstand: Scots, Randall later learned. 'East Berlin without the laughs.'

Randall responded with a laugh of his own as he sat into the car. Jennings raised an eyebrow and pursed his lips. McAuley slammed the door and the least external sound at once disappeared. It was like being shut in an icebox.

'Armoured,' said Jennings and patted the armrest. 'Means if they blow it up it comes down harder.'

Randall nodded, face straight.

'That one was a joke,' said Jennings.

'Maybe if you were to give me a signal in advance.'

Jennings relaxed his lips a little. 'Very good, very good.'

McAuley was behind the wheel now. He steered the car with the heel of his right hand out through the fortified perimeter fence and on to a straight two-lane road, farmland on either side. They could not have travelled more than five hundred yards along it before they encountered an army check: soldiers with camouflaged faces in the middle of the road, others sharing a hedgerow with a couple of inquisitive-looking sheep. Randall averted his eyes.

'The secretary of state is very invested in your Mr DeLorean, speaking figuratively as well as literally,' Jennings said as though their journey had been interrupted by nothing more remarkable than a stoplight. He tapped a fingernail against the glass next to his cheek. 'He told the prime minister that this deal could save the lives of soldiers like these.'

McAuley was showing his papers to a soldier with corporal stripes. The soldier looked past the driver's shoulder into the rear of the car, checked one face, checked two, then straightened up and made a circular motion with his hand: carry on. Jennings turned to face Randall. That parting had the permanent look of a scar.

'You can imagine the prime minister was sceptical. He said, "That's a rather extraordinary claim to make for a motor car," to which the secretary of state said, "Yes, but it's no ordinary motor car, and if it gives people jobs, *hope*, who knows what changes it might help set in motion."'

'I read the briefing papers on the plane,' Randall said.

'And what do you think yourself?'

'I think you should never underestimate faith in the future.'

Jennings pursed his lips again. He handed Randall another newspaper. The same photograph on the front page, but with a different headline: *Outrage at Cardinal's Prison Comments*.

'And I think you ought to remember there are two sides to every story here.'

'As there are where I come from.'

The other man made a noise through his nose, as much as to say have it your own way. Randall looked out the window but found nothing there to divert him save for hedges and fields and the occasional clump of trees. He closed his eyes and for a moment he was back in the lobby of the Sheraton Universal with Jim Hoffman in fatigues, looking down the barrel of an actual gun. He forced his eyes open again, shifted in his seat. Jennings was annotating a document, McAuley steering one-handed and humming quietly. The road stretched ahead straight between the hedges. The second time he did not feel his eyes close at all.

The engine cut out.

Randall's cheek was pressed up against the glass. It made a sucking sound as he pulled away. The car had stopped next to a tubular steel gate leading into a field that was more mud than grass, the imprint, around the gate itself, of many cow hooves. Jennings was replacing the lid on his pen again. He clipped it into his inside pocket.

'Well, here we are.'

'Where?'

'DeLorean Motor Cars Limited... Dunmurry. You said you read the briefing papers.'

'They didn't mention cattle.'

McAuley had come round to open his door. Randall stepped out unsteadily. The sun had broken through, but it still felt more like early spring than high summer.

He leant against the gate.

The field was actually two fields separated by a stream.

On the far side of the second field was a housing project – two-storey houses and low-rise apartment blocks – with hills beyond eaten into by quarries. In the opposite direction – looking south-east, possibly, to judge by the position of the sun – over the roof of the car at any rate, lay a couple of hangar-like buildings, and a little further on another housing development, dominated by two tower blocks, but otherwise in layout and style, right down to the colour of its roof tiles, a virtual mirror-image of the first.

(The names Twinbrook and Something Hill drifted across his jet-lagged mind. He would have to go back and read the papers again.)

And then from a distant corner of the further field, in front of a red-brick building he had not until that moment noticed, movement: a man striding out in the direction of the gate – by his height and his stride Randall recognised him at once as DeLorean – a dozen others stumbling in his wake, photographers as proximity proved them to be, cameras thumping against their chests, film-roll canisters hopping from their bags, their jacket pockets, as they tried, between shaking the muck off their shoes, to keep up.

DeLorean seemed to have found the only route that was not potholed or mined with cow pies.

Randall pulled himself up over the gate and walked out to meet him part way, sidestepping the hazards as best he could. They were to be producing upwards of ten thousand cars a year on this ground within the next two or three years.

'Edmund! Am I glad to see you.'

The moment DeLorean stood still the camera shutters started clicking. He paid them no regard. Jennings was out of the car now too, although he and his high-polished shoes remained firmly on the other side of the gate.

'Has the secretary of state arrived yet?' he asked.

DeLorean pointed back the way he had come to a smaller grouping before the red-brick building out of whose midst rose a couple of sound-boom poles. 'He was just getting set for an interview when I left him.'

More cars and vans were arriving as they walked back, photographers in tow, disgorging more men with cameras and boom poles. This was really happening. Here in Belfast. Any minute now the whole world would know. From that point on there could be no going back.

Liz had the four nearly matching plates lined up on the kitchen countertop ready to serve dinner when the news came on the TV. She stretched out her right foot and with the toe of her slipper pulled the door open another six inches so that she could see the screen in the corner of the living room. As ever it took her eyes a moment or two to adjust. The contrast was gone, or stuck, she wasn't sure which, and there was something wrong too with the vertical hold. Every couple of minutes a swelling would appear right down at the bottom of the picture, like a tear forming on an eyelid, only instead of brimming over it would begin slowly to move up the screen, pulling everything it passed through an inch to the right, turning landscapes into abstracts, people into question marks, twisting their words besides, for there was an aural counterpart to this visual distortion. And the worst about it was while it *was* only every couple of minutes they could not justify the cost of leaving the set in to be repaired again. Fifteen pounds it had cost them the last time (the pincushion correction circuit apparently): fifteen pounds and their marriage almost. Robert had nearly been as inconsolable as the boys without it.

She wrapped a tea towel round the handle of the potato pot and lifted it over from the stove: four pieces for Robert, three each for the boys, two for her.

Roy Mason was on, standing in a field by the looks of it. She couldn't hear a word he was saying. The boys, out of sight (at either end of the settee, most likely), were arguing.

'Ah, she never.'

'She did so.'

'She never.'

'She did.'

'Never.'

'Did.'

'Give over, the pair of you,' Robert said, closer to hand. (The armchair, always the armchair, to the left of the doorframe.) 'I'm trying to listen to this.'

'Have you your hands washed?' she called to all three a second before Roy Mason's voice finally rose above her sons' bickering, if rose was a word you could ever use of something so flat and nasally.

'This is a great day for British industry, a great day for the people of Northern Ireland, and most of all a great day for the city of Belfast.'

Liz took the pork chop pan from under the grill where it had been keeping warm and when she turned back there was the man from the newspaper that time, the car-maker, not in Limerick now, but in Belfast, standing before the microphone that Roy Mason had just stepped away from.

It had to be raised a good foot before he could speak.

'Thank you, Secretary of State...' He sounded a bit like Gary Cooper. 'I can't tell you how good it feels to be somewhere people understand you at last, what it is you are trying to achieve...' Not Gary Cooper: George Peppard. 'I am delighted to be able to announce that following my meetings with Mr Mason and his team over the past few days the agreements have all been signed.' A younger man behind him frowned, looking off to his right. 'You know, they told us in the US we couldn't do this, go right back to the blank page and build a brand new type of car in a brand new type of factory. They told us there were good reasons why no one had successfully launched an auto company since Chrysler in 1923. They are probably still telling us that, but we can do it and we will do it, on this very spot: from cow pasture to car production in just eighteen months.'

Liz looked down. She had put all the chops on the one plate. She used her fingertips to redistribute them. Hot, hot. The boys came in, pushing and shoving, like some strange two-headed beast trying to tear itself apart.

'Not chops,' said one of them.

'Sure, you love chops,' said the other.

'No, I don't.'

'Aye, you do.'

'Don't.'

'Do.'

Robert appeared in the doorway, looking behind him still at the TV. Back in the evening-news studio the industrial correspondent was throwing out figures: three hundred jobs in the initial building phase, twelve hundred jobs when production began, rising eventually to two thousand, in one of the most economically depressed parts of Belfast, a city whose only notable contribution to the auto industry was the invention of the pneumatic tyre a hundred years ago.

Robert shook his head. 'If somebody was giving me thirty grand for every job I think I could see my way to rustling up two thousand of them as well,' he said and went and sat down at the table. Liz strained the peas between the angled lid and the side of the pot and spooned them on to the plates.

'And this,' the industrial correspondent went on, 'is the car that is creating all the excitement, described by its creator John DeLorean' (so *that* was how you said it) 'as the world's most ethical mass-production motor car and the first car of the twenty-first century.'

Liz tilted her head trying to make sense of the image on the screen. Something odd was happening to the sides of the car – for a moment she thought it must be a trick of the vertical hold, but, no, those were the doors opening, rising up, and up, and up.

She set down the slotted spoon she had been using for the peas and covered her mouth with her hand. Honest to God, it was the only thing she could think to do to keep herself from laughing out loud.

The news crews were packing up. Randall rested a shoulder against one of the vans. UTV it said on the side. He was still dazed from the announcement, the flight, the whole crazy whirl of the past twenty-four hours.

For the final few minutes of the press conference his attention had snagged on a group of kids – mid-teens was his guess – watching from a slight muddy rise a couple of hundred yards away. He fancied for a time that they were trying to signal to him (he really was pretty dazed) then that they were involved in some kind of pat-a-cake or hand jive. Finally he twigged that what they were doing was passing something between them – some *things*: bottles, flashing green as heads were thrown back, tilting them towards their mouths.

He felt a hand on his back between his shoulder blades. He turned. DeLorean. His eyes were shining.

'Well?' he said.

'It's going to be something to see when it's done.'

DeLorean nodded. 'About that, I've been thinking, it might be an idea if you were to stay on here, just until we get the place up and running.'

Randall opened his mouth. DeLorean got there before him.

'Oh, don't worry, you'll not be on your own, there'll

be plenty of faces you recognise, but with so many people sometimes it's good to have someone taking care of L & L.'

Randall returned the initials as a question.

'Call it Logistics and Liaison,' DeLorean said. It was a new one on Randall, but then, his prerogative he supposed: his company, his job descriptions.

A cop walked by, part of the secretary of state's team, toting the same model of machine gun as the cops at the airport. (RUC they were called here: Royal Ulster Constabulary.) DeLorean brought his voice down a notch. 'Besides, with that *overseas* experience of yours you're not likely to be freaked out by the presence of all these guns.'

This time, before Randall could muster a reply, Jennings stepped across their path. He dipped his head with practised deference towards DeLorean. 'The secretary of state would like a word before he leaves.'

'Of course.' DeLorean took Randall's hand in both of his. 'I have to get on to London later: a few more papers to sign before they will start releasing the money. We'll book you into a hotel until we can fix you up with somewhere more permanent. Ring me the day after tomorrow, let me know what you need.'

Randall and Jennings together watched him go to Roy Mason's side.

'I couldn't help overhearing,' Jennings said without turning his head, 'and if you don't mind me saying, it's not the guns you have to worry about, it's the government.'

Randall glanced at him sidelong. 'I thought you were the government.'

'Me? Oh, no: civil service. I simply do the bidding of whoever is in power.' This with a small wave to the secretary of state, just getting into his car. 'And, whisper it, Mr Mason and his party are not going to be in power for very much longer.'

Mr Mason's party, Randall knew, was Labour, which stood in relation to its main rivals, the 'Tories' of the Conservative Party, rather as the Democrats did to the Republicans. The Tories had a woman in charge, Margaret Thatcher. Ronald Reagan was a fan.

'The next incumbents, I am afraid, are not renowned for their love of public subsidy, certainly not under the new regime... And certainly not in the tens of millions that it appears Mr DeLorean has managed to extract. If I had any influence I would make sure he stuck to that timetable of his, although between you and me "eighteen months" was a bit of unnecessary bravado.' He shook his head. 'What I would call handing the opposition a goal start.'

The car with DeLorean in it followed the secretary of state's away from the site. He turned a final time in his seat and saluted Randall with a forefinger off the eyebrow.

Randall raised a forefinger halfway to his own.

Jennings shook his head again.

The kids on the rise overlooking the cow fields passed their bottles round.

5

To begin with Randall stayed in a hotel – the Conway – a scant half a mile from the future plant, hidden away in woods on the edge of one of the housing projects that he had glimpsed that first day. Housing *estates*, I beg your pardon. The Conway, way back when, had been the home of some linen magnate, a brother of the owner of the former Seymour (the name that had escaped him) Hill, whose entire house and lands – hence 'estate' – the Northern Ireland government had requisitioned after World War II for public housing.

And 'Northern Ireland'. Not 'North' or 'North of'. They were very particular about that.

As DeLorean had assured him, he was not on his own. As the weeks went by and the transformation of the Dunmurry cow pasture began, the Conway started to fill up with DeLorean Motor Company Limited guests. (DeLorean himself returned to break ground at the start of October but had already checked in his souvenir spade for the flight back to London before the fourteen earth movers that entered the fields as he exited had between them turned over a single one of the seventy-two acres.) One of the first to arrive was Myron Stylianides, the perpetually upbeat director of personnel, who was responsible for finding a managing director in Chuck Bennington. Bennington was as lugubrious as Stylianides was sunny, a trait that Randall attributed in part to his beard and moustache, which looked to be modelled on an Olde English seafarer's – a Raleigh or a Drake – and which seriously limited his scope for smiling, and in part to his Raleighan devotion to tobacco, which in its permanently lit cigarette form similarly limited his scope for speech. On Dick Brown's recommendation Stylianides and Bennington brought in Dixon Hollinshead to oversee the construction of the factory itself and to help swell the numbers in the Conway's residents' dining room.

There were still nights though, particularly towards the end of the working week, when those who could get out did and when Randall had the dining room pretty much to himself.

Dunmurry was not strictly speaking in Belfast at all, but in the borough of Lisburn, whose town centre lay about three miles south along the main road that ran past the end of the Conway's long driveway. The centre of Belfast lay maybe a mile and a half further than that in the opposite direction, although Randall did not often make that particular journey for reasons other than work and scarcely at all at night, the news that he awoke to each morning being a daily renewed disincentive.

(He was particularly alarmed by the recurrence of the term 'coffee-jar bomb'. How could you trust anything if you could not trust a jar of coffee?)

Instead he would have a couple of beers most nights in the lounge bar – two sometimes, rarely more than three – and afterwards take a walk around the grounds or if, as was often the case, the grass was too wet, follow that long, curving driveway down to the main gates. There were a couple of whitewashed cottages opposite, vegetable gardens just visible in daylight at the rear, the whole lot dwarfed by a pair of twenty-storey apartment blocks that might have sprouted from a handful of magic stones tossed out of a cottage window one night in a fit of temper.

The gates themselves stood open throughout the day, but half a dozen yards in from the road was a security barrier operated from inside a tar-roofed wooden hut by some permutation of the same three guards: the small thin one, the tall fat one and the one with the caved-in nose. They never once introduced themselves by name, or asked Randall his, but generally, if he had gone that way, whichever pair was on duty would step out of the hut the moment they saw him and stand a while with him in an informal smoking bee.

He commented one night, early in their acquaintance, on the fact that they were not armed, as guards back home would certainly be.

'Not allowed here,' said the guy with the nose. 'Only cops and soldiers. Afraid of guns getting into the wrong hands.'

'Anyway,' said his pal (it was the small thin one tonight), 'there hasn't been a bit of bother since they had this barrier put in.'

Which begged the question... Randall asked it, 'There was before?'

'Ach, aye.' The guy with the nose tried to make light of it. 'Sure there's hardly a hotel or a bar in the country hasn't had it at some point by now. And, like, we got off lightly: wee bit of damage to the front door, couple of windows broke, no one badly hurt.'

'Mind you, one of the bombers was shot getting away.' The small one had clearly not picked up on his colleague's attempt to downplay the threat. 'Tried to hijack a car belonging to an off-duty cop.'

The guy with the nose could only suck his teeth. 'What are the chances of that?'

But say someone was to drive up now, Randall asked, not entirely hypothetically, someone with an actual bomb. What could they do?

The small one threw down his cigarette and ducked back into the hut (glimpse of a kettle, an electric heater), emerging a couple of moments later with a lump hammer.

'See that? That goes through the windscreen,' he said. 'Then me and him' – jerking his thumb – 'run like hell.'

And his pal laughed, smokily. 'Don't listen to him.'

It was from the third guy, the fat one, that Randall heard the melancholy story of Thomas Niedermayer. He had come with his family to Belfast from Nuremberg at the start of the sixties to head up the new Grundig factory, German reel-to-reel tape recorders then being seen as the answer to the already acute problem of unemployment in the city. The security guard had used to work there – in the hangar-like building Randall had seen on the edge of the DeLorean site – which was how the subject came up. ('How long have you been doing this then...?') Anyway, everything was fine until five or six years ago – 'this time of year as well' (already it had acquired the characteristics of a folk tale). Late one weekday evening, a man had knocked on the front door of the bungalow in another part of Dunmurry ('beautiful houses') where Niedermayer and his family were living and told one of the teenage daughters that he had reversed into their car, which was parked on the street. The wee girl went and got her father who came out still in his slippers and followed the man down the path, chatting away, but when he bent over to inspect the damage a second man appeared out of the shadows and together with the first bundled Niedermayer into the back seat of his own car – all this in full view of his daughter – since when neither hide nor hair had been seen, nor word heard, of the poor fella.

'They'll have taken him over the border somewhere,' the guard told Randall. 'That's where they all end up.'

'*All?*"

'Oh, no, here, don't take that the wrong way. I mean touts and the like – informers.' He clamped the cigarette in his mouth and mimed pulling a trigger two-handed, aiming at the back of a kneeling man's head, removed the cigarette, exhaled mightily. 'There was a whole thing going on at the time they took him about IRA guys in prison down south. Generally they leave the foreigners well alone and, like, even if they didn't they would never in a million years lay a finger on any of your crowd. Can you imagine the stink the Irish Americans...?' He swallowed the end of the last word. 'Sorry, you're not...?' Randall shook his head. The big guy swiped a hand melodramatically across his brow: *phew!* 'Anyway, you can just imagine it, can't you, the stink?'

Which was not quite to Randall the reassurance the big guy clearly thought it was.

He walked back up the drive to the hotel, alert to every rustle from the bushes crowding in on either side, went into the bar and had another drink, his fourth of that particular night. Well, fourth then fifth.

DeLorean returned at regular intervals throughout the autumn and winter, usually with Bill Collins in tow, sometimes with Kimmerly, now and then with a new guy, Bill Haddad, who had used to work for the Kennedys and who had been enticed away from his last job as a columnist on the *New York Post* – a slightly grander newspaper connection than Randall could boast, as Haddad occasionally reminded him – by the offer of Vice President for Planning. PR, from what Randall could see. DeLorean and his job titles.

The itinerary varied little from trip to trip: site visit, presentation from Dixon Hollinshead and Chuck, meeting with Mason and the Industrial Development Board, interview with one or other of the local TV channels ('I couldn't be happier with how things are going, couldn't be happier at all'), then back to the airport for a late-afternoon flight out, because always, whatever his intentions, something would have come up in the course of the day that demanded he return that night to London or, if Kimmerly was with him, go on to Geneva, where it appeared there was some deal afoot, involving a new set of initials, GPD, General Products Development. (There ought to have been an S and an I as well – Services Inc – but they didn't make the cut and Randall, with so much else to occupy him, didn't give them, or the three letters that did, much in the way of thought.)

All of which meant that Randall's opportunities for liaising with DeLorean one-to-one were usually restricted to the walks from building to car between meetings; the car itself, as he had observed in LA, having become a kind of motorised phone booth, where it was impossible – short of having a phone of your own to ring him on – to get a word in.

On one of these walks, early in the new year, after a working lunch with his senior managers in the Conway (left as usual largely untouched: Randall noted that his was not the only appetite to shrivel in the presence of such fastidiousness), DeLorean was delivering his customary apology for having to leave when he suddenly stopped.

'We need a house,' he said.

'Right.'

'Cristina and I, a permanent base here. Somewhere we can put visitors too when we are not around, let them relax a bit more than they can in a hotel.'

'Right.'

'It would need to be...'

'Private,' Randall was about to say. 'Pretty secure.'

'Of course.'

'Some of these people might not have been here before, they might be a little nervous.'

'There is one place I can think of straight off,' Randall said. 'It's not far. I can go with you in the car and point it out.'

DeLorean thought a moment, looked at his watch. 'Tell you what, wire me some pictures. You have experience in this field, right? I trust your judgement.'

And with that he was in the car and away again.

Warren House was not far at all, standing as it did at the northern tip of a more or less equilateral triangle whose other vertices were the factory site and the Conway itself. Randall had caught glimpses of it through the trees – multi-paned sash windows, ivy in profusion – long before he noticed the For Sale sign at the end of the lane that led up to it off the main Belfast road. Only after he had mentioned it to DeLorean and had phoned the real estate company to request a brochure did he realise that it was the same house he had looked at, albeit with a little less ivy, who knows how many times in a book on the hotel's reception desk. Turns out it too used to belong to the family that owned Conway House – all the large houses in the district seemed to have belonged to them once upon a time although few of them had had such a curious and colourful afterlife.

The most recent occupants had been a chapter of the Plymouth Brethren – a sect Randall had hitherto mistakenly imagined was a uniquely American phenomenon. 'They are like hermit crabs, that crowd,' the real estate agent said when he took Randall to see the house. Lee Bell, he had told Randall his name was: 'Three ls, three es and a B and that's me, nine Scrabble points.' He wore large-framed glasses that, when you looked at him head on, had the disconcerting effect (even more disconcerting after his mention of crabs) of making his eyes appear to bulge out at either side. 'They will move in practically anywhere, even somebody else's church building, although they tell me they don't believe in churches. Make sense of that if you can.'

There were still chairs arranged non-hierarchically in a circle in the drawing room, it being another guiding principle of the Brethren, Lee Bell explained ('the things you learn in this job'), that no man had a right to be raised above, or seated at the head of another.

'You're welcome to keep anything here you think is of use.'

Randall was still staring at the non-hierarchical circle. Whatever it was Lee Bell read in his expression – clearly not suppressed amusement (non-hierarchical circles? DeLorean Motor Cars Ltd?) – he started stacking the chairs. 'Not these, obviously, but anything else – fixtures, fittings...' He gave Randall the benefit of his full, distended regard. 'Or you can have the whole place gutted.'

'Are you kidding me? *Gutted?*'

Lee Bell shrugged. 'Well, you never know with people,' he said, as though referring to a species distinct from real estate agents.

Randall roamed the house with his camera while in the

drawing room Lee Bell caught up with paperwork, or tried to think of names with a lower Scrabble value. Several of the six bedrooms showed signs of damp; the plug sockets throughout were mounted directly on to the wooden baseboard and would have to be replaced; the kitchen looked to have been equipped by people who did not believe in food any more than churches or priests, and as for the bathroom, OK, so it was an old house, but Randall had been in more sophisticated outhouses. Nevertheless, those first few photographs were all that was needed to convince DeLorean, although Randall still returned repeatedly over the weeks that followed to take more pictures – of the plaster mouldings and cornices as well as the baseboards, of the door- and window-frames, the mantels and the fire surrounds – which he sent back along with detailed reports of sunrise and sunset (the dining room got the benefit of the latter) and even cuttings from the shrubs growing nearest to the house.

The instructions that he received in return had, he suspected, more than a little of the hand of Maur Dubin in them; Maur at his most whimsical and Margaret-Mitchell-inspired. The bathroom faucets were shipped from Harrods in London, only Harrods in London apparently stocking the style of faucet that fit with his vision, or the DeLoreans', for the house. The label on the box said gold. Randall very much doubted it. They would not have been to his taste, that was for sure, but then Randall did not have to live with them. Or did not imagine he would have to.

It was DeLorean himself on his next but one trip across

– he had flown into London from Salt Lake City, whatever had him in Utah – who suggested that Randall move in, temporarily of course, while the renovations were still being carried out. 'There is nothing brings a house to life like human beings in it.'

'It's a really kind offer, but...'

DeLorean stopped him. 'Really kind offers never require a but. Besides, you would be doing me a big, big favour.'

And big, big favours, Randall knew, did not admit of refusals, however polite.

Friday night in the Conway Hotel was supper dance night. Saturday was wedding day. The former varied little, only the name on the pegboards outside the function room doors distinguished this week's brown suits and fur stoles (Friends School Old Girls Association) from last's (Derriaghy & District Indoor Bowling League); the latter, between the white tuxedos and the blue velvet, the peach organza and the turquoise tulle, to say nothing of the hats, the hats, the *hats*, were an advertisement for the inexhaustible variety of the human imagination.

Randall was sitting in a secluded corner of the lounge bar late on the rainy Saturday afternoon before he moved across to Warren House, reading a magazine he had picked up in the lobby, when a man in a grey morning suit, an arrangement of a white rose and something purple in his buttonhole, rested his whiskey tumbler on the edge of the table.

'Do you mind?' he said, his hand on the back of the seat

facing Randall. He could have had his pick of two dozen others.

'Not at all.'

'I was worried I might be disturbing you.'

He gestured towards the magazine. Randall showed him the cover. *Homes and Gardens.* He laughed. 'Actually, you're saving me. You're with the wedding party, I take it.'

The man looked down the length of himself, as though surprised all over again by his get-up and the reason for it. 'It's my daughter's getting married.'

'Well that's great.'

'Better now the speech is out of the way,' said the man, shaking the hand that Randall had offered in congratulation.

'I should buy you a drink.'

'Thanks, but I'm OK with this. I have a long night of it ahead of me.' He glanced over his shoulder. 'To tell you the truth, it was the wife's sister asked me to come over.'

Randall looked past him, half expecting to see a face he recognised (though whose that would be he couldn't think), half dreading the one he did not. All he saw, though, was the archway through to the rest of the bar, the doors to the function room beyond.

'She's' – picking his words with care – 'on her own.'

'Oh, listen, that's really thoughtful,' Randall said, then worried that even that could be construed as an acceptance. This guy was – what? Fifty? Fifty-five? And he was trying to set him up with his spinster sister-in-law? 'I mean, it's just, I have a couple of calls I have to make back home, to the US.'

The man held up his hands. 'You don't have to say anything more. Totally understand. I told her I would come over and I did. No harm done, I hope.'

'None at all.'

The man pushed back his chair, but only, it seemed, to inspect his shoes. Shiny like he clearly didn't believe.

'Have you children yourself?'

'One,' said Randall, 'but...'

'Wee boy, wee girl?'

'Girl, but...'

'That's lovely.' It was worse than trying to deflect DeLorean in full flow. Randall gave up trying. 'You know though you'll get your eye wiped, don't you? You tell yourself you won't, but you will, guaranteed.' He leaned forward and clicked the rim of his glass against Randall's. 'Girls. They're too well able for us.'

The man returned to the wedding, Randall to his magazine, although he was barely even looking at the pictures. A little later, passing the doors of the function room, he saw the man dancing with his daughter (ivory taffeta with lace neck) and, truly, a prouder man never trod a dance floor. Randall lingered a while in the doorway trying to imagine. Tamsin had still been at the clomping stage the last time he had led her round a floor – round and round and round and round – to... what? 'Our House'? Surely not. Too neat, though she had loved it then: 'Now everything is easy 'cause of you and our la, la, la, la, la, la, la, la, la, la...'

He actually shook his head to wipe the picture.

At a table at the top of the room a woman was sitting alone, wearing the same corsage as the bride's father, but younger than him by a good twenty years, and beautiful. She caught Randall's eye, held it a moment. His hand started up in a wave but before it had arrived she had set her mouth and looked away. Sorry, buster, no second chances.

6

The warren from which the name derived faced his new home across a steep-sided valley, the shallow Derriaghy River making its unhurried way across the bottom. Randall quickly realised that this was the hill where he had seen the teenage boys passing the bottles between them on the day he arrived in Belfast. Most weekend mornings and a fair few mornings in between he awoke to the sight of their debris – theirs or their fellow enthusiasts – the green glass, the empty tins, bent in the middle – and once saw a rabbit, as though remotely conjured, appear out of a striped plastic bag into which it had apparently crawled in hopes of grass greener than that which lay all around it.

On another side of the house work had already begun to clear the ground for a new private road giving direct access to the factory site, in contravention, no doubt, of all Brethren strictures about raising any one man above another, though not – Randall had sought reassurance from Jennings on the point – of the terms of the British government's grants. 'I suppose if it improves efficiency...'

'And security,' said Randall, who could not help but see the lane up from the main road through DeLorean's eyes, although he had once or twice on his own account wished as he turned on to it that he had about him the lump hammer from the Conway's security hut.

He had been in the house little more than a fortnight when the Labour Prime Minister, Callaghan, lost a vote of confidence in the British Houses of Parliament and was forced to call an election for the start of May.

Several times during the campaign Randall, remembering Jennings's warning, voiced his concerns to DeLorean as poll after poll suggested the Conservatives were winning over voters with their ad campaign, a long serpentine line of the unemployed dwarfed by the slogan 'Labour Isn't Working.'

'It is in Belfast,' DeLorean said.

Randall pointed out that, from what he had seen of it, Belfast, Northern Ireland generally, was incidental to the election campaign, aside from promises – stock-sounding even to a newcomer and varying little from party to party – to get tougher with the IRA. Neither Labour, nor the Tories, nor the smaller Liberal Party were fielding candidates in the Northern Irish constituencies.

'Which kind of makes you wonder what they wanted with it in the first place,' said DeLorean.

Randall listened to the radio long into the election night as the results came in, first a trickle then a torrent, entranced by both the place names – the Wrekin, Sutton Coldfield, Epping Forest, Thanet East, Thanet West, Angus South, Clitheroe,

Cirencester and Tewkesbury – and by the repetition of the commentary: Conservatives gain, Conservatives hold, Conservatives hold on an increased majority, swing of 9.9 per cent from Labour red to Tory blue. The outcome was beyond doubt long before sun-up. Jennings and the opinion polls were right. Callaghan – Mason – and Labour were out, the Conservatives, Thatcher and whoever she decided on as Secretary of State for Northern Ireland were in.

Robert did not much like Margaret Thatcher, but he liked that buffoon Jim Callaghan even less. To his mind *anybody* would have been an improvement.

'Even a woman, you mean?'

'Oh, come on, Liz, Margaret Thatcher's never a woman, she's a man in a dress.'

Liz was not sure what to make of it all. She had long ago given up on politicians in this part of the world – take your pick from old men, angry men, or angry old men – and the ones across the water always seemed, and not just by virtue of the water, remote. Part of her responded to the sound of a woman (whatever Robert called her) commanding attention, shouting down the hecklers – encouraging them in order to shout them down was how it sometimes came across – but another, larger part feared Thatcher's certainty. Liz's granny had a saying (her granny had a store of sayings; it was, besides her children, the principal achievement of her life): the higher you build your tower the harder it is to climb down.

Margaret Thatcher by the sound of her was still building and had no intention of stopping any time soon.

Turned out what had DeLorean in Utah earlier in the year was Imps and Sprytes – Thokiol Imps and Sprytes, to be precise: specialist snow vehicles built in Logan by a company that had got a lucky break in the Space Shuttle programme and were looking to offload their terrestrial holdings at a price that was too good to pass up, even for a man with a new high-concept sports car on his hands.

It was in Utah again, on Mountain Time – a couple of hours closer to the start of his day, in consequence, than had been intended – that Randall tracked him down the morning after the election. Despite the time disadvantage he sounded more alert than Randall felt: already had a full workout under his belt, in fact.

'We should have staked some of that money the last government gave us on the result,' DeLorean said. (He sounded as though he was on speakerphone, quite possibly still on an exercise bike.) 'We could have paid the new one back and still have had change to finish off the factory with.'

'About that,' said Randall.

'You are going to tell me that we are nine months into the eighteen. As I have already said to Dixon and Chuck, our glass is half full.'

'Jennings—'

'—inclines to the half-empty point of view, that's why he is a civil servant, a checker of things. We are makers of things.' Randall was ambushed by a tingling up his spine at these words, their conviction and their inclusiveness: *we*. 'At Chevrolet at one point the parts manual was nineteen inches thick: there were a thousand options just for the dashboard. We're giving our owners four options and half a dozen accessories for the whole car. Do you understand what I am saying? We are not just trying to build a factory, we are rethinking an entire way of doing things and, barring something totally unforeseen, we'll hit our target.'

Viewed through the full half of the glass, the foundations of the factory had now been laid. The stream dividing the fields – a tributary of the river that bordered Warren House – had been diverted and culverted and thousands of tons of stone had been brought down from the quarry at White Mountain, which formed – and daily deformed – part of the skyline to the west.

In places the stone was four feet deep. On top of this the skeleton of the factory itself had begun to take shape. There were to be two main sections, the body-pressing building – the word they used here was 'shop' – and, sitting at right angles to it, the assembly or 'build' shop, the two connected by a system of mobile cranes. The bodies aside, no actual manufacturing would be done on site. Instead, as many of the components as possible would be sourced locally, further boosting employment. The stainless steel panels had been sub-contracted to a factory near Limerick, which as Jennings ruefully observed, meant the southern Irish had contrived to get a slice of the pie without having to buy any of the ingredients.

For the moment, all of this was being coordinated and administered from the 'carpet factory' – the red-brick building before which the press conference had taken place the day Randall arrived – or from Warren House itself, where Randall had been joined, now that the refurbishment was complete, by Chuck Bennington. 'Think of me as the son that never moved out,' Randall said, although Chuck was a largely absent parent, with a schedule that could not have been more punishing if it had been handed down by a court of law.

Besides the private access road, the contractors were laying a new road to one of the two entrances they were building into the factory: the first to the south-east for workers who would be coming from the Seymour Hill direction; and the second – to be served by the new road – pretty much due west for those arriving from Twinbrook. Except no one was buying the convenience story (the gates were no more than a couple of hundred yards apart), although to be honest no one was trying very hard to sell it either. The Protestant and Catholic gates was what they were.

'It is the only way you are going to get both tribes to buy in,' was the way Dixon Hollinshead had justified it.

Buy in, mind you, did not look to Randall as though it was going to be a problem. The applications had started coming in the morning after that first press conference – long before there was such a thing as an application form or even a list of job descriptions. By the time the forms were ready and the recruitment ads went into the newspapers midway through the first spring they already had three or four sackfuls sitting in a corridor in the carpet factory waiting to be read.

Then the deluge began.

Some of the envelopes didn't have stamps, so hasty were the senders, or so unaccustomed to sending letters of any sort. A lot of them carried no address beyond DeLorean, Belfast – or Dunmurry, as some preferred, including one would-be worker who had underlined the place name three times to ensure the letter did not go to a different DeLorean. A sizeable number of the forms inside were lacking vital information, like the contact address, *the name*. But even after Stylianides and his staff had weeded out those they still had twenty applications for each of the first nine hundred positions that had to be filled.

Stylianides reckoned that you could probably have learned more from those letters than you could from a whole library of history and sociology books, although for Chuck the only pertinent fact to draw from them was that there did not exist in the whole of that country more than a few score people with the training or the experience necessary to assemble stainless steel sports cars – *any* kind of cars.

'So, think of all the bad habits they are not going to have to unlearn,' DeLorean told him when the matter was raised on his next visit, and Chuck's moustache and beard closed ranks with the perpetual cigarette to keep his mouth from saying anything else.

The interviews took the better part of two months. If you made it that far you still had less than a one in three chance of landing a job. Randall took his turn on the interview panels same as everybody else. Whatever about no bad habits, it was a struggle at times not to give in to Chuck's misgivings.

He lay this side of sleep some nights, playing the interviews over in his head, got up more than once to write something down before it slipped away.

Woman, 45, according to her form (mistake, had to be: tens and units transposed?)

Stylianides: You say in your application that you used to work in a pram factory?

Woman: Well, we called it the Pram Factory, but mostly what it did was bikes.

Stylianides: Bikes? Right.

Woman: And cuddly toys.

Stylianides: Bikes *and* cuddly toys. And what was your own area of expertise?

Woman: The cuddly toys.

Stylianides: So, like…?

Woman: Stuffing, mainly.

Stylianides (slowly): OK.

Woman: It all had to be done by hand, you know. It's a lot trickier than you think.

Stylianides: You realise that most of our upholstering will be done offsite?

Woman (ages another five years): I didn't realise that, no.

Stylianides: The seats and so forth, the 'stuffing'.

Silence… *long* silence.

Woman (smiling, a girl again): What about the canteen?

* * *

Heavy-set Man, buzz-cut.

Hollinshead: You left your last job, let me see…

Heavy-set Man: In 1975. Third of March. A Monday.

Hollinshead: Is it not more usual to work through to the end of the week?

Heavy-set Man: I had a spot of bother.

Hollinshead: Do you mind me asking what sort of bother exactly?

Heavy-set Man: The foreman was always on my case. Didn't matter what it was went wrong, it was me he gave the blame to. In the end I just threw the head up.

Hollinshead: You quit?

Heavy-set Man (absentmindedly flexing right hand): I lamped him.

Self: Just so we're clear, when you say 'lamped'…?

Heavy-set Man: I flattened him. One punch.

Hollinshead (clears his throat): And you don't think maybe you should have mentioned that in your application?

Heavy-set Man: I told myself I wasn't going to let that… *so-and-so* ruin my life.

Teenage Girl (first interview!!): My boyfriend dared me to apply. Here he was, Sure why not, *I* am, and here's me, *Me*…? Aye, dead on, and now here's me has the big interview and there's him sitting in the house moping. He'd probably chuck me if I was to get a start.

Bennington (removing cigarette from his mouth): That's

what you say here for 'dump', 'break it off'? 'Chuck'?

Teenage Girl: Aye.

Bennington (raises his eyebrows): Well we wouldn't want that to happen.

Teenage Girl (a sigh, like here is a man who understands): I know. Six weeks we've been going.

Slouching Man... he slouches, that's it.

Stylianides: Are you comfortable there?

Slouching Man: Fine, fine. Tell you the truth, but, I had plenty to keep me busy on the brew*. You know yourselves, you can always find something to do. I only wrote off for the form to keep Her quiet.

*A drinker?

Twitchy Man (nicotine to the knuckles): I was on the sick there for a lot of years with my nerves.

Hollinshead: I'm sorry to hear that.

Twitchy Man (nods): Some fella in the place where I used to be foreman went buck mad one day and attacked me for no reason at all.

And that was all in the first week.

Somewhere in the middle of the second Randall looked up, a heartbeat after the door opened, from the notes he had been making, to find a woman already installed in the chair across the table. He half expected her to glance away, or even get up and leave. It was *her*: the woman from the wedding reception in the Conway, the sister-in-law. The rest of the panel were looking at him expectantly. He was supposed to lead on this one.

'So.' He found her form. 'Elizabeth, is that correct?'

'Liz is fine.'

It wasn't her at all, he saw that now. He frowned.

'I'm looking at your application here and I see you haven't really worked...'

'Since my sons were born, no.'

'And they are...?'

'Fourteen and fifteen now. I can hardly believe it myself.'

'So what, after all that time, made you decide to apply to DMCL?'

'Funny,' she said, without the expression, facial or vocal, to support it, 'that's exactly what my husband asked me.'

She had been upstairs changing the boys' beds (the joys of Saturday morning!) when she heard him calling from the hall.

'Liz?'

'Coming!' She bundled up the dirty sheets along with the socks and underwear lying about the floor and stuffed them into the pillowcases.

'*Liz!*' Not just louder, but *higher*, from a point closer to her. He did that sometimes, foot on the first stair for extra projection.

'I said I'm coming.' She came. Along the landing to the head of the stairs. Stopped. He was actually on the third step. Straight away she saw what it was that had raised him to such a pitch. The application form was trembling with the force of his rage in his right hand. If she had leaned forward far enough she could have grabbed it off him, or at least have had the satisfaction of taking him with her if she fell in the attempt.

'You left this on the table,' he said.

'I left it in my bag.'

'You left your bag on the table.'

'You have no right to go looking in there.'

'I have every right. Whatever's under this roof is ours together.' He closed his fist tighter around the application. 'So are you going to tell me what you think you're playing at?'

'I'm not "playing" at anything.' She pushed past him, forcing him back against the banister. Forget that form, she'd send away for another one. She would send away for as many as it took.

He followed her through the living room and into the kitchen reading aloud. '"I would consider myself suitable for any position although I would prefer something on the assembly side of things..." You're not serious?'

'Why wouldn't I be?'

'Do you know where that factory is?'

'Dunmurry.'

'It's Twinbrook: West Belfast. Remember the last factory to open around there? Remember Grundig? It's not safe.' He paused, big sorrowful lip on him. She knew what was coming. Pete. 'You above all people shouldn't need telling.'

'Oh, Robert, don't.' She hated him using her brother's

memory against her like that. Pete would have hated it too.

'Anyway' – he wasn't prepared to let this go yet – 'what are you going to tell them at the interview? That the nearest you've come to the assembly side of things is pushing two chairs together for the boys to "drive" when they were wee?' He jabbed the heel of his hand in the air in front of her face. 'Beep-beep, Noddy!'

'Stop it, will you. It's not funny.'

The boys came in the back door at that moment from their football, grown men nearly the two of them, to look at, wrapped up in a smell of sweat and mud and Wintergreen rub.

'What's not funny?'

'Remember the wee cars your mum used to make you?'

'In the dinette, you mean? With the chairs?'

'Flip, yeah!'

'Where was it we were always driving to?'

'The McGillycuddy Reeks!'

Robert howled at this forgotten detail. 'Don't forget to tell them that at the interview as well: your car made it all the way to the McGillycuddy Reeks.' In her face again. 'Beep-beep!'

She went to knock his hand out of the way but she was still holding the damned pillowcases. She threw them on the ground at the boys' feet – 'You're big enough now you can pick up your own dirty laundry' – then turned on the tap over the sink, hard, spraying water in all directions.

'Flip sake!'

'Watch what you're doing!'

She turned the water off again, swung round to face Robert.

'You know what I'll tell them if they give me an interview? That it's the first thing that's made me smile in this bloody country for years.'

One of the Americans on the other side of the table was frowning, the older one: hadn't spoken a word yet. 'Smile?' he said now.

'A sports car made in Belfast?' she said. 'Whoever heard of that? And those doors, the way they lift up... The very first time I saw them on TV, I don't know, I couldn't help myself.'

The man's expression changed. He tossed his copy of her application (the second one she had sent away for) on to the table and locked his hands behind his head. Maybe he thought he was a film director. Maybe he thought this was a couch she was sitting on.

'That's as good a reason as I have heard all day, all week in fact.'

'Then there is the engine, of course,' she said.

'The engine makes you smile too?'

'It intrigues me. The position of it, behind the rear wheels, same as the Corvair and the Porsche 356.'

The man unlocked his hands and sat forward again, picking up the application. 'I'm sorry, I didn't get the impression reading this that you were interested in cars.'

'I'm not, or at least I didn't used to be. I'm interested in getting a job.'

'You had it for me on the "smile".'

'I know.' She gave him one in real time, but not for long. 'But I didn't want it on the "smile" alone.'

The other American, the younger one, who had stared at her almost as though he knew her when she came in, made a noise, a snort, she was almost sure, that he tried to pass off as a sneeze. 'Pardon me.' He reached forward for his water glass.

The older man cleared his throat. 'Yes, well, thank you, Elizabeth.'

'Liz,' she said.

'Of course: Liz.'

Randall watched her go. He wanted to say something, he didn't know what. ('I'm sorry if I made you uncomfortable, staring, you remind me of a woman I wish I had slept with'? 'I'm sorry if I nearly laughed, you remind me of *myself*, many years ago, going for an interview'?) Instead as soon as the door was shut Bennington beside him covered his eyes with his hands. 'I must have looked an ass there, but that line of hers, it completely threw me, and then when she started talking about the engine...'

The engine. That totally unforeseen thing that DeLorean had said in the wake of the election was all that could knock the production schedule off course.

Bill Collins had designed the car with a Wankel rotary in mind – no piston engine came close in terms of simplicity and reliability. DeLorean had seemed to concur, even though as things stood there was no realistic prospect of its running on lead-free gas, an ambition carried over from the Safety Vehicle days. As the months passed, though, and the trials progressed, he began to have concerns too about the Wankel's poor fuel economy. It was bad enough not delivering on one of their promises, a car that was kinder to the planet, but not delivering on a second of them by producing a car that hit owners in the pocket as well…?

An engine like the V6, on the other hand, would not only be adaptable down the line to lead-free, but would have the double advantage in the present of being cheaper for the consumer and for the company, which could buy them ready-made from Peugeot. Collins was quick to point out the obvious disadvantage, present and future: weight. The V6 was heavier by far than the Wankel, on which all the calculations up to now had been based. He had put it through its paces at the workshop DeLorean had established in Coventry, England, while the Dunmurry factory was being built and reported back: it wasn't going to work, their Elastic Reservoir Moulded frame wouldn't be able to carry the V6. They were going to have to revert to the Wankel or find another alternative.

Well, something was going to have to be rethought, DeLorean said, that was for certain sure.

The words 'Lotus' and 'Colin Chapman', which had already been in the air for some time – since the days of Geneva and GPD – began to crop up now with ever greater frequency in meetings and memos.

His name might not have been so obviously displayed – a tangle of initials on the company crest was all – but Lotus was as much Anthony Colin Bruce Chapman (to account for those initials in full) as DMC was John DeLorean. He had built his first car single-handedly in a garage in London at the tail end of the forties – while DeLorean was still playing clarinet in the Lawrence Tech band – and graduated from there, a class of one, to selling kits to other enthusiasts, and from there in a handful of years to managing his own Formula 1 racing team. Lotus was not just a company, it was a lifestyle. There were Lotus umbrellas, Lotus jackets and hats, and who knew what else. James Bond had driven a Lotus in his most recent movie – a fact that DeLorean had repeated several times to Randall. 'That's what you would want: your car in a movie. Can you imagine the sales from that? You couldn't build enough of them.'

Randall had met Chapman not long after the announcement of the Dunmurry factory, by chance, or so it had seemed at the time, just coming into a first-class lounge at Heathrow as Randall and DeLorean left the side room they had booked for a meeting, DeLorean's schedule on that occasion not allowing him to come as far as Belfast.

The man could not have been more English if he had come in kit form himself (albeit a little scaled down – DeLorean was a good ten inches taller): Michael Caine hair, David Niven moustache, BBC-newsreader accent, an air, if not quite of entitlement then at least of expectation that all things in time could be bent to his will. He had a big house – a 'Hall', Ketteringham – in Norfolk: five hundred years old, by all accounts. There were workshops in the stables and outbuildings, a superstitious nod perhaps to his kit-car origins, although the main assembly these days was done a couple of miles away at Hethel, on the site of a decommissioned American airbase (something of a theme it seemed with start-up auto manufacturers).

All this Randall learned from DeLorean who visited Ketteringham, and Hethel, with Bill Collins, a few weeks after that Heathrow encounter, Chapman himself piloting the helicopter that picked them up from central London.

'You have to hand it to the Brits,' he told Randall on his stopover in Belfast the following afternoon. 'They know how to do these things properly.'

Lotuses were the cars DeLorean would have built if he had been born in Richmond, Surrey, instead of Detroit, Michigan.

Collins had said little then, even less when the Geneva company was set up with a view to funding a joint research and development unit, housed 'for the time being' in Hethel. It was from that quarter that the suggestion came to abandon the Elastic Reservoir Moulded frame in favour of a solid steel chassis strong enough to cope with the V6 engine. Something like the Lotus Esprit's chassis, say.

DeLorean said they were bound to give the matter proper consideration. Modifications would have to be made, of course, a new prototype built, which would inevitably lead to delays in the production schedule, but if it meant savings in the long term then to dismiss it out of hand would be beyond foolish, it would be 'asinine'. (The word was a new favourite.) Collins remained silent.

When, however, a short time after that Chapman again floated the idea of ditching the remaining ERM elements and using instead a body moulding system that he had patented – Vacuum Assisted Resin Injection – Collins finally flipped. At the rate things were going all that would be left soon of their original concept was the stainless steel panels and the gull-wing doors. 'I love the Esprit,' was the line that fed back to Randall from the showdown in the offices on Park Lane, 'but I didn't join DeLorean Motor Cars to build Lotuses in drag.'

And with that ended the relationship that had started the whole ball rolling. But on the ball rolled anyway.

More and more the focus shifted to Norfolk. Chuck was serving four days of his seven-day-a-week sentence there. If he could have figured out a way to conjure up an eighth day, Randall didn't doubt he would have spent it there too.

The new secretary of state was, according to Jennings, Not Best Pleased by this change of direction. Randall could all too easily imagine it. Humphrey Atkins sighed rather in the way that a bagpipe droned. (At least he did in the presence of DMC representatives, which was all Randall had to go on.) It was the base note on which his voice was an elaboration.

'Look, Edmund,' said DeLorean, 'the secretary of state is a businessman, isn't he?' Randall had it from Jennings that Atkins had married into a linoleum manufacturing family. DeLorean seemed to set rather more store by this than Jennings had perhaps intended. 'He wouldn't need it explained to him: this way we simplify the supply line.'

'Which will ultimately keep the price down?'

'Which will ultimately keep the price from rising too high.'

'What about the letters of offer we have sitting here waiting to go out?' Randall asked.

'Send them. Get the people in and start training them.'

The letter did not arrive until a full two weeks after the interview, long enough for Liz to think that she had handled the interview all wrong – would it really have hurt her to humour that fella a bit more? – and for Robert to have conceded magnanimously that right enough the extra few pounds coming in might have been handy.

She sat at the table in the dinette for most of the afternoon, turning the page over and over to make sure that she had not misread it. Only when she heard the boys come barging in the front door and charge up the stairs to their room did she shake herself and get the potatoes peeled and the leeks washed and chopped. Then she sat down with the letter again, her eye drawn back time and again to the starting salary: the *starting* salary.

Her last pay packet, from the Water Office, had been eight pounds nine and eleven, after deductions. She had started in there as a trainee clerk-typist three weeks after her final O level, had her photo taken for the school magazine, standing in front of the assembly hall with another girl, Paula, who had got a job in the Electricity Board. The utilities – they had been taught it since they were old enough to spell it – were second only to banks in the jobs-for-life stakes. Or jobs for as much of your life as you cared to work.

Robert had been in the Water Office a couple of years already, one of a group of young lads who used to come into the canteen together at lunchtime and carry on with the women behind the counter – 'Put a few more chips on there for me, Myrtle. Ah, go on, I'm a growing boy.'

'He's a fat bastard, he means.'

'Language now, ladies present.'

'Are you kidding? Myrtle could teach *us* words. Couldn't you, Myrtle?'

'I'll teach you a lot more than words.'

And so on.

Liz knew pretty much from the get-go that he had his eye on her – because you do know, don't you? You just know – and tell you the truth she wouldn't have been a bit shy about saying in those days that she was a worthwhile place for an eye to linger. They were married a fortnight after her twentieth birthday, and two months before her twenty-first – one month before the birth of her eldest – she took home her last eight pounds nine and eleven.

The Water Office closed in 1973, its functions taken over by the Department of the Environment and a third of its workers handed their cards. Robert was straight down to the dole office the next morning and within the week had started in the City Hospital's Purchasing and Procurement department. Less money than he had been getting in Water, but he was in somewhere, that was the main thing. A few of those no longer young lads he chummed around with found themselves all of a sudden out in the cold.

He worked, Robert. Whatever else you might have thought of him you couldn't deny that: he worked.

She did not know he was home until he was standing in the kitchen doorway, an expression on his face she could not read. She stood up from the table, letter still in her hand.

'Guess what?'

'You got the job,' he said, flat as you like. 'Good for you.'

He threw the evening paper down on the countertop and spun it round with his hand so that the headline was towards her. Her stomach turned over. *Body Found is German Industrialist.*

'Now tell me,' he said. 'Why would anyone want to set up a factory here except to make a fast buck and get out?'

Randall had been walking along a corridor in the old carpet factory when he caught the name coming from a transistor on one of the secretaries' desks.

He doubled back, put his head round the door. The secretary – her name was June – switched the radio off. 'Sorry,' she said, 'I just put it on to hear were there any traffic hold-ups before I headed home.'

'No, turn it on again.'

She was trying to put the radio back into her drawer. 'It's all right, I've heard what I need to hear, thanks.'

'Please.'

June did as he asked, though her sideways glance at Sandra who sat at the desk next to hers left him in no doubt: he was acting strangely.

The news of course was over, the next programme begun, blandly.

'That story that was on a minute ago, the German man...' He clicked his fingers as though he could conjure it up again.

'Niedermayer?' Now she understood. 'Poor man.'

'Poor wife. Poor kids.' This from Sandra, who was opening the front of her typewriter to get at the ribbon.

'They found him?' Randall asked.

'His remains,' June said and Sandra shuddered.

'Over the border?' That's where they take them all, the security man at the Conway had said.

June blinked. 'No, in Colin Glen.' Randall had seen the name on maps of the area around the factory: a narrow strip of forest park between the housing estates running back from the west towards the city. 'All this time,' June said, 'he was just up the road.'

Just up the road and, Randall discovered later, reading the newspaper at the table set for one in Warren House, buried face down. Seems as though the men who had beaten him around the head with their guns wanted to make sure that even if he did regain consciousness he never found his way out of the hole they had dug for him.

7

The eighteen months were up on 3 February 1980. The cow pasture was long gone. They had a factory with two gates in and out. They had a workforce of getting on for a thousand to enter and leave by them in almost equal proportion. They had, instead of a car in production, a new prototype to ponder.

DeLorean marked the occasion by requesting a further £15 million of credit from the British government.

Which refused, of course, in no uncertain terms. Until Kimmerly drew to its lawyers' attention a clause in the initial letter of agreement that bound the Labour government *and its successors* not to let the enterprise fail, as fail it undoubtedly would if more time – and therefore money – were not committed to the development work at Lotus.

Besides, the British were getting a $370 cut on the first ninety thousand cars produced: thirty-three and a bit millions. (Dollars, not pounds, but still, thirty-three and a bit million of them.) And what about the other jobs that DMCL's presence was attracting? Not a single cent of US investment in the previous seven years and all of a sudden there were thirty companies lined up. LearAvia was already in, north of the city, with – lest anyone forget – fifty million dollars of new, *Conservative* government grants and loans to make components for its Lear Fan executive jet.

Jennings, who needless to say could not let the day pass, or rather, 3 February being a Sunday, let the day after it pass without paying a call was more rueful than raging at finding himself, and the government whose bidding he did, over a barrel.

'You can rest assured that there will be no such clause in the revised letter that accompanies *this* loan. As for Lear Fan, by the way, there is no comparison. It brought rather more of its own money to the table and it won't see a penny of ours unless it gets a plane in the air before the end of this year, which' – not *quite* under his breath – 'might have been a sensible condition to apply in this instance too.'

Maybe he thought those really were gull's wings.

He had walked with Randall around the assembly shop (still sparsely enough fitted out that Randall had broken up a full-scale lunch-hour soccer game only two days before), nodding with what at moments and in another person might almost have been taken for approval. *Well, if you did have £65 million of public money to spend this would not be the worst way to spend it...*

His parting shot, though, was a reversion to type. 'The problem with making unrealistic promises is that even though people know they are unrealistic they are inclined to hold you to them. Until this point the clock has been ticking down. From here on it is ticking away. You know the principle of the away rule, don't you? Everything against you counts double.'

Randall had not the first idea about the away rule, but he understood the import of the metaphor.

To replace it with one of his own: the longer the delay the deeper the shit they were likely to find themselves in.

The only thing he could do was to help keep the preparations here on track, be ready.

The way it was explained to Liz and her co-workers, they had to be familiar with every stage of the assembly process so that in the event of an emergency – 'Armageddon' was the word Mr Bennington had used, and coming from him you could well imagine it – any one of them could stand in for any other, *all* the others, and finish the cars single-handed. ('Because make no mistake,' Bennington said, 'if anything can emerge from Armageddon other than the cockroaches it'll be our cars.') Hence the months, and months, of training.

To begin with they were in the old carpet factory, watching videotapes and live demonstrations, being introduced to the DMC-12 part by part and to the tools they would be using to put those parts together, *tools*, as Liz soon learned, being a term that covered everything from a wire brush to the enormous dies – the size and shape almost of landing craft – in which the fibreglass bodies were to be moulded. A handful of completed bodies were already in circulation for them to practise on. 'Mules' they referred to them as and approached them to begin with as though they might actually get a bite off them or an almighty and unexpected kick.

As the new buildings took shape and more and more of the equipment was installed the workers were walked through them, group tours, two, three times a week: here – the body-press shop – is where those dies would operate in the fullness of time; there – the chamber with concrete piers and desolate air of a concentration camp that never failed to give her the creeps – would be the ovens for curing the bodies for fettling (a good old-fashioned scrub, the task of the wire brushes) and transport by cranes – for the moment hypothetical – to the assembly shop, which was, or would be, a whole other world again.

They had been shown photographs of the Tellus carriers, which were somewhere between a low platform and a species of lunar vehicle, in length and breadth a foot or two bigger than the car bodies they would move around the assembly shop under instruction from a computer. The track that they would run on (Liz remembered the boys' Scalextric, its cars more often off than on) had already been laid down one side of the shop starting at the point where what they called the trim line – all the internal wiring – and the chassis line were to meet and the body and chassis 'mated', a word that, when it came up in the tours, never failed to raise a laugh and a few choice comments: *how many screws does it take...?*

At intervals along the carriers' route other lines would come in at right angles, bringing the engines, the stainless steel panels, those outrageous doors, and finally the seats and the wheels, at which point the car would be transferred on to another contraption – a rolling road (it went nowhere but round on itself) – to test its brakes before the big roller door in the bottom left corner of the shop was raised and out into the world it would go.

Eight minutes' worth of fuel was all that it was to have in its tank, that being to the precise second what was required to take it through the Emissions and Vehicle Preparation shed, whatever that was, once round the test track and up the ramp of the transporter that would carry it to the docks.

Liz learned it like a catechism, recited every night with the prayer that Robert was wrong, that tomorrow or the next day or the next week at the latest they would start and build a bloody car.

Randall was crossing the open ground between the two shops one afternoon when he saw coming in the opposite direction the woman who had said the thing in her interview about the doors making her want to smile. She wore the grey version of the company coveralls, the collar – deliberately he supposed – flipped up. Her hair was held back from her face by a large clip at the crown.

He slowed as she drew closer. 'Liz, isn't it? I'm…'

'Mr Randall, I remember.'

'I don't usually bother with the "mister".'

She nodded.

'So,' he said, because he had stopped now, he had to say something, 'you've been finding your way round all right?'

'Are you kidding? All those walks? I could give other people tours.'

'I've realised the mistake I made when I moved here.'

'You didn't get out walking enough?'

'I didn't have someone to show me around properly.'

She had been looking over her shoulder – they all did it, embarrassed to be seen talking to the bosses – but turned her head again now, sharply.

'Oh, no,' he said, 'I wasn't suggesting...' Which of course made it sound even more as though he had been.

She nodded again, acknowledgement of his clarification or confirmation of her first suspicion, who knew? 'I should probably be getting on here.'

'Yes,' he said, 'you should. I mean, we should. I mean, I should too.'

She was gone before he got the last word out.

He did not sleep properly that night or the next, now telling himself that the fault was entirely hers, that it had been a perfectly innocent remark, making small talk, now wondering who he thought he was fooling: something within him had quickened seeing her walking towards him. Maybe he *had* meant to leave the invitation hanging.

Gossip was what he feared rather than an official complaint. (He was not so paranoid as to think he had stepped that far over the mark.) He was grateful for the inventory that had started to arrive, the clipboard that as often as not he was obliged to carry with him when he ventured forth, checking, reconciling, pushing everything – everyone – else to the periphery. A busy man at a busy time, head down, focused.

A week this went on. No complaint – he had been right about that – but no sense either out the corner of his eye of workers nudging one another as he passed: *did you hear what your man there's supposed to have said...?*

He was standing late one morning genuinely absorbed in the clipboard at the newly connected Tellus control station when he heard a voice.

'Anyone would think you were trying to avoid having to talk to people.'

'Pardon me?'

She was closer to his shoulder than he had anticipated. He had to take a step back in turning to avoid treading on her foot. She held up her hands close to her face in imitation of him.

'No,' he said, 'I was...' What? *Really* looking at it this time? 'Miles away.'

'Well, you're back now.' She had folded her arms. Defensive. 'I just wanted to let you know... the Botanic Gardens are lovely this time of the year. If you wanted to get out and about more, I mean.'

'The Botanic Gardens.'

'Right. Especially on a Sunday morning.'

'Sunday.'

'Right.'

'Thanks.'

'You're welcome.'

* * *

She had no idea what possessed her. She had been on the point of passing him by – he had his nose stuck in paperwork – and then she thought, no, I'm going to say something here and then her mouth was open and instead of giving out to him she was telling him about Sunday mornings in Botanic Gardens.

Absolutely no idea at all.

There had been a shift in the tenor of their training of late, less now about getting to know the ins and outs of every stage of the assembly, more about getting to know one particular task. Hers – whatever it was the people in charge of the training had observed in her in the previous weeks and months – was seats.

Right down at the end of the assembly line. That was where she had been going when she saw your man Randall at the Tellus control station and suffered the rush of blood to her head.

A pair of seats was sitting there waiting for her, positioned as they would be when eventually the computer brought the carrier to a halt, a fully fitted car mounted on top, doors raised.

For now, though, it was mules and anatomy lessons. She had to learn how to take the seat apart and put it back together again. Thirty named parts, some, like the Nyloc nut, its washer and cap screw, in multiples of four per seat. The seat covers were black and made from the hide of she preferred not to think what, so soft was the leather. (She wouldn't have said no to a pair of gloves made out of it, all the same.) Hand-stitched, she was pretty sure. This wasn't work, she sometimes thought, it was a window on another way of living.

Along with the clearly defined role came clearly defined workmates. Taking the seats apart and putting them back together with her were a fella by the name of Anto Hughes and a wee lad, not much older-looking than her own boys, Tommy Cahill, who went by TC.

Liz had never noticed either of them on the way in in the mornings or on the way out again at the end of the day so figured they must be coming and going by the other gate, the Twinbrook one.

'No kidding?' Robert sarked. 'Tommy *Cahill* and *Anto* Hughes and you *think* they might be from West Belfast? Go to the top of the class!'

'God help us,' she said, 'if our names should ever be all that define us.'

She would have put Anto a year or two either side of her – mid to late thirties. Always had a book sticking out of his overalls' pocket, which he would read, sitting quietly off to one side, any time he had a spare moment.

'Jack London,' she said into one such lull, glimpsing the name on the spine. 'I remember getting him out of the library when I was a kid – *The Call of the Wild*.'

He looked at her, she thought a little embarrassed. 'I haven't read that one.'

'There's another one, isn't there, with a dog in it? What's this you call it?'

'I don't know.' He frowned and folded back the cover on the book he was reading, which she saw in that movement was called *The Iron Heel*. A huge black boot for an illustration. She wondered if she had got the right Jack London. She wondered if some of Anto's discomfort was for her, not him.

TC, the morning after the three of them were first teamed together, was late getting in. 'Sorry if I kept you. I had a pass out for an hour there to go up to the Tech for my exam results.'

'Exam results?' Anto said.

'Level Two City and Guilds, Welding and Sheetmetal Fabrication.'

'And?' said Liz.

'I got a merit. I've already put in for my Level Three.'

'Well done.'

Anto made a face. 'Aye, well done, but in case you hadn't noticed they've been turning us into jacks-of-all-trades since we got here. What are you planning on doing with a Level Three City and Guilds in a place like this, or even a Level Two?'

TC drew himself to his full height, six inches shorter than Anto, a couple shorter than Liz, even allowing for the arches of hair rising up either side of his centre parting. 'I'll tell you what I plan on doing – training to be your supervisor, that's what.'

Anto nodded: *sure thing.* 'You in a union, TC?'

'Of course.'

'Which one?'

'Which one, he says,' said TC to the world at large; to Anto, 'Which one do you think? The big one.'

'Well then, man-who-would-be-my-supervisor...' Anto punctuated each word with a light tap on TC's breastbone, 'I'm your union rep.'

Light or not, TC looked like he was about to return the taps with interest until Liz intervened.

'Hold on, you two chiefs, are you telling me I'm the only Indian here as well as the only woman?'

They turned to face her, but before either of them could speak the safety goggles went up on to the forehead of the worker who had been bent over examining a pressurised cylinder a few feet away.

'If it's any comfort, love, I'm an Indian too,' she said.

In fact, as Liz well knew, there was no shortage of women about the place, and not only where you would have expected to find them in other factories: typing letters, answering phones, though mind you even in DeLorean she never saw a man do either of those things. More astonishing still, there were enough cubicles in the toilet blocks (of which there was one about every hundred yards throughout the factory) that she didn't have to stand in a line reaching halfway down the corridor, watching as any amount of men came and went from the toilets next door. They had been prepared for this, in other words, the management. Her and all the other women, they were not here by chance but by right, on equal footing.

* * *

Randall took a call on Thursday evening. DeLorean in LAX. The irresistible lure of the last phone booth before embarkation. 'I am going to be in London this weekend. I was hoping you could meet me... You're not doing anything that can't be dropped, are you?'

What was he going to say? 'Funny you should ask, I was hoping I might take a stroll in the Botanical Gardens.'

'No,' he said, 'not at all.'

He flew over on Saturday morning, later than intended. The flight was delayed due to the cancellation of the previous night's last inbound flight from Heathrow: a regular occurrence in Randall's limited experience. 'Any time there's an emergency on another route they pinch a plane from Belfast,' the woman who took his ticket said with a smile. 'I suppose they think, sure who's going to notice?'

He rang the Ritz from the arrivals lounge. Mr DeLorean had already gone out, but he had left a message to meet at three p.m. in Soho Square.

'Soho Square?' Randall asked. 'What is that? A restaurant?'

'No, it's a park.'

Randall did not think he had ever seen DeLorean out of doors when there was not a factory to be an announced or a car to get into. He was half expecting to find a film crew in attendance, or at the very least a photographer, but instead the only cameras on display in the square ('park' was maybe stretching it a little) were being wielded by tourists arranging others of their party around the plinth of the statue of the man in stockings and wig at its heart, or trying to get an angle on the curious half-timbered building out of which the gentleman on the plinth might have stepped moments before he was petrified and in the lee of which (and not, Randall thought, incidental to the photograph being composed) stood three bona fide London punk rockers, all spikes and studs and sideways snarls.

He had sat on a wooden bench for almost twenty minutes before he spotted DeLorean coming – *walking... alone* – along the narrow street to his right. He was carrying a paper bag under his arm. A book it looked like. 'Instructions from Maur,' he explained as he sat and placed the bag on his lap. He eased the book out part way. Faded blue slipcover, an eight- or nine-line title, of which Randall took in only the words in larger font: *Morris Movement* and *Fiftieth Anniversary.* 'Hard to come by, he tells me, even in New York.'

DeLorean looked about him, filling his nostrils with Soho Square air, nodded, yes, this was exactly how he had he expected it. 'What I like about London is how inconspicuous it lets you be.' He turned a smile on Randall. 'Even the sex shops I passed are discreet compared to Times Square. You could take your grandmother for a walk around here.'

'Without someone trying to buy her off you, you mean?'

They sat a moment or two more. 'What do you know of Lear Fan?' DeLorean said then.

'The plane?'

'The factory.'

Randall shrugged. 'Only what we have already discussed. I

met Moya Lear at a reception a few weeks back. A handshake, nothing more.'

DeLorean's nod this time was slower, shallower. 'I knew Bill better.' Bill Lear had died a couple of years earlier. His wife had made a mission, at an age when most people were thinking of retiring, of seeing his plane through to production. 'Another guy I know, Morgan Hetrick, used to fly people down to parties in his house.' Randall had heard that name Hetrick somewhere before. He must have frowned trying to dredge it up. DeLorean took it the wrong way. 'Oh, it was quite the thing then flying people in for parties. I guess Moya was just never around for Bill's. I sometimes wondered if that wasn't where he got the idea for that little jet of his... Eight guys bouncing down to the Caribbean for the weekend... Or girls...' A sideways glance as he said this then a shake of the head, he was straying from the point: the factory. 'I'm worried that Thatcher has made it her pet project. I was assured she didn't much care for other women, but she seems to have made an exception for Moya. As long as she doesn't try to use her to make an example of me as well, you know: Good American, Bad American.' He straightened the book bag on his lap. 'What I'm trying to say is you are there day to day, you talk to people, they talk to you, anything you pick up that might be of interest let me know.'

'I think you are maybe overestimating my social circle, but OK, I will let you know if anything comes my way.'

They talked a while longer. Maur wanted some more photographs of the house. Dick and Roy were still racking up the dealer numbers: getting on for four hundred now.

Eventually there was a silence. They seemed to have exhausted everything.

DeLorean looked at his watch. 'How's Chuck?' The question – addressed more to his wrist than Randall's face – took Randall almost as much by surprise as the earlier one about Lear Fan.

'Fine,' he said. 'I mean, I hardly see him. You know Chuck, how much he takes on.'

DeLorean breathed in audibly through his nose: he knew all right.

A heavily bearded young man in a plaid work shirt had crouched down beside an olive drab gear bag on the grass about ten yards away. He proceeded to take from it a camera with a hole where the lens ought to have been. The lens came from a separate smaller nylon bag on his other shoulder: four, maybe five inches in length. He wasn't intending to take tourist snaps with it.

DeLorean clapped his hands on his thighs, tucked Maur's book back under his arm. 'Listen, I have another appointment now.' The young man stood as DeLorean did. So there was a photographer after all. 'I would say stick around, but I fear the next half-hour or so will be immensely dull.' It was as though he had forgotten in the novelty of walking that Randall hadn't just strolled down to this square this afternoon too. He leaned a little closer. 'The only thing that keeps me smiling is the thought that if this winds up on a cover it's worth eight million dollars to us in publicity.'

And he smiled, half, shook Randall's hand, and walked

out to do again what he had to do to make the world want his car.

So that was it. He wasn't expected to stay the night. He got about fifty yards down Oxford Street, vaguely intent on the British Museum, when he saw a London cab coming his way, its roof-light lit. He stuck out his arm. 'Heathrow Airport, please.'

There was a traffic accident just beyond the start of the overpass at Chiswick – a 'proper pile-up' the taxi driver called it. 'I hate to tell you, mister, but you ain't going nowhere at this rate.' Randall looked at his watch twice a minute for a quarter of an hour then resigned himself. An ambulance passed on the shoulder, a fire tender, another ambulance. The taxi driver whistled through his teeth, breaking off every now and then to toss a question into the back. Where had Randall been, then, in London? What did he reckon to the food? The weather? Then, 'Hang on', the car in front rolled forward a foot, braked, rolled forward another two, braked before rolling again, and in that stop-start way they covered half a mile in first gear until the flashing blue lights and the tow trucks were all behind them. He made it to the airport minutes before the last flight of the day was scheduled to leave, although as the airline was still making up the time lost earlier in the day he had another hour to wait. It was well past eleven by the time he got back to Warren House. No sign of Bennington.

No sign either the next morning.

Sunday.

Randall decided to take the train. There were so many restrictions on parking – so few secure car parks – he was surprised anyone drove into the city ever. The train halt (it was no more than a couple of benches and a Plexiglas shelter) was less than a fifteen-minute walk, but once there he stood for almost four times as long without seeing a train in either direction. After the twenty-four hours that had preceded it he would nearly have been surprised if it had been otherwise.

Someone had set fire to the post on which the timetable was mounted; vandal or amateur surrealist, the melted glass had a Dali-esque appearance, *The Disintegration of the Persistence of Hope*, perhaps. The instant I walk away a train will come, he told himself for the last thirty minutes of the fifty-five that dragged by before the train finally arrived: two carriages, the first of which was completely empty, for the very good reason – as he discovered before joining the other eight passengers in the second – that it stank of urine.

(No way was that a single person's doing. There had to have been a gang of them: jump on, pee like fury, jump off again... Or sit in the adjoining carriage as though they had never met one another.)

It was one of those days that could turn up in any of the city's seasons: warm for one, cool for another, about average for the other two. The train window offered him an overview of Belfast's pastimes and preoccupations, garden sheds and vegetable patches, succeeded at length by yard walls – soccer goals here and there etched on the bricks, jerry-built pigeon lofts balanced on top or, more precarious still, kitchen chairs angled to catch the sun.

On the opposite side a goods yard piled high with metal beer kegs gave way to a stadium – as inviting in its concrete fastness as one of their neighbourhood police stations – hard by which was a wall entirely covered with a painting of a man in a scarlet coat and voluminous black wig, smiling blandly astride a white, rearing charger.

I think I might have seen a buddy of yours in London yesterday. Looking OK for his age, but maybe a little off-colour in comparison.

A voice came over the speaker at the head of the carriage: the next stop was Botanic Station, Botanic Station was the next stop (twice they said everything, everything, in a different order, they said twice). Eight pairs of eyes watched Randall alight. He had overheard a couple of the contractors building the factory talking once about Americans and their shoes. A dead giveaway, one of them said to the other, you don't even have to wait for them to open their mouths. He looked down at his own. Florsheim Royal Imperial Oxfords. They might as well have been painted with Stars and Stripes.

They carried him, the Oxfords did, along the platform, at the bottom of a steep cutting, thick shrubs overhanging, and up a flight of steps to street level. Past a ticket booth they went then, through a turnstile, and out on to a shabby avenue of nineteenth-century townhouses – about one in two a shop or office, all, this Sunday morning, closed – with trees not so much lining the pavement as interrupting it, angled like arrows fired blind by a giant in one of their old tales.

(*There* was a thing that no one had explained to him, how a people that claimed such heroes in their lineage had come to be burying fathers of teenage girls face down in shallow graves.)

After a moment or two getting his bearings (away from the city centre: so, left), he strolled up the avenue, passing behind what he assumed was the university and into the Botanic Gardens by a narrow side gate, a sign beside it informing him that after five o'clock this evening there was no way out again. He passed a sunken garden, water trickling nearby, a down-at-heel glasshouse – two long wings with a dome at the centre – and a roofed-in man-made ravine, the doors to which, like the doors to the glasshouse, like the doors to the museum they shared the gardens with, were currently chained shut.

All the same, the woman, Liz, was right, it was – they were – lovely. He spent about an hour, until past noon, just sitting on a bench before the glasshouse, arms stretched out along the back, or forward, resting on his knees, watching the people come and go: the young, it seemed, and the very old, and not much in between.

He tried not to let it harden into conviction, but he felt about getting up from the bench what he had felt earlier about walking away from the railway platform with the melted timetable, that it would make happen – and therefore make him miss – the very thing he was waiting there for, though with even less reason for hope in this instance. (She had said it was a nice place to visit on a Sunday morning, that was all.)

As it was when he could wait no longer – could scarcely physically sit another minute – he looked back over his shoulder every third or fourth step until he had reached the little gate once more.

And it didn't happen. And the train would have come when the train did come whether he had stayed on that platform or walked away.

In the middle of the following week DeLorean sent Chuck Bennington to Coventry. The official line was that he was to start work on the development of a right-hand drive model of the DMC-12 – why shut the gull-wing door on a third of the motoring world, after all? His work in Belfast was done. Randall couldn't imagine, though, that Chuck would have chosen to go before the first cars had even come off the line.

Thinking back to the conversation in Soho Square, he was afraid that he might inadvertently have hastened his departure. It was a short step from taking a lot on to taking on too much, spreading yourself too thin. Chuck, however, on the one occasion that their paths crossed in the house after the announcement, appeared willing to shoulder the blame himself.

'We're more than six months behind. Someone has to take the rap.'

But the circumstances, Randall said, the complete overhaul of the design...

'That's what you say to your financiers, but they still

expect to see you make changes. Anyway' – he paused to crush one cigarette and light another – 'John's right, we need that right-hand model.'

A new managing director arrived – straightway: further proof, Randall consoled himself, that the decision had already been made before the conversation in London – a Canadian, Don Lander, who had done time with Chrysler in Africa and the Middle East. Less edgy than Bennington, more communicative. 'I have been brought in to get the cars out, as simple as that,' he told Randall and the other senior staff, gathered in the newly fitted out boardroom. 'And you are here – thank you very much – to make sure I don't fail in the attempt.'

He took Randall aside. 'I understand from John that you have been here from the very start.'

'Practically the only one left,' Randall said, 'now that Chuck has moved on.'

Lander nodded. 'L & L, right? Logistics and Liaison.'

'Right.'

'Would it surprise you to know that some of your colleagues call it Looking and Listening?' He pre-empted Randall's response with a raised hand. 'Whatever works in this business works and from what I can tell whatever isn't working here just now has got precious little to do with you.'

With all this going on, Randall was not exactly in the best of spirits when the end of the week rolled round again. (Did they really think that was what he did? Looked and Listened?)

The steady rain he awoke to on Sunday morning was just the soggy frosting on a rather unappetising cake.

A rabbit – little more than a kitten it looked like – came out of the warren and, ignoring the lure of the plastic bags and discarded cans, raised its twitching nose to the sky and went straight back down the hole again. Randall might have followed its lead and stayed put had he not while searching in an understairs cupboard for batteries for his shaver come across an umbrella, left behind by Chuck – Lotus F1... well, it would have to be, wouldn't it? – and feeling in that instant as though he had been deprived of that particular excuse; in the next was telling himself he ought at least to give the Gardens one more go.

He timed his setting forth this week so that he was on the platform of the local halt a quarter of an hour before the train had arrived last Sunday, in case it might have been running late then. It arrived at the exact same time, the exact same distribution of passengers, even though the urine stench had gone from the carriage in front: Randall checked then sat in the rear one anyway in case the other passengers knew something he did not.

The rain had eased to less than a drizzle – a spit they called it here – by the time he emerged a second time on to Botanic Avenue. He kept the umbrella furled.

As before not a single shop was open. He remembered, though, having noticed a man sitting on a stool at a corner, selling newspapers. They were covered this week with polythene sheets, held in place by a brick. Randall bought the *Sunday*

Times – the thickest newspaper the man had – and when he had arrived at his spot in the Gardens took out the sections he had no interest in reading and laid them on the wet bench.

Lander's arrival as managing director was accorded a single paragraph – little more than a press release (the hand of Bill Haddad?) – on the bottom left of a front page dominated by more horror stories from inside the prisons. (Women prisoners in Armagh had added menstrual blood to the palette of dirt on their cell walls.)

He had been sitting for less than ten minutes when Liz appeared. One moment she wasn't there, the next moment she was. She wore a fawn-coloured raincoat, darker at the shoulders, the belt's keeper lapping itself, tucking in finally above her left hip. He could imagine its having been given a determined yank.

'I wasn't expecting you,' he said and thought that he meant it.

'I wasn't expecting me either,' she said and sounded as though she thought she meant it too.

He handed her the sports pages. A moment. 'Thank you,' she said then. She folded the pages, smoothed the seat of her raincoat and sat.

'My mother lives just over the river,' she said and nodded, sideways, in the direction of the sunken garden and – apparently – eventually – the river and its far side. 'I take a stroll here the odd Sunday on my way over to see her, get my strength up.'

'Is she very old?'

'Sixty-three, but to hear her you would think she was a hundred.'

They were both taking pains, now that there were only inches between them, to look dead ahead. A dog trotted by with a stick in its mouth, head jerking from side to side, looking for whoever had thrown it.

'Do you still have your parents?' she asked.

'In a manner of speaking. They separated when I was six. I haven't seen too much of my father since.'

'And if you don't mind me asking, have you...?'

'Children of my own? A little girl. Tamsin.'

'Nice name.'

He shrugged. 'It wasn't my choice. Very little to do with her life has been. Her mother and I mainly communicate through lawyers.'

'Carrying on the family tradition.' Now she did turn to look at him directly. 'Sorry, that came out the wrong way.'

'Believe me, I have wondered about it myself.'

Something caught her eye. His followed. The dog again, passing in the opposite direction, faster than before, head jerking more frantically. A church bell rang. Liz stood.

'I had better get going.'

'So soon?'

'Siegfried!'

'I beg your pardon?'

She had clamped a hand to her mouth. 'When we were at school, any time anyone said "so soon" we all shouted "Siegfried!" He was a poet we studied. Siegfried Sassoon.

First World War.' She handed him the sports pages. Warm. 'There you go, don't say you didn't learn anything.'

'Another couple of Sundays I'll be ready for my Literature paper.'

'No, I mean learn anything about me.'

8

Since his arrival in Belfast Randall had not made it back home for more than three or four days at a stretch. That Christmas he managed five. As before it took him the first couple to adjust to *not* seeing soldiers, and cops in body armour, at every turn. More than once he was bawled out by people trying to get in the door behind him after he stopped in the entrance to a store for a search that never materialised. Mark Chapman had shot John Lennon outside the Dakota two weeks before, since when another seventy or eighty men, women and children had been shot, stabbed, strangled or otherwise done to death in New York City. There had in that time in Belfast been a single killing. He was at a loss for how to explain the difference to people. It was not just a question of comparative size for, even allowing for that, New York was ten times more deadly. Something to do instead with the unpredictable nature of the violence, the daily – or at least weekly – reminders that for all the searches in shop doorways, for all the cops in body armour, the soldiers on round-the-clock patrol, there was no guaranteed safe zone. Coffee-jar bombs. Maybe that was what it came back to. Maybe that was all he needed to say. Coffee-jar bombs.

He got to spend three hours of Christmas Eve with Tamsin, who was turning out to be a better kid than he and Pattie had a right to hope after the way they had conducted themselves, were still conducting themselves.

Pattie made him wait on the sidewalk by the car until she released Tamsin on to the porch. He barely even saw his ex-wife's face. Tamsin seemed not to know at first what to do with her feet with so much path to cover. About halfway down she decided to skip.

Randall wrapped her in his arms. 'What would you like to do?' he asked her. 'See a movie?'

He was thinking maybe *Popeye*.

'I'm good just going for a ride and talking,' she said and for a minute or two afterwards he didn't trust himself to say anything in case she took his laughter the wrong way.

Not that she seemed to notice. Whatever spaces he left she filled with her chatter, about school mostly, complicated stories involving groups – 'tables' she referred to them as – named after forest animals and losing good-behaviour acorns because Nate (his name came up a lot) kept making a sound with his hand in his armpit and saying it was someone else, and not their armpit either.

They stopped for a soda. (He remembered as he always did now his first time asking for one in Belfast, the shop assistant directing him to a bakery down the street where his request was this time rewarded with a triangular bread loaf, an inch and a half thick.) The Ronettes were singing, 'I Saw Mommy Kissing Santa Claus'. Tamsin frowned. Here it comes, he thought. 'What is it?' he asked.

The frown deepened. 'Will this ever happen again?'

'Us, you mean? Together?' This wasn't what he had expected at all. 'Of course.'

'No,' she said, 'will I ever pick this soda in this diner, with that song on the radio?'

He laughed. 'Well, not the exact same soda, no, because you already have most of it finished...'

'Will anybody else?'

He tried to find a form of words that would console her, for he knew now that what she was grappling with could not be laughed away. 'Maybe some day you will be somewhere else and you will lift a soda or hear that song and it will be like you are right here again, like we are, together.'

'OK,' she said, as though it was just as suddenly a matter of no importance, and leaning forward to her straw, drank.

He *must* get back here, before she was grown up entirely.

He had bought her a ballet-dancer doll with straps to go over her feet and hands so that they could dance together, face to face, or face, judging by how much his daughter had grown, to somewhere between breastbone and chin. (He had never watched it, so couldn't say for sure, but he had a feeling anyway that face to face was not the way the actual ballet worked.) He took the box out of the trunk, wrapped, when they arrived back at Pattie's place.

'I'm not supposed to open my presents until tomorrow,' Tamsin said.

'That's all right. Take it in and put it under the tree.'

Tamsin looked at it a little doubtfully. How was she even going to pick it up?

'Don't worry,' he said, 'I'll carry it for you.'

She looked over her shoulder at the door. Pattie must have been as precise to her as she was to Randall in her rehearsal of the arrangements. 'I'll just set it on the porch for now,' he said, and she nodded. That would do.

He leant it in the end against the doorframe while he rang the bell then pulled his daughter to him for one last hug. 'Happy Christmas,' he whispered.

The screen door did not open until he was safely in his car once more. A hand ushered Tamsin inside and then a second later the girl came out again, pointing at the package and behind her a man Randall had never seen, dressed in white-T and sweatpants and moccasin slippers. He tucked the box under his arm and turned to look down the path straight at Randall, raising his hand in a no-hard-feelings way, before letting the door swing to again.

The previous day Randall had joined some of the DMC New York staff for drinks in the Waldorf Astoria, on the other side of Park Avenue from two-eighty. Haddad was there and Marion Gibson, the English woman who for the past while had been in overall charge of what she liked to refer to as the 'front of office' operations. It was the first time Randall had been in their company without DeLorean being there.

He had left town earlier that afternoon. 'Cristina and I are taking the kids to the ranch for the holidays,' he explained to Randall. (The face of Jim Hoffman floated across Randall's mind's eye. He blinked it away. If that's what went with a ranch they were welcome to it.) 'If next year goes the way I'm expecting it will it might be the last chance we get to be all together for a while.'

Haddad was one of those guys, whatever the subject, he knew more than anyone else around the table. If he hadn't seen it or done it himself he had learned it from the Kennedys. He interrogated Randall about Belfast, about the factory, about Warren House. Seemed there was no end to his curiosity, or his antipathy. He had something against Roy Nesseth, something even greater than he had against Maur Dubin, whose 'excesses' – to say nothing of his access – were in danger of making DeLorean a laughing stock among CEOs: apricot carpet, indeed!

Disliking Roy of course was not unusual, although in Haddad's case Randall got the impression that he believed Roy was standing in the way of his elevation to a position of greater (and rightful) authority. I mean, he, Haddad, had worked for the Kennedys, the United Nations Peace Corps. What had Roy ever done except hustle people into spending more than they had intended on their new cars and accepting less than they had hoped for on their old ones? (There had been another complaint, from Wichita, an elderly couple had signed a blank lease form on the understanding that the terms they had agreed in the lot would be written in. They weren't.

They said. Roy said he would see them in court sooner than pay them the $9000 they were claiming he had overcharged.)

'Who would you rather have going in with you to a meeting with the British government?' Haddad said.

It was a long couple of hours.

Truth be told, he had spent happier Christmases. Not even much in the way of snow to help create the mood. All in all they had had a pretty easy time of it the past couple of winters. Every cab driver he had while he was in town said the same thing: they were due a really bad one some year soon.

In Belfast too – it was no surprise on his return to learn – it had been mild for the time of year.

He had not been back at work more than a few hours, the bulk of them spent with Don Lander in Lander's office, a sort of 280 Park Avenue debrief, when the devil he had so far avoided talking of (talking of how *he* had been talked of), Nesseth, rang.

'Clear the third week of January,' he said, loud enough that Randall could hear him without Lander removing the receiver from his ear.

'And a very good morning to you too, Roy,' said Lander. 'Third week of January... Can I ask what for?'

'That's when we are unveiling the first Dunmurry-made DMC-12.'

'I would *hope* it would be ready by then.'

'No, it will be. John is coming that week.'

Lander had covered the mouthpiece with his hand. 'Did you know about this?' he hissed. Randall shook his head.

'Don, are you listening?' Roy asked.

Lander took his hand away. 'I'm listening all right.'

'We're just making final arrangements with press on this side. I'll get back to you with an exact date.'

'I await that with interest.'

'Oh, and tell Randall to book into a hotel for that week. Or better still leave the booking open-ended.'

'He's standing right here,' Lander said. 'Why don't you tell him yourself?'

'That's fine,' Randall called towards the phone and Roy hung up.

A half-hour later, by which time Randall was back in his own office, DeLorean himself rang.

'I'm sorry about Roy,' he said, a little wearily. 'Carole told me she was in his office when he was speaking to Don. I didn't know he was going to take it upon himself to call. We had only finished talking and I was going straight into another meeting...'

'No apology needed. Like Don said, I just hope we are going to be ready by then.'

'I have every confidence in you all. And thank you, by the way, for agreeing to move out for a while. It's probably time anyway we tried to find somewhere more permanent for you.'

Randall's shoulders slumped. 'I thought maybe once production started I wouldn't be needed here any more.'

'Oh, sure, when I say *permanent* I'm talking about the end of this coming year.' Twelve months of Randall's life – of Tamsin's – accounted for just like that. 'It's just I'm thinking

I'm going to be spending a lot more time at Warren House myself from now on.'

There was a big meeting called in the body-press shop the first day back after New Year. Managers and union reps shoulder to shoulder at the front. Anto, at the near end of the line to where Liz stood, had had a haircut over the holiday. Short back and sides, possibly DIY. Randall – next to Don Lander – was almost dead centre. It was odd. She knew now his forename was Edmund but she did not think she had once called him by it, nor could she imagine the circumstances in which she ever would.

Liz hadn't seen him since the Sunday before Christmas. He looked, she thought, a little jaded. Who knew what he had been up to over there.

(She had *Saturday Night Fever* in her head. The trailer. Robert hadn't liked the look of it when they caught it before *Jaws 2*, and there was no way, once she had seen the age of the ones in queues outside it, she would have gone on her own.)

Lander started by wishing them all a happy and prosperous 1981. He told them how much he appreciated their patience all these months – their patience and their *application*. It was no easy thing to keep putting in the effort when there was so little that you could point to and say, 'See? *I* did that.' He wanted to ask them though to apply themselves with renewed vigour. These next few weeks were going to be the most important yet. All this equipment they saw around them would have to be tested and retested. All the routines they had rehearsed would have to be rehearsed a few times more. On 21 January the doors at the end of the shop next door would open and a DMC-12 would be driven out. He didn't think it was too much of an exaggeration to say that the eyes of the world would be on it, and them.

She was held up getting home that night. A lorry abandoned under the M1 bridge by Black's Road was the word that filtered down her bus. (Some day someone would give the bombers and abandoners of lorries and cars jobs in the roads department. They knew the network and its stress points better than anybody else.) After twenty motionless minutes outside the Speedy Cook on Kingsway she cracked and got off. Avoiding the bridge, she walked halfway up Dunmurry Lane then hoicked her leg over a low wire fence and climbed a clay embankment into the wood. Robert would have a fit. She would have a fit herself if it was one of the boys attempting it in the dark. Except it wasn't absolutely dark. Lights were still burning in the school on her left and, a little further off to the right, she could see through the trees – thinner than she remembered them – glimmers from the streetlamps at the back of her estate. It was no distance between the two, she told herself. The assembly shop, for goodness sake, was longer. Even so her heart when she emerged on to the playing fields on the other side was thumping. She wouldn't be doing that again in a hurry.

The car was already in the driveway when she turned into the street. She hoped Robert or the boys had had the wit to turn on the potatoes while they waited for her.

Her shoes were caked in orange mud. She went round to the back door and kicked them off on the step. Give them a wipe with a sponge later. No one would be any the wiser.

The glass in the door and in the window next to it was steamed up. She pulled open the door, into the kitchen, and the heat wrapped itself round her face like a wet facecloth. One of the three of them had turned on the potatoes all right, but whichever one it was had forgotten to turn them off again when they came to the boil. The lid was half off. She lifted it with a tea towel bunched in her hand. Mush.

Chumps.

She was turning from the cooker to the living room door when Robert opened it from the other side.

'Do you know anything about this?' he asked and pushed the door right back.

The boys were on their hands and knees on the floor, surrounded by cardboard and Styrofoam packaging, examining a twenty-four inch colour television as though trying to divine the magic of the Big Box of Moving Pictures. (It's called electricity, boys. Try plugging the thing in.)

'They told me they weren't able to deliver it till Saturday,' Liz said, though she had to work at the accompanying scowl. It was a beautiful set. Top of the range.

'Here, look at this!' One of the boys had unearthed a remote control and was holding it flat across both palms. His brother reached out a hand, withdrew it again without making contact.

He whistled through his teeth.

Robert sucked saliva through his. 'Do you not think you should have talked to me first? What are the rental payments, a brand new set like that? You don't even know yet if that place of yours is going to last.'

'Look on the bright side, why don't you? Anyway, there are no payments. I bought it' – his brows knitted before she could get to the end of her sentence – 'in the sale at Gilmore's, half price. It was to be a surprise... Next week? Our anniversary?'

There was another whistle of wonderment from the explorers on the living room floor. 'Ceefax as well... We'll be able to check the football scores.'

Robert stared, trying, she would have sworn, to find something, anything, to be annoyed about. 'I'm going to get washed,' he said at last.

'Can we put it on?' the boys asked as one over their shoulders. They had clearly located the plug.

'You can get into the kitchen and peel some more potatoes for me,' said Liz, her eyes on the door Robert had walked out of. 'Both of you.'

As Randall was leaving Warren House on the afternoon before the day appointed for the unveiling, the landscape gardeners were arriving. Two middle-aged men in tan bib overalls and – her hair hidden under a tweed newsboy cap – a very short young woman who, he quickly realised, was running the show. She directed the men to take two bay trees from the back of their flatbed truck and place them either side of the front door, then knelt herself before the first of the trees, a roll of red satin ribbon in one hand, a pair of scissors in the other, and before Randall's car was even halfway down the drive had the first bow fashioned and attached.

He checked into the Conway again, into his old room. (He was touched that they had remembered.) The residents' dining room was full of journalists ahead of tomorrow's ceremony. The bar – all the bars – fuller still. Randall kept his head well down. Time enough for all that hoop-la in the morning. He went instead for a wander around the grounds after dinner, arriving eventually at the security barrier at the front gate. A guard stepped out of the hut. Tall, well built. Not one of the men he remembered. No more was the man who remained inside, turning the pages of a magazine. Even the uniform looked different.

'New company has the contract now,' the guard said in answer to his first question, and in answer to his unfinished second – 'The guys who use to work here...?' – 'You're asking the wrong person, mister. All's I do is raise and lower the barrier and look in the car boots.'

Randall offered him a cigarette.

'Don't touch the things,' he said and went back into the hut leaving Randall looking across the road at the cottages and their giant concrete offspring, gaudy with lights and TV screens.

The afternoon of that same day Liz and her workmates had had their final walk-through, starting up at the entrance to the assembly shop from the body-press shop. Bennington used to conduct the tours himself sometimes, before his sudden departure. Randall had filled in once, much to his obvious discomfort, and hers. She missed the name of the guy who was doing it today, but he was one of their own, stepping up, *acting* up, half taking the pee out of it, half hiding behind the Americans' manner of speaking.

'Right, let's see who has been paying attention on our little excursions,' he began. 'The cranes bring the bodies through here to the assembly shop...' He pointed to a man in the front row. 'How many square feet?'

'Me? Um...'

'Too slow: two hundred and seventy-two, six and a quarter acres. So, bodies come in, are lowered on to the trim line here, trim being the polite word for the viscera, the guts, all those wires that give civilians the heebie-jeebies when they look behind the dashboard... Pardon me, the *dash*.' He – they – had reached the far end of it as he talked and now wheeled right, round the corner of the parts' shelves that flanked the trim line. 'Round here is the...' He pointed at the same man again.

'The, ah, chassis line.'

'More like it: the chassis line. The end of the chassis line to be exact, where the chassis, all nicely "dressed", is placed on one of these...'

'Tellus carriers,' the man said without waiting to be asked.

'Now you're just showing off... and is carried to where the trimmed body waits to be – ahem – mated with it.'

Cue the sniggers. The guide raised his voice above them. 'I cannot promise you that heavenly choirs will sing, but I can promise that if that body and that chassis do not meet at the time prescribed all hell will break loose. Am I right or am I right?'

'You're right!' the group chorused.

'Good. The chassis and the body, now forever joined, are guided by the miracle of computers on the most important part of their journey. He had stopped next to a double-decker rack of stainless steel panels, or skins. 'The doors get all the press, but you know and I know the stainless steel skins are what make the DMC-12 the DMC-12. Guaranteed rust-proof for...?' He cupped his hand behind his right ear.

'Twenty-five years!' came the cry. They were starting to enjoy themselves.

Your man nodded, satisfied. 'One quarter of a century. So, skins there, then doors here, then all that remains is the seats and the wheels...'

'Here, less of the "all that remains",' shouted Anto, a little to Liz's left.

The guide acknowledged the justice of his complaint with a raised hand and a bowed head. 'Correction, after that there follows the vitally important task of fitting the seats and wheels, then the car is placed on the rolling road, its brakes tested, its headlights aligned, and off on out the doors it goes – to what is no concern of yours. In fact, from the moment you walk through that factory gate in the morning, whichever gate it is you walk through, you don't have to worry about anything...'

The chorus now became a sing-song. This was an old favourite: 'No green, no white, no orange, no red, no white, no blue. We are the independent state of DeLorean, our wages are DeLorean wages, our conditions are DeLorean conditions.'

The guide held up a finger, straight as a baton. 'As long as you keep getting fibreglass bodies in one end of this building and DeLorean motor cars out the other.'

They applauded, him for his performance, themselves for their contribution and for what they were about to do together.

'OK,' he said – he was Jimmy Cagney now, all twitching lip and jittery hands – 'tomorrow we make cars.'

9

Randall left the Conway a couple of minutes short of half past six. The scaffolders were already onsite when he reached the factory, laying out the metal poles for the temporary bleachers – grandstand as they preferred here, if a structure with a mere twenty-four seats could be thought of as grand (as opposed to some of the people who would sit in it). Before it was quite eight o'clock half a dozen outside-broadcast units – ranging in size from VW van through three-axle fixed-body truck to giant semi-trailer – were parked in the loading bay at the side of the assembly shop, thick black cables running from them into a generator provided gratis along with the constant supply of tea and coffee and triangles of toast brought from the canteen by Peggy, who once upon a time had stuffed cuddly toys in the pram factory.

(Did the people in the vans and trucks thank her, or him? They did not.)

Jennings showed up an hour ahead of schedule, looking as ever as though he had dressed according to strict civil service guidelines, right down to the size of the bow on his shoelaces.

Behind him came an advance party of the RUC, bringing with them a pair of Labrador detection dogs, one golden, one black, who were let off their leashes to run around a while, ears up, tongues wagging, noses to the ground, before being called to heel again. In went the tongues, down went the ears.

'I sometimes think I would like to leave something very small for them to find, they look so disappointed,' said Jennings, as the handlers coaxed the dogs into their van.

They were no sooner away than the VIPs began to arrive, or the PIPs at any rate – the pretty important people: the industrial developers, the local political party leaders, doing their level best to be seen to be ignoring one another, a couple of lords lieutenant, Colin Chapman, accompanied by a woman half a head taller and a decade and a half younger, who did not answer to any of the descriptions Randall had heard of Chapman's wife.

Another thirty minutes and a convoy of Land Rovers came through the gates with, at its centre, two long black cars. Jennings made straight for the first as it pulled up, Randall for the second, the two of them opening the doors almost simultaneously.

Humphrey Atkins stepped out of Jennings's car then turned to offer his hand to a woman with the longest neck that Randall – from whose car no one had yet emerged – had ever seen. The press corps as good as ignored her, as they had ignored her husband before her, but as the first size sixteen black chain loafer was belatedly planted on the ground next to where Randall stood they made a sudden and determined charge.

John Zachary DeLorean – for he seemed on this occasion to emerge in three distinct stages – finished unpacking himself from the car (however he *packed* himself his suits never creased) and was followed in one fluid movement by Cristina, towards whom every camera and microphone now pointed.

'Mrs DeLorean, if you would... this way... please... Mrs DeLorean!'

'How are you enjoying Belfast?'

'Had you time for an Ulster fry on the way from the airport?'

Cristina merely smiled, which appeared from the absence of further questions to satisfy the journalists for now.

A few yards to the left Mrs Atkins maintained her smile too in case it was needed any time soon. Randall rather suspected it would not be.

DeLorean dipped his head towards him on his way to shake the secretary of state's hand.

'All set?'

'All set.'

DeLorean squeezed his upper arm.

Don Lander, who had met up with the DeLoreans in London the night before, got out of the car last and least noticed. 'Well I got to the bottom of the choice of launch date,' he told Randall. 'Seems Sonja thought this was the most auspicious day.'

Randall looked at him blankly.

'Cristina's palm-reader,' Don said. 'And there I was thinking it was the interior designer.'

All through the morning they had listened to the crowd gathering on the other side of the assembly shop doors. People returning from outside brought updates – 'The sniffer dogs are here...' 'There's fellas out there speaking German and all sorts' – and questions – 'Anybody know what CNN stands for...?' 'Who's the woman with your wee man Chapman...?'

Liz had a distant memory of a Girl Guide Concert – dear God: *1959* – she and her fellow Guides taking it in turns to sneak a peek through the church hall's dusty black curtains: *What can you see? What can you see?* Then, as now, when show time finally came it took them all a little by surprise, as though the reason for all that activity out front had temporarily slipped their minds. Then it was chords bashed out on the ancient piano; now it was a sound as of the whole factory being kick-started.

They turned their backs en masse on what was happening beyond the doors and strained to see the crane bring the first of the fettled bodies through from the pressing shop and set it, beyond the sightlines of those at Liz's end of the chain, on to the trim line. There was an enormous cheer from that direction, modulating into a buzz – workers combining, talking one another through the tasks in hand – which after a time yielded to something more querulous, something indeed very like a grumble, punctuated finally by a single ringing cry, 'What the *fuck*?'

Anto gave TC a boost and he clung to a pillar long enough to report that it looked as though there might be a ruck. A fella from the engine-dress line had already been despatched to find out more and returned breathless a few minutes later (the clamour had subsided a little) with word that the skins didn't fit – 'curling like the lids of sardine cans', was what he had been told – and that the Tellus operators had been desperately trying to override the settings on the carrier, which kept wanting to move it on to the next stage. People were practically standing with their backs against it, others spreading themselves against the skins to keep them flat, and then some wee man from Rathcoole had produced a fistful of penny washers from his overall pocket (no one asked what he was doing with so many on his pocket to begin with) and started replacing the standard issue washers, or in some cases just firing the penny washers on over the top of them. They seemed to do the trick: the lids were back on the cans. Now fellas from all the sections were running to the stores looking for buckets of penny washers.

'So,' Anto said. 'What are you waiting for, TC? Go and get us a bucket of washers.'

'Me go? You go!'

'Forget it, I'll go,' Liz said and would not hear then of them not letting her.

It was as she was making her way back, slowly (who knew there was so much weight in a bucket of washers?), that the word started going round that DeLorean and his wife had arrived – the secretary of state and his wife too – which would have accounted for the sudden competition again from noise without.

Liz set down the washers, with an inadvertent thump, between her and Anto. The Tellus carrier was moving again, past the doors section now, heading straight for them.

'My palms are sweating,' Liz said.

Said TC, 'My cheeks are.'

'What way's that to talk?' said Anto and seemed to shift uncomfortably inside his own overalls.

And then there it was in front of them and there they were at last, the three of them, hoisting the first of the black leather seats, their tools, the galvanised bucket of washers, and immersing themselves in the interior.

'Wait a second... Wait a second.'

'Watch! No, lift that... A bit higher... A bit higher... Whoa! Whoa! *Whoa!*'

'Where's this supposed to...?'

'Look: down there. Remember?'

'Do you want me to hold it for you?'

'Quick, chuck us a couple more washers.'

'The torque, the torque! Use the torque wrench!'

And, almost before they had time to think, they were out and the car had moved on. For the life of her she couldn't remember the second seat even going in. A couple of minutes after that it was through the wheels section too and up on the ramp for fuelling. (One third of an imperial gallon those eight minutes amounted to. They would have been better off with a dropper than a pump.) There had been talk of Jackie Stewart or Stirling Moss coming to drive the first car out, or even – they should be so lucky – James Hunt. Instead that honour went to one of the test drivers, Barry, Liz thought it was you called him, who walked to the car like the astronauts at Cape Canaveral to their rockets, that same expression on his face of anticipation mixed with dread. As he got in, left side, to the driver's seat, TC and Anto were running to help open the roller doors.

DeLorean stepped up to the microphone, to the right of the grandstand, as though – Randall had observed it before – he moved through a different medium, or was being shot on a different speed, to everyone around him. He had never looked more impressive, his hair spun, you would almost have thought, from the same guaranteed rust-free stuff that sheathed the cars that bore his name. And as for his jaw... it was his conductor's baton, his wand, wherever it pointed there was a reaction, a jumping to attention, a rush of colour to the cheeks, an instant abashed smile.

'Mister Secretary of State' – forget the syllables now: every letter nearly was drawn out to a sentence in its own right – 'Missis Atkins, Distinguished Guests, Members of the Local and International Press, Friends and Well-wishers...' From somewhere at his back there came a muffled thud. His eyes flicked towards Don, then Randall, but he carried on without noticeable hesitation and only a fraction louder than before, '... Ladies and Gentlemen. Thirty years ago, when I was a young man just beginning to make my way in the automobile industry...'

Don being too close to the dignitaries and the cameras that were trained on them, and too far from the source of the thud (for that was what the rapid movement of the eyes had signified: go, one of you), Randall backed slowly towards the assembly shop and, avoiding the main doors, ducked inside. It took him several moments to make sense of what he was seeing.

The car was wedged at an angle between the door pillar and the wall. The test driver stood, hands gripping fistfuls of his hair, at the centre of a crowd of horrified workers.

'The brakes just weren't responding,' he said.

'But we tested them,' said the man at his left shoulder, practically in tears. Randall was not far off joining him.

The test driver's hands tightened their grip, pulling his features into a dreadful grimace. 'They weren't responding. I was pressing and pressing, and nothing... nothing at all.'

'We're fucked,' somebody said. Randall glanced round at him. One of the union leaders. Always had a book with him at meetings. He was looking straight at Randall, who was thinking in that moment *Don*, and how to get him away from those cameras out front without alerting everyone that there was a problem.

Oh, Christ was there a problem.

'Wait,' he said and turned to the driver. 'There are still a couple of those mules around, aren't there? Steering wheels and all already inside? Go and get one of them. And, here' – this to the workers gathered round looking instantly a little less horrified – 'get the skins off this.' He leaned over the hood to have a look at the damage. The licence plate at least was salvageable: DMC1. 'And the licence plate too. Time and a half for everyone if you can get a car out of here in the next quarter of an hour!'

Liz was the first to respond. Not a flicker as she rushed past him. Too focused.

He slipped out the side door again.

DeLorean was still on his feet, still talking (he had only just left the fifties behind for the thrill that was his *first* Car of the Year, the 1960 Tempest), his instinct and his experience telling him that if something was not going right there was every chance it was going very wrong indeed, but telling him too that the best people to deal with it were almost certainly already on the other side of the doors. What else was all the training for?

Randall, ignoring the frown Jennings turned his way, placed himself in DeLorean's line of vision. He showed him the fingers of both hands then of the left hand alone. As before there was barely a pause, although maybe a careful observer would have seen his jaw jut out a fraction further. Fifteen minutes? He could do that. And how. From the Tempest to the GTO – a generous word for Bill Collins, in absentia, who had been part of the Pontiac too, a nod to Ronnie and the Daytonas, who had taken 'this modified little Pon-Pon' to the top of the Pop Charts as well as the auto sales charts – from the GTO to the GM kiss-off (here lightly done: this was not a day for recrimination), to the Vision that had guided him this past seven years and more... Randall could have flashed him a half dozen more handfuls of fingers and the store would not have been exhausted.

On fourteen and a half minutes, though, the mechanism controlling the assembly shop doors kicked in.

'But now, ladies and gentlemen' – you would have thought, so seamless was the transition, that the opening of the doors had been timed to fit his words and not the other way about – 'this is the moment they told us we would never live to see, the moment they told us we were mad to dare *dream* we would live to see, and the moment that, but for the faith of my wonderful wife Cristina' – she pressed a knuckle beneath each eye in turn – 'I might even have got to thinking once or twice myself I was mad to dream I would live to see.' Never more impressive, never more vindicated. 'I present to you all...' A final dramatic pause, or a catch in the throat, 'the DMC-12 sports car.'

Randall uncrossed his fingers to join in the applause, which grew as the doors opened wider then, as the nose appeared (complete with licence plate), lost the run of itself completely. People were whooping and hollering, Irish people, *British* people. The press were whooping and hollering loudest of all. The secretary of state put his hand to his tie, patting the knot, when it seemed from his expression as though what he wanted to do was yank the thing loose or tear it off altogether.

The test driver was steering (hair again smoothed flat), but the engine was silent. The power instead was being provided by the six workers pushing from behind.

'It's basically held together with washers and duct tape,' one of them told Randall out the corner of his mouth. 'There's bits of wood and all sorts in there.' But that was not how it looked at all. The gull-wing doors lifted and every person present smiled.

'You will excuse us if we don't start the engine,' DeLorean said, though it was doubtful that many heard, 'but this is a high-performance car and with so many of us gathered this morning space is maybe a little tighter than is strictly advisable.'

Jennings materialised at Randall's shoulder. 'For a moment when he was spinning us those yarns about Johnny Carson and Sammy Davis Jr I thought he was going to hit us with another delay.' But even as he was saying this DeLorean was inviting the secretary of state and his wife to come closer – to get inside – and Jennings was forced into an undignified shuffle to take Mrs Atkins's bag, which he held as a man might a severed head that had been thrust into his hand, at arm's length, by the hair, that is to say the straps.

Liz sat on the toilet with her head firmly between her knees. It was the only way she could think of to keep her legs from shaking.

Jesus, they had got away with it.

For the past half-hour, since the dressed-up mule had been pushed out the front, she had been waiting for the doors of the assembly shop to burst open again and every cop standing guard outside to come charging in and arrest the lot of them for fraud.

Jesus, Jesus, Jesus.

She squeezed out an excuse for her occupation of the cubicle, hitched up her overall, and flushed. She opened the door and almost closed it again straight away.

Cristina Ferrare was standing at one of the sinks, a small make-up bag balanced, open, between the taps.

She looked up into the mirror, meeting Liz's eyes next to the half-closed door, after which of course Liz had no option but to open the door fully and carry on out to the sinks. (If only she had been a man she could have headed straight for the exit. As Robert said to her once when she called him on it, 'It's not as if we hold the end of it or anything.') She chose a sink two along on the exit side. Cristina Ferrare did not look round, or track her walk, but examined her own reflection for signs of imperfection and incredibly found one, high on her left cheekbone. She went at it with powder from a deep-red tub. Liz concentrated on the action of soaping her hands, folding them over one another, interlocking fingers and thumbs, thumbs and fingers, rinsing them then, thoroughly. Anything to avoid having to meet herself in the mirror, having to make the comparison.

She turned off the tap, shook the excess water into the basin then turned, hands aloft, to the roller towel. Pull a yard, dry, dry, dry, pull a yard again for the person after you.

She watched her feet as they tiptoed towards the door. She saw them stop, as though the decision to speak came from them.

She faced about.

'Don't mind me asking, but he's serious about this, isn't he?'

Cristina Ferrare paused in the act of returning a brush to a bottle of lip gloss. Only her eyes moved, a slight frown forming above them as they sought out Liz's a second time in the mirror.

'Pardon me?'

'Your husband, Mr DeLorean, well, I mean some people' – she made the singular plural – 'still can't quite believe that he came here at all or that he is going to stay, you know, for the long haul.'

And now Cristina Ferrare turned so that they stood finally looking at each other, face to face, woman to woman.

She was more beautiful head on than seemed right or fair. Liz couldn't tear her eyes away.

'Of course he is going to stay, we bought a house here.'

'I know,' said Liz, hardly able to credit it was her talking at all. 'So have a lot of the people I'm working with, the first house they have ever owned, most of them.'

'Well, then.' Cristina Ferrare smiled: a brilliant smile, and despite the reapplied lip gloss, entirely without artifice. 'We are all in this together then, aren't we?'

Liz saw her again a quarter of an hour later, holding tight to her husband's arm as together they tried to make their way through the workers who were lining the corridor between the machinery, cheering and clapping and whistling through their fingers. DeLorean in the end climbed on to a workbench, raising himself still higher above the heads that surrounded him.

He held up his hands, but the cheering and clapping and whistling through fingers for a time only grew in volume. He spread his own fingers, made a tamping motion – *Please* – and now, at last, they let him speak.

'I am so proud of each and every one of you today,' he said, 'so humble in your presence,' and humble was exactly how he sounded to Liz: looked it too, more elbow and knee joints all of a sudden than he knew what to do with. 'That car out front has my initials, sure, but make no mistake, it is your car. A few...' he stroked the side of his nose, a sign that he was in on the secret, '... glitches today, but we can all work on those. We'll write off today's car and the next however many it takes as training exercises, but if you can get me three hundred top-notch cars by the start of April we will have a shipment leaving here bound for the US and the American market. What do you say, can you do it?'

'Yes!' Liz shouted, though she could barely hear herself, so loud and numerous were the yeses on all sides. They could, they would.

Randall held the door for them to pass through back outside. DeLorean paused before him and rested both hands on his shoulders. He didn't say a word. He didn't need to.

Don Lander, coming behind, did have something to say, *sotto voce.* 'I don't think you'll have to worry any more about the Looking and Listening jibes.'

The secretary of state had not accompanied the DeLoreans on their tour of the factory. 'Their moment,' Randall had overheard him tell Jennings. (Perhaps it was time to revise that view of him as a man of constant sighing.) Randall could not imagine that he and Mrs Atkins had simply stood and waited, but wherever they had been in the interim they were here now, by their official car, to hear the last resounding cheer before the door to the assembly shop closed again.

'You appear to have made quite an impression with the workers,' Mrs Atkins said, that same smile on her face she had worn when she stepped from the car ninety minutes before.

'I can tell you,' said Cristina, 'they have made quite an impression with me.'

'Shame!' another woman said – shouted – through a loudhailer, it sounded like. 'Shame! Shame! Shame!'

Cristina's head turned. Mrs Atkins's head turned. Everyone's head turned. The gates it was coming from, Twinbrook side. 'Shame! Shame! Shame! Shame!' The woman with the loudhailer was flanked by two more women, who seemed to Randall to be wearing nothing but blankets. There were other women, children too, holding up large photographs of bearded men – prisoners, of course – clad in the same coarse blankets. 'Shame! Shame! Shame! Shame! Shame!'

'Oh dear,' said Atkins, at the end of a long sigh. 'I think maybe it is time we were going.'

A detachment of cops was already at the gates, trying to keep the roadway clear. Others closed in around the official cars, hands variously clutching radios, baton handles, the stocks and the perforated barrels of the guns angled across their chests.

Cristina's expression curdled. She seemed to stumble as

she took a step towards the car and had to grab hold of her husband's sleeve to keep from falling.

'I don't imagine those shouts are directed at you,' Atkins said, although from the look on her face this was scant comfort to Cristina. She had reached the car now and at once slid across the back seat, almost for the moment disappearing from view. DeLorean got in after her and leaned forward, speaking animatedly to the driver.

There was jostling now at the gates, which the cops were trying to force fully open against the wishes and the weight of the protestors. The jostling became scuffling. A cop had his cap knocked off and he reacted by shoving the woman closest to him on the shoulder.

'Brutality!' yelled the woman with the loudhailer. 'RUC brutality!'

The cars and their police escorts meantime were heading in convoy towards the exit, press photographers trying to keep pace, Randall trying to keep pace with them. As the lead Land Rover went through the gates it took a hit on the left side of the security grille from a bag of flour, which exploded in a white cloud that the secretary of state's car drove through, windshield wipers going at maximum speed. An egg hit the roof, and another, and another.

It was as though someone in the throng was systematically emptying a bag of groceries.

The fourth egg overshot and broke, spreading its mess against a window of the car carrying DeLorean and his wife. Randall, who had drawn almost alongside – close enough that he had managed to get his hand in the way of the lens of the photographer dropping to a crouch to fire a shot off – saw Cristina's head pop up, as though propelled by shock, or outrage. He was not inside the car so had no way of knowing for sure, but he saw the look on her face, he saw her mouth moving, 'Away,' she seemed to be saying. 'Away!'

The news bulletin that evening mentioned the protests only in passing, thank the Lord, preferring to focus on the car, which looked, through the filter of the camera and the television screen, even more convincing than it had when it was pushed out of the assembly shop to meet its public. Robert sat through it, as he had sat through dinner, in complete silence. Actually he barely said a word all night. Liz waited until they were getting ready for bed.

'You never asked me how it went today,' she said when he came into the bedroom from the bathroom. She was already in her nightdress, a jar of face cream uncapped in her hand.

'Sure I know how it went. Didn't I see it on the TV?'

'You didn't see everything,' she said. She was leaning over looking in the mirror on top of the chest of drawers. She saw him glance up. He knew that tone of voice. After all these years he ought to. 'I met the model wife.'

He had his trousers in his hand. He folded them the way he did, using his chin to hold the waistband flat, but there was a greater than usual deliberateness about his movements. And though the mirror didn't let her see far enough down to be certain, well – after all these years – it didn't need to.

'Her?' You're kidding me?'

'Uh-uh. Standing at the sink in the toilets, like this, putting on her make-up.' She set down the face cream and licked the tip of one finger and brushed her lips with it, glossing them. Purely for the purposes of illustration, of course.

'Did you speak to her? What did she say?'

'She said you had better get used to being a kept man.'

'Did she now?'

He was round her side of the bed by this time. The reflection in the mirror now was all his chest in his white vest, rising and falling with the quickening of his breath.

'Like a servant you mean?' Hands on her hips beneath the nightdress, nudging it up, moving her a few inches to the left, getting the angle. (He knew that too of old.) 'A gardener, maybe?'

And – dear God – he was in – as quick as that – right, right in. She could hardly breathe and yet she thrust back wanting even more. The face cream and all the other bottles and jars were scattered. The mirror tilted, toppled. She bit her forearm and the world went white.

The phone call came while Randall was still at dinner in the residents' dining room. Most of the journalists had already checked out, but he went out to the lobby anyway to speak rather than have the phone brought to the table.

'I didn't get a chance to say before we drove off,' DeLorean said, 'but there has been a change of plan.' In the background at that moment a flight was being announced, gate now closing. Randall saw again the expression on Cristina's face as the car drove through those women in their blankets, put the two together. It must almost, in the pause that he left, have been audible – a more-than-mental *click* – because DeLorean at once began steering him towards a different conclusion. 'There is a dealers' convention, starts tomorrow, in Long Beach. I had been thinking on the flight across it would be too good an opportunity to miss with that first shipment coming due.'

'No, you're right. It makes perfect sense.' And it did, of course. It really did.

There was a further and final call for passengers intending to travel.

'I'll talk to you from Long Beach,' DeLorean said. 'And, Randall... thank you.'

He moved back into Warren House that same evening, with – cold though it was – the familiar firefly-dance of cigarette tips across the valley to greet him. The red satin bows were still attached to the bay trees at the front door. Inside, not a grape had been dislodged from the pyramid of fruit in the crystal bowl on the sideboard, not a petal had dropped from the white peonies in the vase on the console of the bathtub beside which Randall undressed, letting his clothes fall to the floor where he stood. He reached into the bath and turned the dial to close the plug before opening the hot tap all the way. Steam billowed around him. He watched himself in the mirrored tiles disappear from the knees, the thighs, the waist up, knowing that all he had to do was pull the cord on the fan to begin to reverse the trick, but not yet (chest now, shoulders, neck, chin... bye-bye eyes), not just yet.

10

The Botanic Gardens rendezvous continued through what remained of the winter and into the spring. Liz told herself she was doing nothing whatever wrong. She would have been there on a Sunday morning anyway, or not a million miles away, and it wasn't as if they did anything apart from talk, sometimes not even that, just sat, a careful distance apart, people-watching.

One February Sunday, caught in a sudden downpour, they fled to the relative shelter of the sunken garden, and straight away wished (his body language echoed hers) that they had taken their chances with the rain, and took them, in fact, the moment the rain stopped bouncing on the paths above their eye level.

Her sister Vivienne in Melbourne was having an affair, Liz was pretty sure, with a man at her work. She had not come right out with it in her letters – they had never been the type of family to come right out with anything – but it was there between the lines, even just in the frequency with which the letters had started to arrive: she needed to be talking, just as she had on those nights in her teens, coming home from dances, shaking Liz awake (Vivienne had five years on her little sister, was already bringing home a wage before Liz had finished primary school), spouting nonsense about everything under the sun – the *moon*, make that – when the thing she really wanted to tell her, the thing she could not come right out and say, was whose arms had wrapped themselves around her, whose hands when the lights had gone way down had found their way *up* – defying elastic and latex and metal underwiring – *there*.

Liz had taken to ripping the letters up and burying the pieces in the bin, several bins even, the minute she was done reading them for fear that Robert would pick one up, (accidentally it would have to be, but still, accidents did sometimes happen), and read into it the same thing she did.

Because if he was to ask her to her face – 'What does that sister of yours think she's at? And what about Ivor? Do you not owe it to him to write and let him know?' – I mean, seriously, how could she fail to give herself away?

The odd Sunday she went straight to her mother's, skipped the Gardens altogether. Show him he wasn't to depend on her coming. Show herself she wasn't dependent on seeing him.

Monday to Friday and half of every other Saturday she built cars.

Eventually they would be turning out seventy or eighty a day, but for the first shipment they had a shade over eight weeks to manufacture three hundred they could swear by on the American market. The same car could come around two, three times, sometimes more, before the inspectors were content to let it out, or out as far as the Emissions and Vehicle Preparation shed at any rate. She knew what the shed was for now. EVP was their A&E. There weren't many cars that didn't come out of there better than they went in.

They were all still learning.

An assembly line is an exercise in rhythm, individual and collective. Like an orchestra, she was chuffed with herself for finally saying the day she tried to put it into words (tried to put it into words while simultaneously wrestling with a tension spring). Aye, said Anto, or like galley slaves.

The important thing was to distract all but that part of the brain required for the task in hand. Some people whistled – no: a lot of people whistled, a disproportionate number of them through their teeth – some people sang, or made noises approximate to singing in words only occasionally approximate to the ones committed to vinyl.

Anto had a game – 'Where in the world?' Where in the world would you be if you travelled five hundred miles west of such and such a place, then veered north for five hundred more?

Liz thought he must have invented it himself, for it was always him that won it. TC hated it – 'Change the record, will you, for fuck sake' – but he knew that the rhythm was better in the pit, or the galley, if they were all distracted by the same thing.

(Car arriving.)

'You've come out of Stockholm, heading due south, you

hit land… Where in the world would you be? Liz?'

'Stockholm, you say?'

'Stockholm.'

(Passenger seat in position.)

'Stockholm, Stockholm, Stockholm…'

'Due south.'

(Upper and lower shields aligned.)

'It's not Denmark?'

(Cap screws through the slide runners.)

'Correct, it's not.'

(Washers, nuts.)

'I give up.'

'After one guess? Come on! TC?'

(Tighten, tighten, tighten.)

'Bangor?'

'Ha-ha.'

'Not our Bangor, the other one.'

'Tell me' (Driver seat in) 'you're not serious.'

'If I wasn't serious I wouldn't have said it.'

'Wait! Is it Poland?'

(Cap screw one, cap screw two.)

'The *land*'s right, the *Po*'s wrong.'

'What other land is there around there?'

(Washers, nuts again.)

'Gotland.'

'*What* land?'

'Got. It's an island, smack in the middle of the Baltic Sea.'

(Tightening.)

'Why's it not in the World Cup, then?'

'Because it's still part of Sweden.'

'That's cheating!'

'Cheating how? I never said anything about countries: I wanted the name of the piece of land, simple as that.'

(Car gone.)

Deep into the second month she was still able to count the cars lined up in the car park as she walked towards the gate at night. When she could no longer do it without breaking stride – somewhere around the hundred mark – she quit bothering. It would be tight all right, but they were going to do it, they were going to get the shipment out on time.

Randall had already decided that he was going to press the issue of his returning to the US as soon as the first shipment was delivered. From there on in it was all production. He had by now, he hoped, something to offer elsewhere in the company. He had a daughter he needed in every sense to be closer to. In comparison to which the business with Liz was a small consideration indeed. But even there the conviction was growing that things could not go on indefinitely as they had been going on. Nor could they – whatever thoughts to the contrary he had once entertained – go any further.

Sundays now getting off the train at Botanic Station he found his feet occasionally dragging: what if this week he was the one who did not show up? OK, next week then...

Across the road from the station was a broad building out of keeping with the rest of the street: flat-roofed, red-brick, metal window frames; a sign at the end nearest the station proclaiming it the home of the Belfast Arts Theatre. Maybe upstairs it was. Downstairs for almost its entire length it comprised single-window businesses: a laundromat, a bric-a-brac store in the guise of a gift centre, and, between these two, a dingy-looking record store.

Randall had peered through the security mesh a couple of times – in those feet-dragging minutes after disembarking, or again on his return to the station with minutes still in hand before the next train – and had been intrigued to see among the album covers beginning to fade behind the glass a fair number of jazz artists.

On the one occasion that he had found himself, by chance, on the street during the hours of business, however, there had been a crowd of school kids – schoolboys – around the door, blazer lapels basically backdrops for their button badges and safety-pin collections, and he convinced himself he was in too much of a hurry anyway.

Then the sole on his right shoe started to go. 'American?' said the man in the Heel and Key Bar in Dunmurry to whom he showed it first. 'We don't get a big lot of these in here. Don't get a big lot of shoes at all, tell you the truth. It's mostly the keys. I don't know what people do with them.' He picked up the cigarette from the ashtray next to the cash register, squinted and blew a thin jet of smoke at the sole. Wisps of it came out through the eyelets. 'Here.' With the world's smallest pen he wrote an address on the back of a docket. 'You'd be better off taking them into Belfast, get them done right.'

It was a fortnight before Randall found the time. A Saturday afternoon. He could only imagine what it would be like trying to find a place to park. He took the train again, carrying on through Botanic this time to Central Station, although to what exactly the windowless bunker of a building he stepped out of was central he had for several disorienting moments not the first idea. Dereliction wherever his eyes lit.

A man approached him, red hair sprouting sideways from beneath a flat cap. 'Taxi?'

Randall nodded, fist closing tighter round the Heel and Key Bar docket. The man trotted to a black London cab parked twenty yards away. He held the rear door for Randall then, as soon as he was inside, shut it again and disappeared in among the passengers emerging, scratching their heads, from the station. A minute passed. Two. The man in the cap returned with three other lost souls and admitted them to the rear of the cab with Randall. He went round then to the driver's side and got in, turning in his seat once he had settled himself, and speaking through the sliding window between front and back.

'City centre, all of you?'

The four strangers – two men, two women, two greyheads, two in the prime, one with worn shoes wrapped in a bag on his lap – looked at one another and nodded.

'Flat fare, two pound each,' the driver said, and shut the window on the matter.

He set them down a quarter of a mile and a couple of turns in the road later (a couple of turns impossible to divine from the sidewalk before the station) at the back of the City Hall.

Randall and his temporary travel companions split without once having broken their silence, aware that they had been taken for a ride that could not be measured in distance alone.

Come the time to leave again, therefore, Randall opted to walk to the station he knew best and found himself at the entrance to Botanic two minutes late for one train, twenty-eight minutes early for the one after.

He looked over the road at the record store. No schoolkids today.

There was a crosswalk a little way up the street, but having by now had ample opportunity to observe the Belfast road-crossing etiquette – a hand raised in apology (or admonition) to the oncoming traffic – he decided on the more direct route and, hardly breaking stride, pushed open the shop door – halfway.

'I beg your pardon,' he said.

A kid was hunched over a box of records on the floor behind the door. In fact, looking about (it didn't take long), he realised there were at least as many kids inside as he had previously seen outside, only out of uniform now and twice as rowdy.

Something or other, the one behind the door was saying emphatically (neither the bump or Randall's apology having interrupted him) was a load of balls. Randall spotted a Yes album cover in the boy's hand. He forgot now the name of the artist, but Stafford in his unit – the memory broke surface, blinking from long submergence – Stafford had been a huge fan, painstakingly stencilling his artwork for Gun on to the back of his flak vest: all hellfire and opened-maw ghouls.

Randall was about to take back the one step he had taken inside, pull the door quietly behind him, when the man – fifties maybe – working the counter called over the top of the heads between them.

'Something you're looking for there?'

Randall raised the hand with which he had moments before deflected the traffic. 'I saw the LP covers in your window.' He tried to make it sound as though it was his fault for imagining that there would be any connection between what was on display there and what was to be found on the shelves. 'I was kind of wondering whether you maybe had anything by Artie Shaw.'

The man's face lit up. 'Arthur Jacob Arshawsky! Now you're talking.' He came out from behind the counter – a little more hesitantly than Randall would have expected: perhaps he had misjudged his age – and taking Randall by the arm guided him to the adjacent aisle. His fingertips skimmed the top edges of the sleeves, stopping now and then as though guided by touch alone to pull out an LP. That one? On second thoughts... *That?* No, wait: *this* one.

'Let me show you,' he said, and turned back to the counter where he slipped the vinyl from the third sleeve, displaying it front and back beneath a lamp. 'First pressing. See? Not a mark.'

Randall laughed awkwardly. 'All I need to know is does it have "Nightmare".'

'They nearly all have "Nightmare". Do you want to have a listen?'

He still had better than twenty minutes before his train was due. 'All right.'

The man had already raised the lid of the turntable behind the cash register. He positioned the record on the rubber mat then bent over to place the stylus on the groove – an operation as precise as cutting the diamond the stylus had come from. He took an untipped cigarette from the box in his shirt pocket – this too appeared be part of the operation – and with a nod of his head – for that was not mere hiss they were hearing, that was the sound of the forces gathering and could not be talked over – invited Randall to join him. Randall nodded back – he would, sure – and lit up with him, two sides of the same flame.

The kids looked over their shoulders curiously at the first funereal notes from some enormous horn. A whole shipful of bad news. Trumpets came in, harsh as sirens, then a clarinet – Artie himself: the sound of one man trying to steer a course through the confusion.

Randall remembered the night sitting in the grillroom in – where was it? – Manhattan Beach – DeLorean's hands making the shape of the clarinet, though perhaps it was something far more intangible he was trying to conjure... those stories of his childhood on Six Mile Road – parents striving to live decently, clarinet lessons and a piano in the parlour, despite the goons and the summer lay-offs – his first days at Packard and the awe he felt in the presence of the actual makers – not the machine-operators – the craftsmen, who knew, and knew that everyone from the goddamned president down knew, their proper worth.

The track ended at the same time as the cigarette. Randall's head was whirling with the strength of the tobacco, the intensity of the music, the combination of the two. The man lifted the stylus with even more care than he had set it down.

'Imagine someone with that much talent just walking away.'

'Who walked away?'

'Artie Shaw. Hasn't played in twenty-five years. Story is he couldn't bear the prospect of hearing his powers diminish night after night.' He eased the vinyl back into its inner sleeve. The barest whisper of a contact. It would still have been pristine in 2001 if he never let it out of his hands.

He laid the LP flat on the counter. 'What do you think?'

'I'll take it,' said Randall.

'Buy or borrow?'

'Oh, listen, I couldn't borrow it, thanks all the same.'

'Read the sign,' the man said and pointed, and sure enough, there it was, black on fluorescent yellow: *Record Library*. 'Ten bob to join and ten bob up to three LPs a week.'

Randall already had his pocketbook out. 'Ten bob is…?'

'Fifty new pence.'

So Randall gave the man a hundred of them in the shape of a Bank of Ireland pound note, took the first pressing just demonstrated, another slightly more dog-eared Artie Shaw, plus a Stan Getz potluck (*Groovin' High*) and crossed the road again – by the lights this time: never mind it had only cost him a pound, he had a valuable cargo under his arm – to the station.

A couple of days later, just before noon, with Don in Hethel for a meeting, he was passing his office window on his way to the filing cabinet when he noticed a large number of workers weaving between the cars in the parking lot, headed in the direction of the Twinbrook gates. His first instinct was to pick up the phone to June in the office down the hall. 'Did I miss something? Has there been a fire drill?'

She hesitated before replying. 'A fire drill...? No.' There was a lot of background noise, chair legs scraping across the floor, footfalls in the corridor. He checked the window again – still men and women leaving in their scores – then put down the phone and made his way across to the assembly shop. For a moment he thought it was completely deserted, but then his eyes lit on a worker here and a worker there and somewhere else again two or three where he would have expected to see six or more, tinkering, all of them, rather than working.

Two men came round the corner from the chassis line intent on the door.

'Can one of you tell me what is going on here?' Randall asked, but the men only put their heads down and carried on around him. He turned. 'I am talking to you!'

They didn't stop, if anything speeded up. He began to jog. And then the next thing he was running, back through the shop, out the door, calling out to people who continued to ignore him. 'You do not have permission to leave this factory in working hours... I insist that you return to your work station immediately!'

He spied Stylianides at his office window and followed the direction of his gaze. Placards were being waved outside the gates – the same placards that were waved as the car carrying the DeLoreans sped through – *Victory to the Prisoners*, *Support the 5 Demands* – except there was something almost jaunty in the motion today, the workers as they exited being greeted with clapping and cheering. The loudhailer was there again too, although the voice that came from it on this occasion evidently belonged to someone (Randall from that distance, with that distortion, could not have said who) from within the workforce.

'Volunteer Bobby Sands refused food yesterday morning in his cell in H2 of Long Kesh. We, the workers of the DeLorean Motor Company Limited, wish to express our solidarity with him and with all the brave men and women willing to sacrifice themselves for political status in the British concentration camps here.'

Randall had heard enough. It was only with an effort that he kept his whole body from shaking as he marched back to his office. He met Stylianides at the head of the stairs.

'We need to get the name of every woman and man who walked out of that gate,' he said, pointing back the way he had come.

Stylianides shrugged. 'Sure, but maybe to save time we could collect the names of the ones who didn't.'

* * *

It had to have been prearranged. Liz did not hear an actual command, but all at once, from all corners of the factory, there was a sound, beyond the simple downing of tools, of labour being definitively withdrawn.

Liz glanced over her shoulder, back up the line, and when she turned around again Anto and TC were walking too.

'Here!' she said, as in 'Come back... *now*.'

Anto held up his hand – I hear you, but I'm not going to heed you – kept walking, on up past the Tellus terminal, left, out of sight.

She looked about her and registered it almost at once, the ones left standing – standing like her, like spare parts – they all came in through the Seymour Hill gate. She knew then right away. Robert had said to her this morning that there would be bother, just wait and see, but there had been a hunger strike at the tail end of last year and things had carried on in the factory as normal. To be honest Liz had hardly paid it any attention at all. There had been a couple of awful incidents in England a few years ago – they didn't stand for any nonsense there, Robert said – hunger strikers choking while being force-fed – but in her experience these things usually petered out, as that last hunger strike did in... Do you know, she couldn't even have told you when exactly.

The protests, right enough, had not let up – she had seen that first-hand – and the priests and what have you that were always in and out of the prison had been saying every opportunity they got that next time they worried it would be 'for real', but she had thought that was just the prisoners upping the ante, hunger-striking at one remove.

But now here it was again. For real.

The word soon filtered down through those that remained that Randall been ranting and raving out the front of the assembly shop. She blushed to hear it, for him, in part, for making a show of himself, but more than anything for her and this whole grotesque spectacle that passed for politics here.

The heat had not entirely left her face when half an hour after they walked out Anto, TC and all the rest walked back in, picked up their tools again and re-engaged their labour.

Liz leaned into the car that she had for the last thirty minutes been left to deal with on her own.

'Do you want a hand there?' Anto asked.

'I'm fine.'

And wouldn't you know, it was one of those: the bloody seat wouldn't line up right. She hit the track a whack with the heel of her spanner.

'Are you sure?'

'I said' – another whack – 'I'm fine.'

TC was crouching down on the other side of the car, rattling around in his tool bag. 'Anybody see my lug wrench?' He tossed everything-but-the-lug-wrench about noisily. 'Why is it always the lug wrench you can't find?'

Anto interposed himself in the aperture between TC and Liz, resting his arm across the doorframe, sealing their conversation in.

'Is everything all right?'

'What could possibly be wrong?' She didn't trust herself to look at him, but it was impossible in such close confines not to see anyway his head drop forward an instant then snap back up again.

'Wait till I tell you,' he said, quieter. 'It's all very well these Yanks coming off with stuff about us being a country apart in here, but there are people in this factory who would take note if anyone who came in through our gate didn't go out it in support of the prisoners. Do you understand what I'm saying?'

She shoved the seat with her shoulder: that would have to do. EVP could sort it out.

Only then did she meet his eye. 'Nice speech,' she said, 'but maybe I am not the one you need to be trying to convince.'

Stylianides had obliged Randall with the personnel files and payroll lists and then had withdrawn, pleading a plane to catch for a meeting previously postponed – on two occasions – with Bennington in Coventry.

Randall, surrounded by pages with photographs clipped to the top corners, by folders containing more pages, boxes containing more folders, was coming to the realisation that he had not the faintest notion where to start, which was enough to cause his cooling anger to boil again.

He picked up the phone and at once set it back on the cradle and, standing up (his chair nearly toppled with the suddenness of it), walked down the hall. June was sitting side-on to her desk chatting to Sandra.

'Haven't you got that line for me yet?'

She faced front again. 'I'm sorry: Monday, everything's busy.'

'Except in here obviously.'

He slapped the wall on his way out and swinging back into his own office nearly collided with the union guy, Hughes – Anthony, only it wasn't Anthony he called himself, not Tony either...

'This really isn't a good time,' Randall told him. (*Anto*, that was it.)

'I know it isn't, that was what I wanted to talk about.'

Randall gestured to a chair, trusting that that casual flick of his wrist set the tone for the proceedings: this was not a discussion, this was an audience granted under sufferance.

Anto considered a moment before sitting. 'I just think it would be a grave error to overreact,' he said then.

'This would be to over fifty per cent of the workforce staging an unauthorised walkout in the middle of the day?' Randall threw himself back theatrically, for the second time in a matter of minutes almost causing his seat to topple. It only added to the effect.

'For half an hour,' Anto said. 'They're all back now.'

Randall came forward again, elbows on the desk. 'Yes, but for half an hour they were out, five hundred of them, that is at least two-hundred and fifty man-hours lost, that is *cars* lost, seven weeks before we are due to send out our first shipment to the US, and over what? The radio is saying this guy Sands is in prison for blowing up a furniture store, for Christ sakes – destroying jobs.

'I know, but that "guy" Sands also happens to be from around this way. He's a neighbour of a lot of the people building your cars. He's not Sands to them, he's Bobby. Bobby who persuaded the black taxis to put on a route out to Twinbrook because there was next to no public transport.'

'Which wouldn't have anything to do with the IRA's habit of burning every bus its members can lay their hands on.'

'Look, you have to understand what a hunger strike means to people here.'

'Some people here: there were quite a few who didn't follow you out the gates.'

Now it was Anto who sat back, slowly, though, shaking his head. (Reviewing the moment later Randall thought of a grandmaster who had drawn his opponent into the trap he had for several moves past been laying.) 'Oh, I don't think you want to go down that road,' he said.

'What road?'

'You know rightly what road. The Protestants didn't walk out so the Protestants keep their jobs? I'm sure the headlines that made would be as welcome back home as a cargo ship without cars: *DeLorean purges Catholic Workers*.'

Randall's phone rang. He snatched at it. 'Yes?'

A somewhat sulky June. 'I've got that line to Mr DeLorean for you.'

Anto was watching him closely from across the desk.

Randall cleared his throat, of anger more than anything. 'Put him through,' he said and the next moment there was DeLorean, Edmunding, asking if things were all right.

Randall turned his chair round to face the window. 'Things are just fine,' he said and a moment later heard the door close as Anto let himself out.

'That's what I was hoping you were going to say,' DeLorean said. 'Everything depends on us making that shipment. We are drawing up plans at this end for the launch schedule.'

And he went into detail then about how field operations were to be divided, four geographical areas, Eastern, Western, Southern and Central: Edison New Jersey, Irvine California, Atlanta Georgia and dear old Detroit. There were to be two Quality Assurance Centres besides, at Irvine again serving all dealerships west of the Mississippi and Wilmington Delaware serving everywhere to the east.

'And these Quality Assurance Centres would be...?' Randall had until mention of them been regaining a little of the confidence that had been haemorrhaging over the previous two or three hours.

'To be sure, to be sure. Isn't that what they say there? Besides, the cars will have been at sea for a few days. We'll put them through their paces one more time before we deliver them to the dealers. Means all you have to do there is concentrate on the numbers.'

Randall did not really take in a lot of what came after that – the text of the letter that was to go into the owner's pack along with the Scotch-Brite pads and the stainless-steel shampoo, praising the faith – make that the courage (maybe he wasn't talking to Randall at all, maybe he was dictating) – the *courage* manifest in purchasing a revolutionary new product such as the DMC-12... It was the numbers he kept coming back to: all else for now was of secondary importance to getting the numbers out.

That did not sit well with Don – for you can believe that there were many calls to his line too in the days that followed – nor would Randall have expected it to. Still, there was a date, there would be a ship leaving with space in the hold for three hundred cars. What else was there to say?

Randall was scarcely in his office at all the rest of that month, but toured the shop floors, the stores, the holding tanks for the resin, chivvying, encouraging, asking questions, on the spot or on the phone: those pallets arriving at the dock levellers – *stacking up* at the dock levellers – was there any way of speeding up the inspection? Yes, this was Mr Randall, yes he was ringing – for the fourth time now – to enquire about the automated fettling tool... *Where in God's name was it?*

He was not above donning coveralls and pitching in, starting in that fettling room where, in the continued absence of the damned tool, they needed all the help they could get. (And needed too more than just a set of coveralls: they needed hoods, a personal air supply.) God it was grim: every particle of excess fibreglass – 'flash' – to be removed by hand, and to hang, most of it, in the air, before the bodies were fit to leave the body-press shop. He helped cut the mats for the moulds (another process that had not yet been automated), he stripped the plastic coverings from the panels as they were being stacked on their racks (a process he doubted ever would be), he took a blowtorch to dents, sandpaper to scratches; once, while one of the men who usually did it was at the restroom, he had a go at centring the first – and crucial – roof panel to see if it could be done faster. It took the man on his return ten minutes to repair what he had done.

He did everything but switch out the lights at night.

At the end of each day he dragged himself back to Warren House and stretched out on a sofa positioned between a pair of tall, narrow speaker cabinets, listening, eyes closed in concentration, to whatever records he had that week borrowed from (or – as most often was the case – had not had time to return to) the record library. More than once it was the hum of the speakers that woke him – shivering, disoriented – hours after they had last emitted a pre-recorded note.

And so March passed. Two more prisoners – a soldier-killer and a guy caught on a street with a hand grenade – joined Sands on hunger strike. The lots continued to fill with cars.

11

April nineteenth, Easter Day, crept in through a damp mist that lingered into the morning and low to the ground with the curious effect that when the sun did at last appear the maisonettes looked like skyscrapers, breaking through the clouds, the hills beyond them virtual Himalayas.

The rigs had been travelling back and forth since nine o'clock the night before, but there were still, twelve hours on, scores of cars waiting to be transported to the docks.

Even though it was a Sunday – even though it was Easter – there were also, by nine a.m., scores, possibly hundreds of workers gathered. Unlike previous red-letter days theirs, today, were the only cameras in evidence. They snapped away as the cars were loaded, posing their workmates by the tailgates then passing the camera to someone else whose place in the group they took, arms folded, grinning. As each fully laden rig headed towards the exit some of them ran alongside, taking more pictures. Others stood and cried. Randall, once or twice, had to widen his own eyes to keep them from filling up. (It was, despite the sun, a watery kind of morning.) Refocusing after one such moment he saw Anto break away from a group of half a dozen women and men and walk towards him, eyebrows knitted.

His heart sank.

'A word?' Anto said.

'What is it?'

'A few of us have been talking.' This with a jerk of the head back the way he had come. Randall couldn't be doing with the theatrics.

'And?' he said shortly.

'And we're not happy.'

'Well there's a surprise.'

'Some of the cars have been parked out here so long they're filthy.'

Randall looked long and hard. The man was right. How many times had he stood at his window watching the clouds tumble over the brow of the hills, bringing the next weather front? Whatever soot and dirt they had picked up on their race across country to get there this lot took the full force of it.

'We were thinking maybe we would go down to the docks later on before they were put on the ships, give them a bit of a wash.'

Randall turned to face him, struggling for words.

'It's all right,' Anto said to him, 'we're not going to be looking for overtime for it... Just this once.'

* * *

Liz watched from a distance. Anto had told her what he and the others were planning on doing. 'Can't have those Americans thinking we're all a load of dirt birds.'

'I'd love to help,' she said, 'but we're having people over later.'

'I know: Easter.'

'Have you no plans yourself?'

'Me?' His voice went up as though the very thought of it was absurd. 'No.'

It occurred to her that she didn't know a single thing worth the knowing about his life outside the factory, other than that he was wearing out his library card. (*The Jungle* was his latest book. Something told her there were no talking animals in it.) Not that he could have known a big lot about her life, having never bothered his head to ask.

When the last of the lorries with the cars on them had gone she raced home and got the roast on – silverside – with onions cooked in the juices until they were practically caramelised. Robert's mother and father came, along with his unmarried brother Hal-God-Love-Him (it was said so often it sounded like part of his name: there was something not quite right with Hal... God love him) and an aunt of Liz's who had just lost her husband of forty-seven years. Everyone commented on the television. Robert showed them how you used the remote control, ran through a random Ceefax selection: TV listings, share prices, a recipe for hollandaise, the weather in Kuala Lumpur.

Didn't say a word about how they had come by the set, which suited Liz fine: it had been fully incorporated into the household – it and the job that had put the money in her purse to give to Gilmore's.

When the last guest had gone – the aunt, reluctantly... sure, what was there for her at home now? – and the boys had disappeared up to their room with what remained of their eggs (what age were you supposed to stop buying them?), Robert switched the TV on again to the big film: *Murder on the Orient Express*.

About twenty minutes in he turned to her.

'Was it those onions?'

'Was what those onions?'

'You're squirming in your seat there like I don't know what. I thought maybe you had a touch of indigestion.'

She blushed. What it was, she realised, she had been miles away, down at the docks with Anto and the rest, washing cars. She tried to focus on the film. Richard Widmark was showing Albert Finney the small silver gun he slept with under his pillow. His life had been threatened, he said: his secretary could show Finney two letters he had on file.

'It's nothing,' Liz said.

Robert looked at her looking at the film a moment longer. 'Well I'd hate to see you if it was something.'

Randall stood in a canopy of sodium light watching, heart in mouth, as the crew gathered in the ropes and the ship gradually detached itself from the dockside. The cargo doors did not burst open as he had feared, in some grotesque Easter parody, they might. The cars remained, gleaming, in the hold.

The channel was broad and straight from the port into Belfast Lough and the open sea beyond. On the far side of the water from him was the shipyard. Those two enormous yellow cranes, stamped with H & W, Harland and Wolff – gateways they looked like, triumphal arches: *Forget the City Hall, forget the factory chimneys and the parades of shops, this is where the real power resides.*

Resided.

How many decades had it taken for shipbuilding to be established here, DeLorean had asked him, for Belfast to be able to claim this as the biggest, most productive yard in the world?

Exactly.

Little more than two and a half years it had taken to get these cars out. Not eighteen months, sure, but even so, two and a half years where no cars had ever been made before.

Don Lander came and joined him in the light, watched a while in silence. 'Of course,' he said at last, 'the best thing that could happen is for that boat to sink halfway across, assuming the crew got picked up, of course. That way we'd get to say we got the cars out on time and no one would ever know at what cost.'

Randall glanced at him. Don was looking dead ahead, inscrutable.

* * *

The word Liz heard was 'dogs'. Washers – as he had been known since he saved the day, with the world's press waiting, by calling for a bucket of them – carried the word with him from the trim line where he had heard it spoken – spat – by his Big Mate, who had got it straight from a fella he knew on the boat. The only difference being, said the Yanks who had been tasked with unloading them on to the docks, *actual* dogs in that kind of shape would have been put down. Instead these dogs of cars were being sent straight to a Quality Assurance Centre to be taken apart and put back together at two thousand dollars a pop.

'Cheeky gets,' TC said.

'Come on, you're the one wants to be a supervisor,' said Anto. 'Don't tell me it wasn't obvious to you.'

'Well, maybe the odd one was a bit iffy, but the whole lot...? Cheeky fucking gets.'

Washers' Big Mate on the trim line also brought the word that the management was going to be looking for volunteers to go over to the States and find out how to do it the American way.

'There you go, TC,' Liz chipped in. 'Stick your name down and tell them when you get there that the next lot of cars will be better, and the next lot after that. And see by next *year*, they'll be sending people from there over to us to find out how *we* do it.'

TC sucked saliva through his teeth. 'I wouldn't give them the satisfaction.'

'Not even for a wee holiday?' Washers said and anticipated his next sentence with an expansive hand gesture. 'Broaden your horizons, sort of thing?'

'I've been there once already,' TC said, mainly to his toolbag: lug wrench again. 'Got sent when I was at school with this kid from the other side, you know, see if we could stop fighting.' He sat back on his heels. 'Pittsburgh. What a hole. The only thing we had in common, him and me, was that we couldn't wait to get the fuck out of it and back home.'

'I nearly moved there once myself,' Anto said.

Lord, thought Liz, they were coming like buses now, the revelations.

'Pittsburgh?'

'Schenectady, upstate New York. Had a job all lined up.'

'Doing what?'

'I don't even remember now, cement factory or something. Tell you the truth I couldn't have cared less about the job, even then, it was the name I loved.' He got full value out of it: 'Sche-nec-ta-dy.'

'So why didn't you go?' Liz asked.

'The usual reason, I met a girl...'

'Don't sound so miserable about it.'

'... the girl met somebody else...'

'Ah.'

'... by which time things had kicked off here and the notion went off me.'

'Some would say that things kicking off here was all the more reason for going.'

'Yeah, but it would have looked like I was running away.'

'And you wouldn't want to look like you were running away, even if it killed you?'

'What can I say?' Anto shrugged. 'If I had another brain it would be lonely.'

Washers cracked the knuckles of each hand in turn against the opposite palm: time he was getting back to work taming skins. He checked back. 'What about that other fella, TC – the one you went to Pittsburgh with. You ever see him again after you got back?'

TC picked up a seat. 'I saw him all right, a couple of years ago, in the paper. Got life for dropping a breezeblock on a fella's head out the back of some club. Thought he was the "wrong sort".'

He had the tact not to say what sort that was.

'Jesus wept,' said Washers under his breath.

'Yeah.' TC dumped the seat into the car, eyes averted from Liz's. 'Jesus wept.'

Johnny Carson got his car. Johnny. Carson. Got. His. Car. A week more and he had been going to tell them he would hold on now for the hearse model: at least he would be guaranteed one ride in it.

It broke down the very first time he took it out. Pressure regulator. The dealer had to rush a spare out to him and fix it at the side of the highway. Johnny seemed genuinely not to care, any more than the two hundred and ninety-nine people below him on the waiting list cared about, or even registered, the difference between the $12000 they had been quoted way back when and the $25000 they ended up paying. Most of them anyway would have been prepared to pay a premium for the kudos of driving one of the first three hundred to come off the boat. 'Say, is *that* what I think it is...?'

As Johnny said, after sitting out there on the highway waiting for the repairman, the damn thing was getting more looks than he was.

It was not only more expensive than originally intended but, thanks to the Lotus makeover, heavier too, slower off the mark (they had had to *down tune* the engine to 130 horsepower to meet emissions standards), and when it did get going it was able to deliver just nineteen miles a gallon, ten short of projections and not far above federal minimum standards. The doors now and then, and despite the offices of the Quality Assurance Centres, had an alarming habit of jamming open, or (more alarming still) shut. Randall's erstwhile colleagues in the auto pages and the specialist trade press – the same people who had fallen over themselves to praise the '73 Vega – reported all this with an amount of malicious glee, adding for good measure that the bodywork showed up the pawprints of every one of those 'slack-jawed gawpers'.

Yet withal it was thing of beauty. (A thing of beauty – critics note – with anti-pawprint shampoo in the glove box.) No one but no one could fault it on that.

DeLorean telephoned at four in the morning, forgetting for once in his urgency the hours between them. For the first half a minute, during which DeLorean could get no further than 'Edmund' – ten, maybe fifteen times – Randall thought he might be high, but that wasn't what it was at all. He had driven – he got the words out at last – *driven* his own DMC-12 out from the ranch that afternoon, deep into the desert beyond Palm Springs. He must have sat for two hours with just the driver-side door open watching the sun's declension, from ragged white hole to blood red disc, played out on the hood.

'I'm not a man for hearing voices, Edmund, but I swear something spoke to me out there: "Don't rest on this. Keep going… Keep going." Does that sound crazy?'

Randall told him he had had enough testimony from good and perfectly sane army buddies – one who had turned to answer a question (there was no one behind him who could have asked it) a split second before a bullet passed by right where his head would have been – not to discount anything.

Later there would be stories – most of them put about by DeLorean himself – that he was in fact no stranger to supernatural interventions of this kind, that the palm-reader who had conjured up 21 January as the day when the first car would come off the line had been guiding his every decision since he turned his back on Puerto Rico, that much of what he was still to do – doubling production, floating on the stock market – was at her prompting too, or at the prompting of whoever spoke through her, palms being the least of her psychic talents.

Randall never bought it, any more than he bought the conversion to Christianity that caused DeLorean to confess it.

Every time the subject came up he thought back to that early-morning call, DeLorean's embarrassment almost at what he thought he had heard out there in the Californian desert.

Anyone who had been receiving messages from a 55th Street medium for the previous however many years could have taken something like that, you would have thought, in his long-legged stride.

12

Up to now the money had all been flowing in one direction: out. From here on, though, it would start to flow back in again. The overheads too, now that they were in full production, would come down dramatically. The Hethel presence, for a start, could be scaled back. No need, with the initial research and development phase over, for a separate DMCL office onsite. Randall travelled across to Norfolk to oversee the winding-up of operations. Chapman apologised that the helicopter was otherwise engaged, and sent a car instead to meet him off the train up from London at Wymondham, a place that took half as long again to spell as it did to pronounce, lodging him in a wing of the hall (my God, the hall) with a view from his lead-paned window of a nine-hundred-year-old church.

DeLorean was not wrong about the Brits.

Chapman himself could only spare a few minutes the afternoon of Randall's arrival. It was the Grand Prix season, he had just got back from Buenos Aires, where Elio de Angelis had – to Chapman's evident disgust – finished 'only' sixth, and had another three races coming up in quick succession (three opportunities for de Angelis to make amends): San Marino, Belgium and Monaco.

Randall had got the feeling on the previous occasions he had met him that Chapman always had at least one eye out for someone more important approaching. Meeting him here, however, on his home ground, with no one else around, Randall realised that importance was not relative to situation: even for a few minutes he was never going to command Chapman's full attention. Even as he was saying hello, shaking hands, Chapman was already looking *beyond*.

Indeed, though he thought at first it was just another facet of that famous English reserve, the longer Randall was there, the more polite hands that were extended, the greater was his sense that there was a distinct coolness towards him, or rather the car that he represented, as though it and he were eating up time that could be better spent handcrafting Esprits and Elans.

As for the office equipment whose repatriation he was here to effect, Randall had no idea where it was all going to go. The Dunmurry offices were full to overflowing as it was: Portakabin for now was all he could think. There were still a couple behind the body shop, left over from plant's construction.

He had toyed with the notion of driving across to Norwich by himself to finalise the arrangements with the shipping company, take a detour through a few of those villages in which the countryside abounded. At least in this part of English-speaking Europe he was unlikely to encounter soldiers in hedges or discover on arrival at his destination that one entire sector (the one, wouldn't you know, where he had been intending to park) had been evacuated because of a telephoned coded warning. When the time came, though, he found a car waiting for him at the door, a driver already at the wheel.

It had since his earliest DeLorean days been part of the package, but it had got to the point here where he half expected a Lotus man to be waiting to walk down the corridor with him when he stepped out of his room at night to go to the bathroom. He had heard of things like that happening to people on trips behind the Iron Curtain, only it wasn't service they called it, it was surveillance. Not that he was complaining by the end of that day, quite the reverse: without the driver to call on for help he doubted he would have understood a word that the guy in the shipping office was saying. As accents went it was at the atonal end of the sing-song spectrum.

Still, when he had returned to Ketteringham Hall later that afternoon and packed his bag and nodded one last time to the driver holding the car door for him (no sign at all of Chapman), he was not exactly heartbroken to be leaving.

The following Sunday was as beautiful a spring day – as beautiful a day period – as Randall had seen in all his time in Belfast. When he arrived in the Botanic Gardens mid-morning, the grass between the paths was already colonised by students from the university next door, books open before them, some of which were even being read.

A quarter of an hour after he sat down, Liz dropped into

the seat beside him, the briefest of smiles to acknowledge that she had seen him, hand shielding her eyes from the sun as she scanned the student faces, or perhaps, it only occurred to him afterwards, shielding her face from any return gaze.

Up to now they had met in public, but without much in the way of the public to witness it.

Randall had spent the evening before reading over lists of names. 'I see no one from your section has put themselves forward for the retraining programme,' he said in lieu of a hello of his own.

Her mouth side-on looked lipless. 'It appears America holds bad memories for some of them.'

'I'm sorry to hear that.' Taking on the unspecified sins of an entire nation. 'What about you?'

She turned to face him, her eyes as narrowed almost as her mouth, though the sun was at her back.

'*I'm* not going, if that's what is bothering you,' he said, because something evidently was. 'I just thought maybe if you were thinking in the future of advancement...'

Liz shook her head. 'You still don't get it, do you, the way things work in this country? Men earn more than their women, that's the deal. It was enough for my husband to swallow me getting a job at all, never mind bringing home more than he was. I can just imagine how he would react to me "advancing", and as for me waltzing in and telling him I was taking off to the States for a couple of weeks on my own...'

'Hardly on your own.'

'Do you seriously think that makes it *better*?' She stood up suddenly. He was reminded of the very first time they met here, all those months of Sundays ago: same raincoat, despite the improvement in the weather, same belt, which she tugged on, hard, before offering him her hand. He didn't know whether to laugh or not, but in the end followed her lead: not. He put his hand in hers (a vein in her wrist pulsed). She shook it once.

'Goodbye,' she said.

'Wait a second, you're not telling me...'

'I'm telling you we'll not do this again.'

He felt an odd sense of relief. He had thought at first she meant goodbye to the job and everything.

'If you say so.'

'I do say so.'

He went to get up.

'Don't,' she said. 'Please.'

He sat back, spreading his arms as wide as they would go along the top of the bench: look at me not getting up. He watched her walk along the path in the direction of the river, take a quick step back to avoid an errant Frisbee travelling between students who had given up all pretence of study, then carry on, shoulders even from a distance set, round a bend and out of sight.

Randall let out a long, slow breath and hauled himself to his feet.

So that was that, whatever it was.

* * *

She had said his name the night before. Robert had stopped dead, mid thrust, pushing her back off him, holding her at trembling arms' length. '*What?*' His chest was heaving, hers too: hers even more so. God, she had been so nearly there, so caught up she didn't know she didn't know what she was saying. But the echo of it reverberated now. She moved his palms from her shoulders on to her breasts, pressing down hard. 'Hands all over me,' she slurred the words. It wasn't all put on. She raised her hips an inch, raised them another, took him by the right wrist, fitted his fingers into the gap she had made, as much on him as in her. 'I want your hands' – guiding the left one the length of her back, shoulder blades to tailbone, on down from there – 'all over me.'

He started again – couldn't help himself – took back the inches she had temporarily denied him, strained then to find one... inch... more. It was over in seconds. Her before him.

That's how close she was.

And that's how close she was.

She couldn't risk anything like that happening again.

The Frisbee, checking her stride, nearly broke her resolve, but she put her head down, held tight to the strap of her shoulder bag and ploughed on.

Randall awoke two nights later from a nightmare of scudding over jungle scrub taking fire on all sides to find that it was no dream at all – he was actually there or it was actually here – the clatter of the rotors, the sky's untimely orange, the fizzes, the pops, the dreadful bangs. He rolled off the bed on to the floor, and kept rolling, looking for a place to hide.

What Liz heard first was bin lids. She swung her legs out of bed and crossed the floor barefoot to the window, opening it a fraction, as quietly as the latch would allow, which was not quite quietly enough.

Robert sat up, knocking over the bedside lamp as he tried to switch it on... righting it again at the second attempt.

'What is it?'

'Listen.'

'What?'

Distant, distant.

'*Listen*. Bin lids. He must be dead.'

Robert reached for the lamp again, still squinting against its light. 'If he is it's nobody's fault but his own.'

'I know, but...'

'But what?' He rolled over. 'You have your work in the morning. I have mine. Close that window and get back into bed.'

She listened a few moments longer then did as he said.

When he had reoriented himself sufficiently to understand that he was not under direct attack Randall ventured to wriggle out of the corner into which he had rolled and raise the window blind an inch or two with the backs of his fingers. All was confusion: overlit, overloud confusion, much of it concentrated on a point about five hundred yards to his right, beyond the trees, corresponding to the Twinbrook entrance to the factory.

Six feet to his left, at the other end of the window, the telephone sat on a glass table. He felt along the join of the baseboard and the carpet for the cable, yanked, bringing the handset crashing to the floor then reeled it in, dial tone buzzing angrily.

It took ten minutes and four numbers – the last passed on to him by the housekeeper in Pauma Valley – to get through, to another house – ranch, Randall supposed – where a party was in full swing; a further ten while DeLorean was located, the phone so far as Randall could tell brought to him, elbowed through a dozen bellowed conversations and sudden bursts of laughter, rather than he to it.

'*Edmund?*' he said, and you just knew he had a finger in one ear.

'I'm sorry to be phoning, it's all gone crazy here.' Randall pushed the receiver under the blind, held it to the window for half a minute. The glass throbbed. 'Did you hear that?'

'It's hard for me to hear anything with this music,' DeLorean said, or shouted. Randall was getting it too. Yvonne Elliman, if he was not mistaken, singing as though she was standing by DeLorean's side.

'Hold on, hold on, let me see,' he said. A door slid open in California, slid shut, and Yvonne was gone, the backing track of voices, ice against glasses, pool water being efficiently displaced, was gone. 'There.'

Randall did not bother a second time with the phone to

the window. 'I'm guessing two, three hundred people, right in front of the gates. It's to do with that hunger strike,' he said. 'Has to be.'

He thought for a moment or two that DeLorean still hadn't heard properly, so unhurried was his reply.

'You know that's why I have you there, right? I figured if anyone knew what to do in a situation like this it would be you. This is your moment, Edmund. You call it.'

These last words were barely out of his mouth when he spoke again, over his shoulder as it sounded, and as though taken entirely by surprise. 'Oh, I'm sorry, I didn't mean to intrude.' Then 'Hey,' he said, 'is that...?' The rest of the sentence was smothered by his hand on the mouthpiece. When he removed it again – a matter of seconds – the pitch of his voice had changed.

'I'm back in New York tomorrow,' he said, chords stretched tight, something more immediate he did not want to betray: whoever, or whatever, it was he had seen trumped for a moment the spectacle Randall was trying to describe. 'We'll talk then.'

Randall sat a full minute after DeLorean had (abruptly) hung up, the phone still in his hand, then he pressed a finger on one of the black buttons, summoning the dial tone back, and called the only Belfast number he knew by heart.

'I was wondering when I might hear from you,' Jennings said, as though it had been an overdue social call he was taking.

'We need help,' Randall said.

'I have a feeling you are not the only ones,' said Jennings.

The help, however, arrived at the factory within the quarter hour, a mere minute or two after Randall himself, which, given, as Jennings implied, how much else was under threat that night in Belfast, was beyond better than might have been expected, though there again few places under threat that night in Belfast had quite as many millions of government money tied up in them.

The captain to whom Randall opened the Seymour Hill gate could not have been more than twenty-one, a voice as clipped as the prince whose soon-to-be bride was hogging the headlines everywhere in Britain but here. Randall had met his West Point cousins, young men passing through the military on their way to high office. He shook Randall's hand, more gentleman than officer, then waved through four armoured cars, from the rear of which a platoon of soldiers dismounted. These were the men whose lives the DMC-12 was supposed to be going to save. They walked beside their vehicles in the lee of the body-press shop, trying to come at the Twinbrook gate unseen.

Randall went a few feet ahead of them, rounding the corner of the building nearest the gate on his own. The drive was a mess of rocks and broken glass though it was not quite the catastrophic vision Randall had imagined when he inched up the blind in his room. He quickly realised that there was not *a* group of people gathered outside, but two groups: the one closest to the gate itself, with their backs to him, trying to hold the other, much larger group at bay.

Seeing Randall come round the corner – or sensing

somehow what was coming round the corner behind him – this group found new and more aggressive voice. They surged forward, pressing the small group back, causing the gate and the fence flanking it to shake. A man looked over his shoulder – red-faced even at that distance and in that light – lips stretched tight with the strain of trying to hold the line.

'Are there Brits in there?' he called to Randall.

'Brits?'

'Don't fucking give me that Dumb Yank crack. These ones are shouting they seen soldiers. Did they?'

Randall glanced behind him, which was all the proof the man needed. 'They did see them! They're fucking in there.'

'They're protecting the factory.'

The red-faced man's face got redder, closer to the fence between them. Randall recognised him now. One of the storemen. An index finger poked through. '*We're* protecting the factory, telling these young bucks it's supposed to be neutral. Do you not understand? It's in more fucking danger with the Brits in there.'

Then suddenly from somewhere further back there was a shout – a cheer almost – and Randall looked up to see a black object arc overhead, trailing flame.

Instinctively he went into a deep crouch, which only delighted the shouters and cheerers and missile-throwers more. The man at the gate turned back to face them. 'Which one of you wee fuckers threw that?'

Randall, stumbling as he tried to get to his feet again could only watch, prone, as the missile – the petrol bomb – struck the flat top of a Portakabin and spread its flames all over the tarred surface.

A voice that must have been the captain's, though it sounded shriller, issued an order and a soldier broke cover, dragging a hose, which pulsed a couple of times, convulsed, and finally shot out water in a silvery crescent that seemed only incidentally to take in the Portakabin and its flaming roof.

Even the men who had been holding the young bucks back bellowed at this. More rocks came over the fence, more bottles. Here now was the cataclysm. Another three soldiers emerged from the shadows, short wide-barrelled guns already braced against their shoulders.

Someone had a hold of Randall by the collar and was trailing him back towards the armoured cars.

The captain had a megaphone now. 'Move away from the gates.' Royal command. 'My men are under orders to fire baton rounds at identified targets only. Please, move away from the gates.'

He handed the megaphone to a soldier twenty years his senior and several ranks his junior.

'You did the right thing requesting assistance,' he told Randall. 'Those men would not have been able to hold back that crowd another ten minutes on their own.'

The rocks and bottles continued to come over. The trio of soldiers continued to move their guns across the face of the crowd, trigger fingers twitching. The Portakabin roof, despite the water that was now, with two more soldiers helping hold the hose, being properly trained on it, continued to burn.

Stylianides was there, shouting, 'I am supposed to be head of security.'

The captain laid a hand on Randall's shoulder. 'Try not to worry, everyone freezes their first time.'

Randall, his first time, he could not find tongue to tell the captain, did not freeze, he fled, somewhere very far inside. His helicopter had made an unscheduled landing in a clearing in torrential rain. Aftermath of an ambush. The radio operator whose call had brought them was sitting splayed-legged on the ground bleeding through the dressing on his stomach, alternating between crying and laughing. A medic was dressing a head wound nearby, the body to which the head was attached already to Randall's eyes inert. The definitively dead were under capes, seven of them. Randall's commander was arguing with a lieutenant, pointing at the corpses – 'We're supplies, we can take the wounded, but we can't take these guys' – and then from the edge of the clearing as the lieutenant ducked back out of the range of the rotors there came a bright light – that was all Randall could remember of it – a bright light getting brighter, brighter... blinding.

Then it was one week later and he was under a bed in a hospital in Saigon. A nurse was looking in at him through a gap in the blanket draped over the frame to make a canopy. She smiled. 'Are you ready to come out now?'

His commander had wanted to have him put on a charge, refusal to obey an order, specifically the order to get out of the chopper when the mortar hit the clearing and the lieutenant disappeared along with the wounded radio operator and the medic winding bandages round a dead or dying comrade, who disappeared too, his head at any rate.

Dissociative fugue, was the diagnosis of the doctor who had, all unknown to Randall, been monitoring him since he had been brought in and sought sanctuary on the floor. He literally had not been himself from that moment to this.

'Fuck fugue,' was the commander's reaction relayed to Randall when he was transferred at length to another supplies unit. 'I have been in this army long enough to know cowardice when I see it.'

Liz heard it on the shop floor a couple of days later that, contrary to what he had told her the last time they talked, Randall had in fact gone to the States with the volunteers for retraining. Washers had phoned his Big Mate before he had even left Aldergrove for the connecting flight. Your man Randall, he told him, had weighed in while they were queuing at the check-in desk taking the piss out of each other's passport photos: Was that before you'd the operation…? Did the cops not ask you for their photo back…? Anything to take their minds off the fact that they were to be locked in a metal cylinder for seven hours six miles above the Atlantic Ocean.

'First class, of course. Gave us some crap about it being the only seat he could get by the time he booked. I tell you, I said to him, if it was me and I could I would do it every time and wouldn't give a monkey's what anybody thought of me.'

'Imagine going away and missing all the fun and games

here,' Big Mate said, winding up his report.

The fun and games had kept the factory closed the whole of the first day after Bobby Sands died. Practically the only buses moving in town were being pushed by the wee lads who had hijacked them, under instruction from the not so wee lads standing in the wings, to reinforce their barricades.

Even now on the second day only about one worker in three had been able to plot a way through the mayhem, or had attempted to.

Robert had astonished Liz this morning by proposing that he drive her right up to the gate. 'It isn't right, other people dictating to you when you can and can't work,' he said and she resisted the temptation to point out how rich that was coming from him, because she was genuinely grateful – touched – and then too maybe some of his reservations about her being here had not been entirely unjustified. Forget for the moment those Sunday mornings in Botanic Gardens (and what did they amount to really?): imagine she had told Robert that she did want to put her name down for the States; imagine she had insisted on it – as she had insisted, despite him, on applying for the job in the first place, on going for the interview and accepting the letter of offer; imagine she had wound up in a hotel somewhere over there with Edmund Randall?

'Fun and games,' Washers' Big Mate said again as he walked off, slapping his *Sun* against his thigh. 'Fun and games.'

13

Randall had left the DeLorean workers at the airport, one group waiting for an onward flight to California, and the Santa Ana QAC, the rest for the buses that would take them to the centre in Wilmington, and carried on by himself to Manhattan. (One of the Wilmington-bound workers told him with many accompanying winks he didn't blame him not taking the bus with them. 'But I'm going in a different direction,' Randall said and the man winked again. 'You don't have to explain to me.') Rain was falling when he got out of the car in front of 280 Park Avenue. A doorman ran down the steps to the sidewalk opening an umbrella. 'Came right out of nowhere,' he said and sure enough in the time it took Randall to cross the lobby to the elevators and the express car to deposit him on the forty-third floor the skies had cleared so much you could have been forgiven for thinking it had never rained at all.

Carole had been taking instruction from Marion Gibson when he entered, head bowed over her desk, and was barely able to get out from behind it in time to announce him.

'Edmund!' DeLorean looked up, took off the spectacles perched on the end of his nose and gave Randall his broadest smile. 'The way the news was reporting it I'm surprised there were flights leaving there at all. Luckily I have been in the news often enough myself to know not to believe everything I see or hear.'

'We had to get the army in.' (He could hardly get the sentence out.)

'Isn't it good to know we have support?' DeLorean was round in front of his desk now, buttocks and feet firmly planted.

Randall was pacing, right to left, left to right. 'And there's still the funeral to come. There could be more trouble at that. A whole lot more.'

DeLorean spread his hands. He was a giant bird against the window of sky at his back, riding the currents.

'Think back to the very beginning of all this, Edmund – think of the hurdles we had to overcome. And look where we are now.'

He did not, Randall knew, mean the office per se, but that inevitably was what he found himself focusing on, the apricot carpet, the bust of Lincoln, the life-size photo study of father and son, the telescope through which in rare idle moments, DeLorean liked to look down on to the street below.

'Whatever the next few days throw up we will get through that too. I feel it in here.' He gripped his shirt front, held it till his knuckles whitened. Then let go and pushed himself up off the desk. 'Now, Carole, can we get some coffee for this man?'

The coffee arrived a few minutes later in a pot with an exaggeratedly belled base. DeLorean insisted that Randall take the first cup. 'They are lovely people, the Brits, but they don't know the first thing about making coffee.'

And Randall thought as he sipped (thought *through* the recognition that it was true about the coffee) how far indeed he had travelled since he last heard that particular B word used.

DeLorean toasted with this cup: 'The Brits' – smiling – 'and the Irish.'

The phone rang in the outer office. Carole was already halfway there. She answered it on the third ring. A few seconds later the phone on the desk at DeLorean's back rang too.

'Excuse me,' he said and leaned across to answer, one long leg rising in counterweight. 'Hey... Yes, it was swell running into you.' Randall was struck by the contrast between the 'swell' and the strain in the voice. Maybe he had reached back further than he had anticipated to pick up the phone. 'Of course, next time I'm at the ranch... Well, that's good of Hetrick to offer, but it's really no bother... No, no, I will, I'll keep it in mind.'

He replaced the phone on the cradle and swung his body round again, frowning slightly, as he searched for something on his desk... found it: a sheet of paper. 'By the way, I want you to start proceedings for a compensation claim when you get back, for the riot damage.'

'The Portakabin?'

'"Additional Office Accommodation" – that is where the Hethel inventory was being relocated, isn't that what you told me?'

'Well there was very little actually in there yet. Most of it is still in transit.'

'So we'll have to pay for storage somewhere else. I've had finance here run the figures.' He gave them a final check. 'Ten million sound about right?'

Randall shook his head slowly. 'I don't know...'

'I mean, I told them you were right there on the spot, but maybe, you know, in the hurly-burly of the moment' – he had Randall's eye now; held it – 'you were nearly too close to form any sort of rational judgement.'

Randall took temporary refuge behind his coffee cup. Did he know? (Stylianides?) Was he guessing? Was this part of what he had seen in him the day they met in Kimmerly's office – the man who had never shipped overseas looking into the eyes of the man who had shrunk from danger – that, never mind the bullshit detector (itself a piece of undetected bullshit), here was someone with something still to prove to himself? Or, worse, here was someone who at a crucial juncture could be relied on to capitulate again?

DeLorean selected a platinum ballpoint pen from the desk tidy, clicked the top, and made a bold blue tick on the page.

'So, ten, then.'

First thing Randall did on arrival at his apartment was shower for half an hour trying to get the smell of the place out of his hair. He made a phone call, standing with the towel draped over his shoulder, then went to bed and slept until twenty after two the following afternoon. He got up and showered again, faster this time, and whistling. His appointment, subject of yesterday's phone call, was for four o'clock. Nothing so formal as lunch or dinner, they had agreed. A civilised mid-afternoon cocktail. Crowne Plaza: Randall's suggestion. Might as well lay more than one ghost.

With that in mind he stopped in too at the bar across the street for a shot of Polish vodka and might easily have persuaded himself of the wisdom of a second were it not for the television set in a corner of the room, across whose screen, at the precise moment he set down his empty glass, moved grim-faced people – thousands and thousands of them – following the coffin of a man who had starved himself to death to make the point that leaving a bomb in a furniture store was a political act.

He felt a secret shame. He was almost afraid that if he risked opening his mouth again his voice, inflected by his time there, would betray his complicity. And that was before he saw the banner off to one side. A DMC-12 smashing through a giant capital H: *DeLorean Workers Against the H Blocks*.

He entered the hotel lounge more assertively than he might otherwise have done. Seated at a table to the left of the door, Dan Stevens got to his feet hurriedly and a little more shakily perhaps than the first and last time Randall had met him at the *Daily News*. (Well, the man *had* been around since the days – a couple of thousand further away now than then – of Walter Chrysler.)

'Randall.' He indicated a seat on the other side of the table. 'Please, sit.'

Randall did. The waiter was on him almost instantly. 'Vodka martini,' he answered before he was even asked, and Stevens nodded his approval – of the drink, the unhesitating way it was ordered, the combination of the two, who knew?

His own drink was something bourbon based. He centred it on the scalloped paper coaster. 'It was good of you to make time to see me on your trip. Tell you the truth I wasn't even sure you would call. I know we didn't exactly get off on the right foot last time.'

'I was probably a little hair-trigger that day.'

'You had every right to be. You were taking a big step. I got to tell you, there are a lot of people in the industry who are surprised – a little upset some of them – that the factory has lasted this long.' He lifted the glass, turned the coaster over, and went through the business of centring again. 'John as ever is taking all the credit while saying he doesn't want to take all the credit. So far as we can see, though, looking in, a lot of it is down to you.'

Randall tried to deflect the praise. 'For the longest time I was used to people asking what it was I actually did,' he said, to which Dan Stevens replied that sometimes the most important jobs were the hardest to explain.

Randall went to interject again. Dan Stevens held up his hand: hear me out here. 'There has been a pretty high turnover at executive level, which is no more than was to be expected, working with John, but it can be destabilising. It could have – should have – been even more destabilising and because it wasn't people start looking at who or what is keeping the ship steady, who has been there throughout... And we heard about what happened at the unveiling: quick thinking.' He drank, ran his tongue over his teeth behind closed lips. 'If that's what you can do there in, let's be honest, pretty hostile conditions, think what you could do here with all our expertise and experience behind you, and on twice the salary you are on at the moment.'

'*Twice?*'

Stevens shrugged. 'Three times. We will hook you up with our real estate people in Detroit, find a property out in Bloomfield Hills.'

The martini arrived, lemon rind bobbing like a kiss curl.

Stevens addressed his glass to it, but stopped short of drinking. 'You have to remember, John is a gambler... Oh, not with his own money... His instinct is to keep raising the stakes – scares people off: *he must have something*. But sooner or later someone will call him on it, and then...'

'A whole lot of people in Belfast will lose their jobs.'

'Well, that's true too, although John wouldn't be alone in thinking of workers as chips.'

'Chips!'

Stevens tilted his head a little to one side. He seemed almost embarrassed by the reaction.

'I've got to say I didn't have you pegged as the sentimental type. It's the product that has to be protected, the brand. That goes, it creates a void and there's no telling what will get sucked in. I wouldn't want to be standing too close to the edge.'

Randall nodded. For all kinds of reasons it was time for him to put as much distance as possible between him and DeLorean Motor Cars Limited. He nodded again, more firmly.

Dan Stevens smiled and went to take a drink. He didn't like what he saw in his glass, or what he didn't see. 'What do you say we have another of those?'

Randall made a show of looking at his watch. 'Sure,' he said.

Stevens returned to Detroit with the promise to 'start the ball rolling', though discreetly for now, and Randall a couple of days later travelled down the I-495 to the Quality Assurance Centre in Wilmington. The cars in the compound on Ferry Road, right on the edge of the Delaware River, were the first DMC-12s he had seen since leaving Belfast. He told himself that pang he felt was only natural: he had no quarrel with the cars themselves.

The guy who met him wore shorts with socks pulled up to just below his knees, which flexed as he stood before Randall talking, like a pair of sensate potatoes (where did *that* come from?) struggling to escape the neck of a sack. Randall was relieved when they started walking to the workshop – 'Lead the way,' he said, and the knees did – and he was able to relax his face, strained from the effort of not looking.

'I'm not going to lie, it was pretty hard going the first couple of days,' the guy said over his shoulder. 'I don't know how many times I had to step in to stop a fight breaking out. Mostly your guys accusing our guys of going out of their way looking for problems, taking a wheel off just to check it had been screwed on right kind of thing... It's settled down a bit since then.' He turned with his hand poised to open the workshop door. 'Don't tell them I said this, but they are good workers.'

Good workers and, it appeared, genuinely pleased to see Randall walk in the workshop door, crowding round telling him this thing they had discovered about the alternator, this other thing about the door hydraulics. Even invited him out for a drink with them that night.

'Probably not what you're used to, like,' said the one they called Washers, he of the winks of understanding at the airport. 'You have been warned.'

'I don't know what you think I'm used to.'

A dive bar, a couple of blocks from Riverfront Market, beer by the pitcher, a stage at one end of the room on to which in due course a young woman in satin hot pants walked and without preamble pulled off her T-shirt to reveal shamrock nipple tassels. The law of supply and demand made barely covered flesh.

No one seemed to object to the failure to give a more rounded interpretation of *northern* Irishness (two of the women did pick up their purses and head for the door, but only, as they said, because there was a fella doing the same thing down the street, and no tassels) and when a tape recorder belatedly struck up 'Danny Boy', a group standing by the corner of the bar formed a circle and ignoring the now twirling shamrocks entirely sang along into one another's faces, glasses raised and touching.

'I needn't ask if you have been enjoying yourself here,' Randall said to the guy nearest him.

'This? Sure it's a bit of fun, isn't it? But I have, aye, I've been enjoying it rightly. Be glad all the same to get back.'

'Homesick?'

'Not exactly. I'm not just saying this because you're standing there, but I miss the work, you know, the cars constantly coming down the line at you – keeps you on your toes.'

There was a loud cheer from the front. The satin hot pants had come off now too. A pair of even smaller pants underneath, *Slainte!* across the behind, which was presented in a swift, toe-touching finale.

'What about you?' the worker said. 'Will you not be sorry when you have to head back to Belfast again?'

Randall frowned. The man drew his head back. 'Wait, you are coming back with us to Belfast, aren't you?'

And the look in his eyes, it was as though he fully expected the answer to be no, because that was what life had taught him to expect, that just when things seemed as though they might actually be starting to go well something always happened to throw them into doubt.

Randall slipped out of that look by turning to the bar and ordering another pitcher. Pitchers all round, make that.

* * *

It was quite possible that he was still drunk the following afternoon when he rang Dan Stevens. Certainly the woman whom he had rung a couple of minutes before *thinking* he was ringing Dan Stevens told him that he was, or at least she did the second time. 'Read the goddamn number, or get someone sober to read it for you.'

(It was the third three, for some reason he kept seeing it as an eight.)

Stevens cautioned him not to be too rash. It would be understandable if he was feeling a little conflicted. Hell, if he wasn't he wouldn't be the man Dan took him to be. So by all means vent some spleen – let rip, in fact – but promise Dan this, that he would call back in a couple of hours when he was...

'I am fine just as I am.' He held up a random selection of fingers in front of his face. Three, not six, or eight. He thought maybe he let a laugh escape, much to Dan Stevens' audible displeasure.

'I am bound to tell you you are doing a very foolish thing. Some doors you will find do not open twice.'

'I appreciate your concern, Dan, really, but what can I tell you? Turns out I am the sentimental type after all.'

He was betting his stash on the same square as DeLorean.

There were still army-issue hoses in the corridors of the administration building when he got back to Dunmurry, sand-filled fire buckets stationed outside the doors, one of which now bore the name Bill Haddad.

Whatever had happened to change his mind in the days since Randall had spoken to him in his office (the funeral pictures might not have been incidental), DeLorean had decided that the image of the factory at least was under threat and accordingly had dispatched Haddad from New York to oversee PR. Randall had not seen him since the un-festive Christmas drinks in the Waldorf Astoria, in the course of which Haddad had repeatedly pulled rank, dropping names (mostly Kennedys) and boasting of his in-depth knowledge of the Northern Irish political scene. So obviously he reacted to actually being there as though it was some sort of punishment.

Or that at least was the impression he gave at the meeting that Don, at Randall's suggestion, called between management and unions to try to minimise the impact on production of any future hunger strike deaths.

'Let's not beat about the bush here,' said Randall, 'how many more do we think are going to die?'

Haddad pushed his glasses up on to his forehead and with the same three fingertips massaged the bridge of his nose. *Has it come to this?*

One of the union guys, taking his lead, threw his pen down on the table. 'I object,' he said.

'And I am only trying to be rational. The worst thing we can do is to leave ourselves unprepared.'

'Well...' Anto broke the silence that ensued, 'there's the three boys who started in March... Hughes, McCreesh and O'Hara... And then there's Joe McDonnell who went on' – he cleared his throat of nothing – 'who went on as soon as Bobby died, and presumably if any of the other three die there will be boys go on after them.'

Randall had been writing all this down. He stopped a second after Anto did. 'Do you really think Thatcher will let it go that far?'

The guy who had thrown his pen down grunted; at least he was still in the room.

'Nobody thought she would let it go this far,' Anto said. 'And I can't see the hunger strikers backing down now. They're inside. It's like its own wee world, prison. Their loyalty is to each other before their families or even the IRA.'

The other men nodded.

Randall readied his pen again. 'So, what are we saying... Four? Five?'

Anto shuddered. 'It doesn't bear thinking about.'

'But we have to think about it.'

'Maybe five, but after that... wiser heads would have to prevail, wouldn't they?'

'Let's say six,' Randall said. 'Worst-case scenario. And if we were to allow half a day per funeral, all those who wanted to attend, that is...?'

The men looked at one another. Anto again spoke into their silence.

'They'll not all be in Belfast. Hughes and O'Hara are both Derry, McCreesh is South Armagh. The like of those I think we could keep down to a symbolic walkout – two minutes' silence on the road in front of the gate sort of thing.'

Randall nodded. Finally they were getting somewhere. 'I

am sure we can work around that. Just one thing… You see that banner they've been carrying – the car smashing through the big H Block? Do you think they could lose that?'

For the first time since they had walked in the door the union men smiled. The guy who had thrown down his pen was slipping it now into his inside pocket. 'What if they just kept it out of sight of the cameras?'

Haddad sat forward. 'Point of order, that is a PR matter.'

'Well what do you want them to do with the banner?'

He gathered up his things and headed for the boardroom door.

'Bill,' Randall called after him. 'They're waiting for an answer here.'

'Keep them out of sight of the cameras, of course,' he said angrily.

One of those who joined the strike after the first few deaths had been a member of the IRA gang (they would have preferred 'unit') that bombed the Conway Hotel. The car they were making their escape in had broken down before it was even out of the driveway. That was when, as the security guards at the Conway had told it to Randall, they burst into the off-duty police officer's house, demanding the keys of his car. (What were the chances of that, indeed?) This particular guy had managed to get away when the shooting started, but only a few months later he was out again, right in the heart of downtown, on his way to plant a bomb, again, when who should appear but the cops – again – and give chase to the van he was driving. He ditched that and tried to hijack another car, but the engine at the crucial moment cut out on him.

It could happen to anyone with any car. Ask Johnny Carson.

On such small mechanical details did fortunes sometimes turn.

He died after seventy-three days without food. Twenty-five, he was.

A waste, whatever way you cut it.

14

The one thousandth car came down the assembly line in the second week of June. Men and women were kissing it before they passed it on to the next section. By the time it got to their end of the shop there were balloons attached to the wing mirrors, streamers hanging off the rear bumpers.

'Didn't we do well?' said TC, an unconvincing Bruce Forsyth, barely even in the same language group, said Anto.

Like the nine-hundred-and-ninety-nine that had come down the line before it, the car, its streamers and balloons catching in the wind, was driven straight out of the assembly shop doors and into EVP. 'Fine-tuning' was the term used now, to minimise the work required when the cars were taken off the ships at the other end, because, despite the weeks of retraining, work 'Stateside' was still needed, although listening to some of the stories the men brought back from over there Liz didn't wonder at it. The ones the women brought back were even more lurid. (They all of them, women and men, sported badges on their overalls, given to them by their American co-workers: Honorary POG. Look like a Pig

Work like a Dog, it stood for. There were no letters for Party like a Wild Animal.) If you were to believe even the half of it they must only have gone into the workshop in the mornings for respite from the nights.

The fifteen hundredth car passed almost without comment. When it came through their section in fact Liz was on a comfort break. It was one of the Americanisms that she and Anto and TC had readily adopted, not to save them the embarrassment of admitting they sat on, or stood before, porcelain, voiding their bodies of waste, but because it better conveyed the amplitude of the 'timeout', incorporating as it often did a dander round the factory harvesting news and what passed in there for jokes (sample: what do you call a female chipmunk? A chipnun), a stop-off at the vending machines behind the chassis line, now and again a fag. (Liz's official line – to herself – was that she didn't smoke. Neither did the other two really. All the same every couple of weeks some one of the three of them would turn up with a box of ten, like they might with a box of Jaffa Cakes or a bag of Wine Gums: a wee change.) There were times when she didn't even have to ask, when Anto and TC would look at her and seem to read the thought before it was fully formed in her mind.

'Comfort break?'

'Do you know, now that you mention it... But don't one of you...?'

'Nah, listen, go on ahead.'

'Aye, do.'

'All right then, I will.'

That was the sort they were. That was the sort the factory was: a happy worker was a productive worker, even if she wasn't productive every last minute of the working day.

Randall wired the photo of the two-thousandth car off the line to New York. The workers had posed it themselves, out in the parking lot, cramming as many people as they could fit into the frame. Some of the ones higher up Randall had no idea what was supporting them unless it was sheer elation.

He received a call in the middle of that same afternoon.

'Congratulations! I have the picture right here. Now there's a sight to brighten a fellow's morning.'

It sounded as though he was on speakerphone, at the limit almost of the device's range. Randall had witnessed it many times, the way he conducted conversations, moving about the office, signing papers, reading unrelated files, communicating with Carole, Maur, Nesseth, Randall himself on occasion, by hand gesture or scribbled note or simply by holding down the secrecy button for tens of seconds at a time and talking over (or was that under?) whoever was talking to him.

He had carried on one very detailed set of negotiations with the Puerto Ricans while having his hair cut and his ears and nostrils trimmed.

'When I am in New York I live in this office. How else am I going to find the time?'

'I have been thinking, though,' he said now, from over by the window maybe, eye to the lens of his telescope, 'this is the moment we really need to push on.'

'I don't see how.' Randall's own view was of ranks of cars, serried rooftops, a renegade Irish flag among the television aerials, a rubble chute in the distant quarry. 'Unless...'

'We bring on a night shift? My thoughts exactly: double the workforce at a stroke and raise production to eighty cars a day.'

It had always been the intention, of course, but still the suddenness of the proposal caught Randall on the hop.

'What does Don think?'

'I'll let you know when I've spoken to him.'

'I told him we would need at least eight weeks to train up the new intake,' Don said later. (DeLorean had not rung back. From the way he was talking it was pretty clear Don did not know that DeLorean had phoned Randall at all.) 'He told me to "stop being so Canadian". They could learn on the job. "Hell, Don," he said,' – the accent was borderline at best – '"you have built two thousand cars with the people you have there already – let them take care of the training. We have the orders, we just need the cars to fulfil them."'

Early the following week Randall looked up from his desk to find Jennings standing in the doorway.

'Don't look so happy to see me,' the older man said.

Randall opened his hands. 'What can I say? You are just occasionally the bearer of some very bad tidings.'

'Actually' – sitting – 'I was rather hoping that you might have some tidings for me.'

'About the night shift?'

'About the stock market flotation.'

There was no use pretending when his expression had so clearly declared that he knew nothing whatever about it. Jennings, though, did pretend that he had not noticed Randall's surprise. He flicked at a speck of something on his lap. 'I am assuming there is a connection between the two,' he said. 'Entirely logical: the higher the output the greater the share value the faster the loans are repaid.'

'I can only speak to the production side,' said Randall. 'The dealers want more cars than we have been able to supply them with up to now.'

'Of course, I forgot, you were over there not so long ago. I suppose' – that speck on his lap again – 'you must have seen quite a few on the roads.'

Randall pulled open a drawer and found a roll of Scotch tape. He pushed it across the desk. 'For your trousers,' he said in answer to Jennings's quizzical look. 'Wrap it around your hand sticky side out: it works like a clothes brush. And for your further information most of the dealers hadn't even had their first deliveries when I was there. Not much chance me seeing too many cars. It's a big place, the USA.'

Jennings frowned. Randall almost felt sorry for him. It couldn't be fun having your lance blunted like that. Jennings picked at the ragged edge of the tape with his thumbnail.

'Oh,' he said, 'the compensation claim... You will be pleased to know we are offering to buy a new Portakabin and to cover the cost of transportation and installation. We expect to have change out of four hundred thousand pounds.'

He bowled the tape across the desktop with the flat of his

hand. Randall moved to his right to catch it, but the roll hit a pencil and flew instead past his left elbow.

'Unlucky,' Jennings said. 'It looked like you had that covered.'

The moment he was gone Randall was up and doing. So they were floating on the stock market. That had always been a part of the plan too. The timing had changed, was all. As Jennings had just unwittingly proved, or proved in a way he had not intended, it was all about how you reacted to sudden changes in circumstances. Whatever was required of them at this end they must be prepared to carry out, and fast, starting with the doubling of the workforce.

It made no sense to put all the new starts on the nightshift, otherwise who would there be to provide the on-the-job training? Stylianides sent a letter round those veterans of the first two thousand cars offering them the chance to volunteer. Volunteers for permanent nights were offered the further inducement of dinner – date to be arranged – with Mr DeLorean himself. *Dates* to be arranged, it was going to have to be, so many at once signed up.

Randall ran into Liz the morning after the letters went out, the first time in going on two months he had seen her face to face. An empty passageway. (There were, even before the new starts were drafted in, a thousand people working in the place, no passageway was *ever* empty.) They both checked their stride then both realised they had no option but to carry on. She tucked her chin into her chest as they drew level.

'Liz,' he said.

'Oh, hello.' As if the act of tucking in her chin had wiped her memory of having seen him two seconds before.

'I just wondered if you had got your letter.'

'I did thanks. I left it in the bin back there.'

'I don't understand.'

'No, you don't, do you? And I explained it to you so carefully the last time.'

'Oh, yes, that's right.' He couldn't understand where this hostility was coming from, hers or his. 'The man owns the wife in this country.'

'Who owns you? At least I am somewhere that I want to be.' She dipped her head in towards his as a door opened at the far end of the passageway. 'And at least I am still getting great sex.'

From her smile it must have looked to the people coming their way like a brief pleasantry. Randall had no time to come back, to tell her that she was wrong on both counts: this was where he wanted to be, for now, and in fact...

In fact.

Since coming back from the States – choosing to come back – he had been dating June from the office down the hall. Not dating so much as sleeping with. Not sleeping with so much as fucking. It was the worst kind of cliché (worse by far than chaste talks in public parks), but with the hours he worked where else was he going to meet someone? Her fiancé was working on the North Sea oil rigs. She told him the first time they fucked that she had wondered how many times she was going to have to drop that into the conversation before he twigged. She showed Randall one of the videotapes she had found in her fiancé's luggage the last time he was home: unbelievable stuff, unwatchable, nearly. 'That's all they do out there when they're not working, it's a wonder there isn't a giant geyser of come...' *Please*, he had said: *enough*, which thrilled her almost as much as the film to judge by what she did next with his hand. 'People look at me and think butter wouldn't melt, but we all do it and we all do it to get to the same place' – she provided the sound effects. 'The only thing that's different is what we do to get there.'

He was sure she was right. He just didn't think he had ever met anyone as dedicated to getting there as she was.

And when she made it...

Pandemonium. Absolute pande-fucking-monium. Anto said, no kidding, it reminded him of August '69, the streets full of people running here there and everywhere, not a clue any of them whether they were running into trouble or away from it. He said he had heard one fella asking another fella if he knew where the experimental workshop was and the fella said sorry, mate, I'm only new, you'd need to ask a supervisor that, and the first fella said to him I *am* a supervisor.

'Are you telling me there are people coming straight in as supervisors?' asked TC, whose own ambitions in that direction remained unfulfilled. 'How can that be right?'

'Maybe they have more City and Guilds than you.'

'Cunny funt.'

'Cleaner mouths,' said Liz.

The Honorary POGs walked around shaking their heads. 'Wait till they see over there the state of the cars this lot are going to turn out.'

At the end of the first week of the expanded workforce one person in every three received an empty pay packet: system overload. One person in every three on the dayshift dropped what he or she was doing and marched on the administration block. Word of their coming and the reason for it had gone ahead of them – actually one in three of the people in the administration block were marching out to join them (You too, June? You too?) – and Randall responded by setting up a table in their path and installing Gardiner from wages behind it, pen in one hand, chequebook in the other.

You could nearly hear the brakes being applied as the crowd wheeled round the corner and saw him.

'The bad news is the computer's brain wasn't big enough to cope with all the extra names,' Randall said into the temporary silence. 'The good news is Mr Gardiner here has a bigger brain than any computer outside the Space Programme, not to mention a good old-fashioned ballpoint pen.' Gardiner showed them it. 'So, if you could bear with us and form an orderly line...'

Which was the signal for a renewed free-for-all.

'It's OK! It's OK! He has a spare pen in his jacket pocket, he's not going to run out of ink – or money.'

It was like a scene from *It's a Wonderful Life* – order was miraculously restored, and the ink didn't run out, neither did the money, and – five, four, three, two, *one* – they reached the end of the working day, the first shift of it anyway, with everyone more or less content.

One of the other consequences of the doubling of the workforce was, it stood to reason (one nine-hundred-strong cross-section of the population – any population – being, morally speaking, the same as another), a doubling of the instances of petty larceny.

Bill Haddad showed up in Randall's office one morning fit to be tied. He had taken a cab the night before – black, of course, it being next to impossible to find anything more regulated – and the radio in the dash – he recognised it straight away – it was one of theirs.

Randall suggested it might just have been *very like* one of theirs.

Not very like, Haddad insisted: the exact radio, a Craig. Who else used Craigs here? Anyway, he had just been down to the stores to double-check: absolutely no doubt. He jabbed Randall's desk with his middle finger. 'We are going to have to put extra people on the gates, introduce random searches.'

'Slow down, slow down,' Randall said. 'I share your concern, obviously, but this isn't a prison, it's a factory. Things go missing now and again.'

He was thinking of the tale he had heard – one cigarette in length – down at the Conway's security hut, about the man who left the shipyard every evening with a jacket draped suspiciously over his wheelbarrow, and every evening this one foreman would pull him over and look under the jacket and find nothing. Only when the pair had retired and met on the street did the labourer put the foreman out of his misery by telling him what he had been pilfering all those years: wheelbarrows.

Haddad's finger was still pressing down on his desk. He didn't look as though he was in the mood for stories.

'John doesn't hold with searches,' Randall said simply.

'Why does that not surprise me?' said Haddad, then changing tack, 'Have you any idea what those radios are worth?'

'I know what every single thing in this factory is worth, and I know what our workers are worth too, and it's more than a toolkit or a couple of pairs of coveralls, or even a Craig radio.'

'That's a very fine sentiment, I'm sure,' said Haddad and leaning all his weight on that single finger pushed himself upright, 'but you forget that until we start to turn an actual profit the money that paid for those things isn't John's and it sure as hell isn't yours.'

It was bad enough having to take one lecture from Haddad, but to have to take another, just a few days later and this time have to admit that he had a point…

There had been a spate of bomb scares, middle of the night: middle of the night *shift*.

Three times in as many weeks Randall had been woken by a phone call telling him to get down to the plant double-quick. (On the second of these occasions he had been surprised to see Liz among the workers standing at the assembly point, though with the threat of an explosive device in the building this surprise was – *un*surprisingly – short-lived.) It was the police who pointed out after the third alert had been declared a hoax that all three calls had been made not just on the same day of the week – Wednesday – but at the same time of night, exactly a quarter after two. A couple of days later they confirmed what had begun to seem obvious: that all three calls had been made from inside the assembly shop, from one particular phone, near the Engine and Gearbox Storage area, whose calls – and the list of them was staggering: Australia and everywhere – for some reason did not appear to be going through the plant's own operator system. With the cops to back him Haddad was not about to be dissuaded. Never mind the bad press if the story was to get out, this was effectively sabotage, this hurt everybody: they would have to mount a stakeout.

Under cover of running repairs to the ceiling a tiny camera was installed high on the wall facing the phone. Randall did not even bother going to bed the following Wednesday, but killed the time until half past midnight (Erroll Garner *Concert by the Sea*: not one he would be sorry to return) then took himself down to the factory.

They had set up the monitor in a corner of Stylianides' office, its bluish greys the only artificial light in the room. There were plates of sandwiches under Saran wrap on the desk, two large thermos flasks of coffee and half a dozen mugs: one each for Stylianides, Haddad, Randall (Don had been more than happy to delegate) and the three cops who had arrived a little ahead of Randall wearing boiler suits with the name of a pest control company on the back.

'You'd be amazed the places these will get you into,' the cop in charge said. 'I've had people shake my hand and then seconds later they're on the floor with the cuffs on them.'

At two-fifteen precisely a figure appeared, a man, moving at improbable speed. They all sat forward at once, heads almost meeting in an arc around the monitor. (Mingled breath of coffee and cigarettes and egg salad.)

'How tall *is* that guy?'

'Wait a second, is he...?'

'What does he have on his feet?'

'He is: he's roller-skating.'

He was, and wearing a child's Stan Laurel mask. He skated out of the picture and a few seconds later skated across it in the opposite direction, and out again. When next he appeared he was balancing on one leg, changing over then to the other on which he performed a passable pirouette before exiting a final time backwards, thumb to Stan Laurel's nose and fingers wiggling.

Randall didn't know about the rest of them, it was all he could do to stop himself applauding.

'You don't suppose, do you,' he said instead, 'he knew he was being watched?'

Liz never heard the words counter-surveillance used, but she did on several occasions overhear conversations to the effect that you had to keep an eye on the bosses to make sure that they never found out they weren't the ones running the factory.

The bomb scares were a breach of that protocol as much as anything else and, worse still, they had drawn attention to the open phone line next to the storage area whose existence to that point close on two thousand people had managed to keep secret from a couple of score.

She had used it herself for the first time a few weeks earlier to phone her sister in Melbourne. It was tantamount to stealing, she knew, but she had been growing more and more concerned about the tone of Vivienne's letters and couldn't think when she would ever get the privacy at home to have the conversation they needed to have.

Mind you, half of the conversation they did have was taken up with her having to explain how she was able to phone at all. Vivienne sounded as though she had been drinking. Liz saw her framed in the doorway of the bedroom they had used to share, swaying, as though she had brought the night's music home with her. Drink had added to her lightness in those days.

No more.

'What time is it there?' she asked thickly.

'Half eleven.'

'In the morning? I thought you would be in your work.'

'I am, but it's OK.'

Ten thousand miles away a cigarette was lit. Liz took the full force of the smoke jet in her ear. 'What kind of place is that?'

'Truthfully? I think it might be the best place I have ever in my life worked.'

'And you have so much to compare it to.' Liz was nearly grateful for the dig, or the speed with which it was delivered. That was more like her big sister.

'You know what I mean,' she said. 'But what about you?' She rested her head against the wall, making sure the circuit was absolutely closed. 'How are things in your place?'

'My place?'

'I just thought from some of your letters that maybe, I don't know, maybe there was something you wanted to talk about.'

Vivienne laughed sharply – the cheek of you! – then started to cry.

Liz made up her mind the minute she hung up the phone that she was going out there to see her. Later, when the dinner things were all cleared away and the boys had taken their perpetual argument up the stairs, she set a cup of tea on the arm of Robert's chair, a chocolate digestive balanced on the saucer.

'Do you remember when the boys were in primary school and that wee P1 boy – Thompson – was knocked down and killed? Do you remember they became obsessed the two of them with dying?'

Robert paused stirring his sugar. Flip, yeah, now that she mentioned it, he did. The father worked in the hardware shop, had a harelip...

'And do you remember' – she must not let him stray off the path she was laying – 'what we said?'

Robert resumed stirring thoughtfully. 'Probably something like it was a one in a million chance.'

'Anything else?'

'They had to make the most of every moment… we all had to.'

'Exactly,' she said. (She did love him.)

He smiled and took a bite from the biscuit where it had been softened by contact with the cup.

'I'm signing up for nights one week in every two. I'm putting the money away to go out and see Vivienne next year, in case the opportunity doesn't come around again.'

He had practically fed her the line. Anyway, she thought later, that great sex thing worked both ways. He was hardly likely to go and change the locks, was he?

It exhausted her, of course, the work, the switching between the two routines, the near impossibility of a full day's sleep. A couple of weeks in she didn't know which end of her was up. By half past ten on her second Tuesday back on days she was dead on her feet, or at least her knees.

She gave the wrench a twist on the last nut of an uncooperative passenger seat and slumped forward in an attitude of prayer.

'I'm never going to last till my tea break,' she said into the soft leather.

TC, working on the other side, spoke to her across his seat and hers. 'Sure, why don't you take ten minutes now?' There were no hooters or whistles to work to, you took your break when you needed it, always supposing your workmates could spare you. 'Me and Anto can manage. Can't we, Anto?'

'Certainly.'

'Ah, no, I couldn't do that on yous.'

'It's not a bit of bother. Tell her, Anto.'

'It's not a bit of bother.'

'Well...' She had pulled herself up on to her feet. 'If you're absolutely sure.'

She walked away wiping her hands on a rag. God, it felt good to be able to turn your back. And to think Robert didn't trust those fellas. The things they did for her, because actually, now she thought of it, it wasn't just the comfort breaks, they were forever letting her take a couple of minutes here and there – You go on ahead, save us a seat in the canteen, we'll just finish tidying up.

She stopped in front of a vending machine full of sweets and chocolate bars. She felt in the pocket of her overalls and found two 10p pieces. It was fate.

TC was standing with his back to the car, looking off in the other direction, when she returned barely two minutes after she had left, a Curly Wurly dangling from each hand.

The seat that had caused her all the grief was on the ground next to Anto's legs. The rest of him was inside the car, from where a scratching sound was coming – a sound she could not associate with any part of the assembly process that she had ever been involved in – a *gouging* sound was probably closer to the mark.

'What's that seat doing on the ground?' she said.

TC nearly did himself an injury he spun round that fast. 'Liz!' It sounded more like a warning than a greeting.

'Is that not the one I just finished putting in?'

The gouging sound stopped. TC had come round to place himself between her and the open car door.

'I, ah, wasn't happy, there was a wee problem with the, ah, what-you-me-call-it.'

Liz pushed past him. She could have knocked him right over without much difficulty. 'Anto, what are you doing in there?'

As he was withdrawing his head from the seat well she was sticking hers in. There were metal shavings in a small heap below... she wasn't sure at first *what* exactly: a candle it looked like, twists of something thorny – barbed wire? – around it.

'What the hell is that?'

'A hunger strike candle,' Anto said matter-of-factly.

'What's it doing in our seat well?' TC opened his mouth to say something, but the penny for Liz had already dropped. 'Wait, are there other cars with "hunger strike candles" hidden in the seat wells too? Is that what all the "go on ahead, Liz, take ten minutes there" is about?'

'No.' TC finally got to speak. 'Some of them have the candles behind the dashboard and some of them, you know, depending on the section have Celtic or Rangers or No Pope Here.'

'Anto?' She was conscious that she was talking to them the way she talked to her own boys, switching her gaze from one to the other in order to winkle out the truth; conscious but powerless to stop it. 'Are you not the one who told me you had to walk out and take your place on those pickets because you never knew who was watching? And now here you are doing something that no one will ever even see?'

Anto was still sitting on the ground, hands dangling over his knees. They made a gesture, a half-hearted attempt at flight.

'You can't build a sports car in the middle of Belfast, in the middle of all this, and not expect it to carry some sort of a mark.' His eyes slipped off her face. 'I don't think you can have any idea.'

'About what? About anger? About people dying?' She was slapping her thighs with those stupid fucking chocolate bars. 'I lost a brother to one of your martyrs' comrades. Dragged him out of his lemonade lorry just up the road here and put a bullet in his head. Put out an apology the next day saying they had mixed up his lemonade lorry with another one that delivered to army barracks.'

Anto's eyes were locked on hers again. He had the grace to look stricken. 'You never said.'

'You're right, I never did. I never did because I made a promise early on that I wasn't going to go through life thinking of myself as a victim.' Vivienne in contrast had resolved never to set foot in the country again. 'Anyway,' her anger was ebbing, turning back on her for breaking even for a moment her promise to herself, and her brother, 'Pete wouldn't have wanted me being bitter on his behalf. That wasn't the type of him.'

'But still...' Anto was on his feet now, TC beside him.

'Listen, Liz, we'll not do any more of them,' TC said and reinforced it with his thumb on his breastbone: down and across. 'Swear to God.'

'You can do what you like, TC, but the first car that comes through here after lunch is all mine. Now, get that seat bolted back in, and here' – she shoved them into their hands – 'enjoy your Curly Wurlys.'

She entertained all kinds of possibilities, trying a few of them out on paper napkins in the canteen – a lemonade bottle with her brother's name on the label seemed particularly apt, but she doubted she would have the time or the skill under pressure to do it justice, and like she had told Anto it was a long time ago now. Six years, a thousand other deaths. She tore that napkin to shreds, and all the others she'd drawn on, and shoved them deep into the wastepaper bin.

It would have to be words. There was something to be said for No Pope Here. The form of it rather than the content. Short, to the point.

The boys (my God, she had even begun to think of them like that) had given her a wide berth while she deliberated. It was clear, on her return, that they had resolved to keep the mood light-hearted.

'Are you ready for your first act of vandalism?' Anto said.

'I had a long life before I came to work here,' she said and was surprised herself at how convincing she sounded. 'Just keep watch.'

They stationed themselves at either end of the next car that came down the line, letting on to be searching for a spanner, inspecting the bodywork for a non-existent scratch (always the hardest to detect).

She knelt, took out the little metal file she always carried in the back of her purse, leaned in and got to work.

She had been dead right not to attempt the lemonade bottle. Christ, it was hard enough to manage a simple straight line. Aagh! Straightish.

'Coat!' Anto, under cover of a cough, barked the code they had agreed for manager and she nearly brained herself on the dashboard before he said in his normal voice, 'False alarm, he's away the other way.'

Back to work she went. Scratch, scratch, scratch.

'Are you nearly done there?' TC whispered.

'Nearly.' She was barely started, but so what, he could flipping well wait.

Another half a minute. The point of the nail file was bending with the effort of bringing a curved line back to the plane from which it had without her intending it deviated. Shit, shit, shit.

'Would you for crying out loud come on!' TC said and could not have sounded more strangulated if someone had indeed had their hands about his throat.

She dragged the file down the metal then started on another letter.

'Seriously,' Anto said from the other end, 'you're going to have to get out of there now.'

'Right,' she said, 'right,' and wrote four letters more. 'OK, give me a hand getting this seat in.'

From the colour of his face as he trotted round to help, TC even looked as though he had been throttled.

'So,' said Anto, 'are you going to tell us what you did?'

'Do you really want to know? Do you really *really* want to know?' Liz gave the rear nut a wrench. 'It'll cost you most of your year's wages to find out.'

15

DeLorean that late summer and early autumn was consumed with the proposed stock-market flotation. Jennings had not been altogether wrong. Here was the opportunity to unburden the company almost overnight of government debt. 'Set sail into open water,' was a term DeLorean used more than once and Randall did actually picture the shares as so many tiny vessels corralled in a harbour, waiting for the wind to fill their sails, or the waves outside to subside a little.

DeLorean had recently completed the purchase of the Lamington Farm estate at Bedminster, New Jersey, preparatory, as Randall understood it, to selling the Pauma Valley ranch, bringing his work life and family life closer: a seventy-five minute drive at the week's end (in so far, with a stock-market flotation imminent, the working weeks ever ended) instead of a six-hour flight.

Midway through September Humphrey Atkins was whisked away to become Lord Keeper of the Privy Seal. (Centuries, it took, to perfect job titles like that.) A new secretary of state, Jim Prior, arrived and, looking, in the television reports, slightly puzzled that no one had thought of doing it before (although a look of puzzlement, Randall soon learned, ranging from slight to extreme, was habitual with him) made a point of going into the prison to talk to the prisoners refusing food. Within weeks the hunger strike was over. The six deaths that the management and the union leaders had, as an absolute maximum, been preparing for had been exceeded by four. Randall who went over it and over it in his head hundreds of times then and in the years that followed could not decide which of the parties to the dispute was the more fanatical.

The mood in the factory the morning after it ended was subdued, sombre even. Only the announcement of the five-thousandth car off the assembly line lifted spirits. Actually, such was the release, it nearly lifted the roof off.

Randall stopped by Don's office shortly after the announcement was made.

'I didn't see that coming.'

'That's because it's the four thousand eight hundred and ninetieth... I thought today might be a day for rounding up,' said Don and clasped his hands behind his head. 'I don't understand it. I thought they would have been glad, all of them, that madness in the prisons was over. Unless of course they're thinking the same thing I've been thinking.' His gaze had drifted off towards the window, but returned now. 'This government seems to like a fight. Who is it going to pick one with next?'

Two days later a member of Thatcher's party accused DeLorean in the press of misuse of public funds, citing the example of Warren House, whose bathroom taps he claimed were made of solid gold.

DeLorean was en route to Daytona Beach when Randall rang him.

'Who is this fucking guy?' DeLorean wanted to know. Nicholas Winterton was the answer and Randall by now had enough experience of the British political classes to further identify him as one of the 'hang 'em and flog 'em brigade'. Hang 'em, flog 'em, anything at all but subsidise 'em.

DeLorean's first instinct was to hire someone to investigate Winterton's own expenses. He didn't care what country you were talking about, nobody walked very far in public life without getting some shit on his shoes.

'And what's Haddad doing? Why isn't he on the phone to me?'

'Well, you see, that's the thing, Winterton's taken all this stuff from a memo Bill sent you last Christmas.'

'Bill sent me a memo about faucets? The hell he did. If Bill Haddad had sent me a memo it would be sitting in my office not that asshole's.'

'It was in your office,' Randall said. 'Marion leaked it.'

'Marion?'

'Seems she landed in England the day before yesterday and went straight to Winterton's constituency.'

He could nearly hear the blood pulsing in DeLorean's temples. 'No,' he said at long last. 'It's not possible.'

'It's in the newspapers, the London *Times*, the *Daily Express*...'

But DeLorean had decided. He said it again, 'It's not possible.'

Randall awoke next morning to photographers camped outside the gates of Warren House. They were still there – if anything had swelled in numbers – when he returned from the factory that evening, there when he picked up the phone at gone eleven o'clock to call DeLorean again.

'I think we should let these guys in,' Randall said.

'Why in the world would we do that?'

'To let them see we have nothing to hide.'

'Edmund, you ought to know better than that. We don't capitulate to asinine gossip in this country.' By 'this', Randall assumed, he meant 'that', which is to say not the country from where he was speaking but the one where Randall stood listening while looking out at the spark-spark-flare of the press photographers' lighters. 'And we don't let people bully their way into our homes either. If anyone does think we have something to hide let them get a warrant.'

So then early the following evening the police arrived, two armoured Land Rovers of them, very apologetic. *Doubly* apologetic: 'We need two Land Rovers these days just to check a dog licence,' said the inspector who dismounted from the back of the second, warrant in hand. They had been asked, he went on, as part of the investigation into the allegations made by Mr Nicholas Winterton to examine certain fixtures and fittings…

'You mean faucets?'

'Gold painted,' the inspector said to Randall when his

examination of the f-words in question (it had lasted for several silent minutes) was complete. 'Gold painted,' he said to his men, distributed about the sitting-room sofas as comfortably as their holsters and body armour would allow. He turned again to Randall. 'That's not really the same thing at all, is it?'

'No,' said Randall, 'it isn't,' and he heard all around him the sound of heavily armed men struggling to lever themselves up from soft furnishings.

Nicholas Winterton was not so easily satisfied, or as eager to quit his cushion on the sofa of a Breakfast TV set, which he had been inhabiting, it seemed, non-stop since he had set the misuse-of-public-funds hare running. Well, parliament was, for all that it was October, still in summer recess. Where else did he have to be?

There had been further 'revelations' in the papers about DeLorean's track record with expenses at General Motors: the highest claims in the entire company – highest in the entire *history* of the company.

Which finally brought the man himself into the fray, in an Italian-suited, Breakfast-TV-sofa, thank-you-for-giving-me-the-right-of-reply kind of way. 'I am proud of my expense claims at GM,' he told the interviewer, with a corroborating tilt of his chin. 'Do you know why? Because I never once disguised them the way executives did who were spending three times as much as me, and I never – ever – freeloaded on dealers out in the field who were already getting a hard time over *their* expenses. I settled all my bills and brought the

receipts back to head office where everyone could see them.'
As for the memo that had started all of this the police had
already investigated some of its more outlandish accusations,
but the fact that such a memo existed proved how open and
transparent the DeLorean Motor Company was. He did not
think there was a single shredder in the whole organisation.

Sure, some people who worked for him asked questions.
That was their prerogative: more than their prerogative, it was
their duty as DeLorean Motor Company employees. Frankly,
the more of these sorts of memos there were in circulation the
better. We all liked to think we were going to be around for
ever – and he sure as heck wasn't planning on going anywhere
any time soon – but 'All Things Must Pass', wasn't that what
they said? At least he could be sure he would be leaving some
pretty well informed people behind. If anybody was looking
for some DeLorean *gold*, meanwhile, they could enter the
raffle that American Express was planning on running for
two specially commissioned DMC-12s: not painted, but
24-carat-electroplated.

The interviewer, hands dangling between his knees now,
cross-examination over, segued into a question about Cristina
Ferrare. Actually, a volley of them: She was back on the small
screen in the US, was that right? *The Love Boat*? Was he a
fan of the series? How much influence did he have on her
choice of roles?

'With respect, you obviously don't know Cristina if you
think I could influence the parts she chooses. Of course' – a
smile as he said this – 'I had a few ideas for improvements

to the *boat*, although' – the smile turned rueful – 'I thought maybe I ought to confine my observations to the engine-room and the *exterior*...'

Even the cameraman could be heard to chuckle.

A week and a day after it broke Winterton's story was officially a non-story. Police on both sides of the Irish Sea let it be known that they would not be making any further enquiries.

All the same the announcement of the stock-market flotation was put on hold for a few weeks to allow the scandal that wasn't (because despite the retractions there were always those who were slow to pick up on the 'wasn't') time to fade from the share-buying public's consciousness.

You only got one chance with something like this. Even a dollar below the optimum could jeopardise the entire issue.

Marion, meanwhile, to no one's great surprise, did not return to New York. Haddad too was gone, though in the opposite direction, his name removed from the door in Dunmurry as quickly as it had gone up, and letting it be known that his departure at any rate would not be quiet. He had served the goddammed Kennedys, the UN, it would take a hell of a lot more than a moral pygmy like John DeLorean to shut him up.

June's fiancé had been home from the rigs on an extended leave, in the course of which he had landed an interview at Lear Fan through a friend who worked there. He had the funniest story, she said to Randall in one rather snatched conversation, which she must remember to tell him next time they had 'a proper chance to talk'. Although speaking of that, she had also, while he was home, spent a lot of time discussing the wedding, less than six months away now. It had put manners on her – she smiled – well a wee bit anyway. Maybe when the honeymoon and all was over and her *husband* was back on the rigs – somehow she couldn't see him settling to a job in a factory – she and Randall could, you know, pick things up again, assuming he was still around himself. Randall suggested she might feel differently once the ring was actually on her finger (June: 'I can't think why'), but, for what it was worth, yes, he thought there was a fair chance he would still be here. He had caught himself a couple of times lately actually making plans predicated on that fact. Maybe come the summer he would have Tamsin over, fly out there and bring her back with him, or at least as far as Dublin if Pattie was nervous about her coming north. He could take her to the Ring of Kerry, Connemara, Blarney Castle. Her face when she saw that: an actual castle, Tamsin... or when she went into a café and asked for a soda... Thoughts to raise the spirits as the autumn days turned darker, danker.

On one such day – the darkest and dankest yet – Thursday, towards the end of November, three transporters, each carrying twenty-four cars, left mid morning, on schedule, for the docks. Some time after two that afternoon Randall took a call from one of the drivers. All three of them were parked up in a lay-by about a mile from the harbour, pointing back towards the factory. 'The fella at the gate said he had instructions not to let us in. Said there were dock fees outstanding. I saw the phone box here and thought maybe I would ring before we drove back through the town to the factory. I mean people are always waving when they see us and they'd be wondering, you know, was there something the matter.'

'Thank you,' Randall said. 'Sit tight, we'll get this sorted.'

Randall had no clear idea himself what the matter was, why the fees had not been paid. He knew only that spending time now trying to get to the bottom of it risked exposing more than just the driver and his colleagues to scrutiny.

Without a moment's further thought he pulled out his contacts book and phoned the harbour master.

'I understand we have a small problem here.'

'There is a problem, certainly. As for the size of it, I suppose in the scheme of things it is not particularly large, no, but if you put yourself in my place...'

'How much exactly?' Randall asked. He listened. 'It'll be with you by the end of the afternoon.'

He sat for a second or two with the receiver in his hand – this was the right thing to do – then phoned the bank where he had his personal account.

'Mr Randall!' the manager said. He sounded as though he had food in his mouth and was trying desperately to swallow. Finally. 'To what do I owe the pleasure?'

'I wanted to arrange a temporary overdraft facility.'

'Of course, of course.' Dabbing at his mouth now, with sandpaper, as the phone made it sound. 'And what had you mind?' Randall named the figure. The manager stopped dabbing, collected himself. 'I would need to ring head office for approval.'

'It would be very temporary indeed,' Randall said, sorry that he hadn't just come straight out with it when he had the man at a disadvantage.

'I am sure it will just be a formality.'

While he was pacing the floor waiting for the call back, Randall overheard two guys passing beneath his window, talking.

'Here's what I'm wondering,' said one. 'All parts are guaranteed for twenty-five years, right? And we're going to be building eighty cars a day for, what – two hundred and fifty days a year? So what's that?'

'I don't know.'

'I'll tell you what it is: twenty thousand cars a year. Multiply that by twenty-five, that's half a million cars before anyone has to buy a new one. Do you get what I'm saying?'

'I think so.'

Randall looked out, but whoever they were they were gone.

The phone rang. The bank manager, preening himself. 'That is all arranged,' he said. 'I will just need a signature from you, if you wanted to call first thing in the morning.'

'No.' Whether the cars shipped out today now or not they had to be got on to the portside of the harbour gates. 'It has to be this afternoon.'

'That might be cutting it a bit fine, getting in from Dunmurry. You know we close at half-past three.'

'I have my coat on,' Randall said, taking it down from the rack.

On his way out to the car he took a quick sideways step into the experimental workshop. It reminded him of that first visit to the Kimmerly offices in Detroit. The car disassembled, parts numbered and recombined. In one corner a hammock hung. The guys working there looked like they not shared a decent night's sleep between the three of them, here or anywhere else, in weeks. They were grouped around a chassis with the steering column on the right-hand side. They barely glanced at him even when he coughed.

'From Coventry?' he asked. 'How close are they with that, do you think?'

'Could go into production spring of next year,' said one.

'No problem,' said another.

Which was, Randall thought as he hurried on out, at least half a million more to keep them all going over the next two and a half decades.

The bank's commissionaire already had the key in the lock when he arrived. He turned it behind Randall's back. 'We stop letting them in after about a quarter past,' he said. There were about fifteen of 'them' in the line for the tellers, two-thirds clutching bags of coins for deposit. The commissionaire raised an eyebrow at Randall beneath the peak of his white-covered cap – 'It all has to be counted,' he said, 'every last half pee of it' – and led him, smartly, across to the manager's office. The manager – rather unimpressive, rumpled even, in comparison – had the papers laid out on his desk. He uncapped his pen.

'Here,' he said, 'and here...' Randall wrote his name twice. 'And that's us.' The manager smiled. 'Can I offer you a drink, perhaps?'

'I had better not.'

'Of course, of course.' The manager looked despondently at the ground before Randall's feet. At his feet themselves, maybe, his shoes. He had made an error of judgement – an error perhaps of national judgement.

'In other circumstances, mind you...' said Randall.

'Of course.' The manager's face brightened, but only a little. 'Of course.'

Randall was offered a drink at the docks too, by the harbour master, 'a small drop of something', to show there were no hard feelings.

'I understand entirely,' Randall said, breaking off to blow on the cheque to make sure the ink was dry. 'I think I would be happier if I knew the cars were safely through the gates first.'

A harbour-police car was already on its way to where the transporters were parked up to tell them to turn around again. The drivers sounded their horns as they passed Randall standing with the harbour master.

It was by now approaching a quarter to six and thoroughly dark. 'OK,' said Randall and clapped his hands under his arms – he had only now remembered that he had nothing heavier on than a sport coat, 'I'll have that drink now.'

He stopped in the town centre afterwards, emboldened

by the generous measure of whiskey the harbour master had poured for him (the Lord only knew what a big drop would have looked like), and by the larger than usual number of people abroad on the streets.

It was the night, he quickly gathered, of the Christmas lights 'switch-on'. The ceremony was over by the time he arrived, the tree before the City Hall – tall and rangy, teenager-ish – already illuminated. The stores were still open, which, he had been here long enough now to know, was something of a novelty, the practice of the last decade being for everyone, shop workers as well as shoppers, to get the hell out the moment the clocks struck five.

Some of the civilian searchers at the security gates straddling Donegall Place, the main shopping street, had attached sprigs of mistletoe to the metal grilles above their heads. Tonight at least the people who presented themselves before them, bags already open, arms half raised, did so without too much of a scowl. Randall had just emerged, level with the doors of Boots the Chemist, from the customary, perfunctory frisk – a couple of pats on the sides, a palm swept up the back of the jacket: *on you go* – when a firmer hand on his shoulder arrested his progress.

'I had been hoping to bump into you some time soon, although I hadn't quite pictured it like this.'

Jennings – for it was his voice, his hand – was dressed in his off-duty clothes, camel hair coat folded over the arm of a navy blazer. His shirt was the palest blue and open at the neck from which an actual cravat – silk, naturally – puffed out.

'If it's about the business at the docks,' Randall said (was there anything in this city the man *didn't* know about), 'that has all been taken care of.'

For once, though, it was Jennings whose face betrayed his ignorance. 'The docks?' He shook his head and steered Randall a few feet to the left to the ornate entrance to a narrow, yellow-lit shopping arcade.

'He has made enquiries about deferring the first interest payment.' If there had been any doubt who the pronoun referred to, the mention of an interest payment dispelled it. 'I don't know what influence you have with him, but whatever you have I would urge you to use it to dissuade him. There is still time.'

At several points in the course of their exchange he had glanced over his shoulder, to ensure that they were not being overheard, Randall assumed, but now Jennings as he took his leave fell into step with a tall and equally well-groomed youth who had been standing all this time behind him. Son, could have been, or nephew, or... Randall realised that what he knew about the man would fit on the back of a postage stamp.

He realised as well that the pleasant effects of the harbour master's whiskey had suddenly worn right off. Ho-ho-ho, to you too, Mr Jennings.

DeLorean when they spoke the next day made much of Randall's initiative in the docks' 'mix-up' – twice what he had paid out would be lodged in his personal account before the close of business there today – and made light of Jennings's concerns over the interest payment. It was pretty much standard practice to miss the first one, although frankly – a little firmer now – it was not Jennings's place to bandy about the details of a private conversation, in fact he had a good mind to take it up...

'I wouldn't if I was you.' They both paused. He had never before said no to anything DeLorean had proposed. 'At least, not just yet,' he added quickly.

Nothing from the other end of the line for several seconds more, then a long breath out. 'All right, in December then, face to face.'

'You're coming over again?'

'For the Christmas party. We have come through a hell of a year. I want us all to celebrate together.'

The way Liz heard it (she was on nights that week) the choice of hotel was decided by the toss of a coin, the workers who used the Twinbrook gate not being best keen on the Conway, nor the Seymour-Hill-gate users on the Greenan Lodge – aka the (Oh, the wit of it!) Fenian Lodge – on Black's Road.

A large crowd had gathered in the canteen to watch. Randall it was who stepped forward with the coin, which was taken in turn by a representative of each gate – this one biting down on it after checking it wasn't double-sided, that one pretending to slip it into his pocket – before being returned to him for tossing, best of three. No prizes for guessing who called (crowned) heads. It came down tails the first two: Greenan Lodge. A groan for every whoop, but then, as the whoopers all said as they walked back to work, side by side with the groaners, sure it was Christmas, one place was as good, or as bad, as another.

The Born Again set said there was no good about any of them, ever, and let it be known that they would not be attending.

Like they would be fucking missed, said Steve, who was telling all this to Liz. Steve's wife, Niamh ('we're the perfect couplet'), was working days. They had one hour a day in which to swap news 'and other stuff', which Liz assured him she would rather not hear about. What she was interested in hearing that particular night was that DeLorean was coming over for the party too, that he might even have an important announcement to make, which was reassuring because a rumour had run round the factory one afternoon the week before that three of the transporter lorries had been refused entry to the docks – a huge wodge of cash owing.

Even the fact that no lorries arrived back at the factory didn't put paid to the rumour entirely. There were still one or two who maintained they knew what they knew and that was that, but maybe there would always be one or two, just like there would always be a Born Again set getting their knickers in a twist about people having a few drinks and singing sentimental songs every December.

16

Randall had noticed the last time he had seen him that DeLorean was carrying a Sony Walkman, not playing music on it, *carrying*, turning it over in his hands at idle moments in the back seat of the car, examining the internal spindles, the mechanism that opened the cassette-tape drawer. *Why didn't I think of this?*

He thought it might be a nice gesture to make up a tape of the records he had been taking out of the library on Botanic Avenue, evidence of how his education was proceeding: Lester Young and Mezz Mezzrow, Barney Bigard's 'Nine O'Clock Beer' and 'C-Jam Blues'.

He spent hours over the selection and sequence (open with the drum fill in 'Concerto for Clarinet' – Artie had to be in there somewhere), hours more over the recording itself, lying on his stomach in front of the hi-fi waiting for the right moment to press pause and minimise the hiss between tracks. (The only other tape he could remember having made was for Pattie, her first birthday after they met. Sitting with a small cassette recorder on his lap, microphone pointed at the record player. 'Laughing', by The Guess Who. 'You took away everything I had you put the hurt on me.' In retrospect maybe the writing had been on the wall there from the very start.)

He even had June help him print up a custom-made liner, track-listing on the inside and on the outside a DMC-12 flanked by a clarinet and a tenor sax, the title arcing in a banner overhead. *Sounds of DeLoreland*, he called it, in imitation of Birdland.

Kept it in the top left-hand drawer of his desk, sneaking looks now and then, half the time not even aware he was doing it.

All in all, he was pretty proud of it.

Tinsel hung all about the assembly shop. There were shoe-whitener snowflakes on the bathroom mirrors and cartoons pinned up of sleighs with gull-wing doors. Anto told Liz there had been an agreement between all the union reps: they were to inform their members that only Christmas trees and Santas were permitted behind the dashboards and in the seat wells from now to Epiphany.

He and Liz were sharing the dayshift with another woman, Amanda, TC having booked a week's leave for his latest City and Guilds exams.

She had moved from the north-west of England specially, had Amanda (a typical Amanda sentence structure was that), her and her husband and their three wee girls. Lasses, she called them. Gracie Fields, Anto called her, until she started calling him Bert Lynch, after the James Ellis character in *Z Cars*. 'I don't sound anything like him,' Anto said. 'And did you actually listen to Gracie Fields ever?' asked Amanda.

There was no work to be had anywhere over there, at least no work to compare with this.

'You may hope that the word doesn't spread too far or there'll be a whole lot more like me come the New Year.'

'The more the merrier,' said Liz.

Anto on that occasion said nothing.

DeLorean flew in via Prestwick in Scotland late on the afternoon of the day of the Christmas party, looking as he always did at the end of those transatlantic flights as though he had ridden a couple of blocks in a cab.

'We have to go to Stormont Castle,' was the first thing he said at arrivals. First thing to Randall: he had already stopped to pose for a photograph with a woman and her baby daughter and had answered good-naturedly the inevitable shout of 'Here, give us one of your cars', from a man egged on by his friends, with the line that his particular car was getting the extra-special treatment and would be another few weeks yet.

'Secretary of state?' asked Randall.

'Actually, I was hoping to speak to his boss: conference call.' DeLorean had already in the time it took him to say this over his shoulder (Randall as ever was half a pace behind) strode two-thirds of the way down the Plexiglas corridor to the exit. He paused at the end to allow Randall to catch up. 'A few loose ends I'd like to get tied up before the holidays.'

There was a point on the journey in from the airport where the motorway bent to the right and the city opened up like a child's pop-up book, the commercial core on the right-hand page and on the left the docks and the shipyard, with low green hills on the far margin, the underused parliament building standing out against them, elephant white.

They crossed the river – the spine of the book – into a neighbourhood of cramped houses and single-window shop fronts, with here and there a derelict-looking factory to relieve the monotony. The Christmas decorations – green, red and gold – competed for space and attention with the year-round displays of the British flag and coordinating bunting. After the initial exchanges in the arrivals hall DeLorean had withdrawn into an almost meditative state, gathering his thoughts maybe for the conversation ahead. Randall had the *Sounds of DeLoreland* in his jacket pocket and once or twice reached inside to take it out, but, no, this wasn't the moment.

They approached the Stormont grounds by the side gates. The driver wound down his window. 'I have Mr John DeLorean here,' he told the policeman on duty. (Mr John DeLorean dipped his head and smiled over the driver's shoulder.)

'Is that right?' said the policeman and proceeded to sweep the outside of the car with a bomb detector, squatting to reach up into the wheel arches. He checked the trunk and under the hood, drumming his fingers on the latter when he had closed it again. Stopping suddenly. 'OK.'

'What was that about?' DeLorean asked as the car pulled away.

The driver shrugged. 'Some people, the wee bit of power goes to their head. Also' – he changed from second gear to third – 'it's cold out there. He's probably saying to himself why should I be the only one to suffer.'

They bypassed the parliament building entirely, following the road between the trees to the castle, which to Randall's eyes more resembled the home of a Hollywood star of the Douglas Fairbanks era, and which for the ten years of what the British called Direct Rule was where the real power resided.

Randall turned as he got out of the car and slipped the cassette to the driver. 'Maybe you could put this on when we come back.' All the loose ends tied, the holidays about to begin.

More security awaited them at the top of the steps up to the front door – a chrome wand with a loop at the end, which traced the outline of their jackets and pants with profuse apologies from the policeman wielding it, who was obviously having a better, or at least warmer day than his friend at the gate.

'Will you both be going in to see the secretary of state?' asked the functionary who issued them with their passes.

'Yes,' said DeLorean before Randall could say no. DeLorean gripped him by the elbow and added out the corner of his mouth. 'You don't think I'd go in without my best man, do you? Besides, it always pays to have someone with you in these circumstances. You would be amazed how often a collective amnesia strikes them otherwise. "Did we *really* say that?"'

A door opened at the end of the corridor that the functionary directed them into and Jennings appeared, restored to his pinstriped suit and tie knotted just-so.

'Jennings!' DeLorean said. It sounded a lot like delight. Jennings merely nodded. Behind him the secretary of state emerged, broad face, hair swept back.

'I believe you have already spoken,' said Jennings.

'A pleasure to meet you at last.'

Prior took the hand that DeLorean offered. 'I was about to say the same thing.'

'You know Edmund?'

Prior smiled blandly in Randall's direction. 'You are most welcome.'

They entered a room with tall windows at one end looking across a lawn to a rather fine-looking glasshouse and, at the room's very centre, a table on which sat a telephone twice as large as any Randall had ever seen and around which they took their seats and waited. Five minutes. Ten.

Prior made a show of consulting his watch. 'The cabinet meeting must have overrun.'

DeLorean held up both hands in a gesture of magnanimity. 'Who are we to curtail the exercise of democracy?'

Jennings pursed his lips and went to the door, opening it and almost immediately closing it again. 'I thought I heard the tea trolley,' he said, a second before a light began to flash orange below the telephone's dial and a voice – *that* voice – seemed to fill the entire room.

'Gentlemen, I do apologise for keeping you waiting. I trust I haven't missed anything.'

The gentlemen, one and all, jumped to, sitting up in their seats, squaring their shoulders in their suit jackets. (Randall could still not quite believe how quickly he had been admitted into this: *the prime minister of the United Kingdom was virtually in the same room.*)

DeLorean spoke before any of them. 'I was just telling Jim, Prime Minister, that we have an order coming in from the United Arab Emirates.'

It was the first that anyone seated around the table had heard it, but it was said with such conviction that Prior actually looked to Jennings as though to make sure he had not suffered an actual bout of amnesia.

'So' – Mrs Thatcher's voice did not waver – 'we can expect to see you start to pay back... *how* much is it exactly we have advanced you?'

Prior – trying to get back on the front foot, or at least return the discomfiture – leaned in towards the phone. 'Sixty-five million pounds, not counting the ten million compensation claim.' (Which was never paid in full, Randall wanted to remind him, but missed his moment.) 'About eleven thousand pounds for every car that has been built to date.'

He sat back, folding his arms. DeLorean carried on as though he had not spoken at all.

'The thing is, Prime Minister, we are on the point here of a major – and I mean *major* – breakthrough. The market is primed.'

'The market, I've heard, is stagnant,' Prior said and could not have sounded more the sulky English public schoolboy.

'Well if you don't mind me saying, you maybe need to get your hearing checked. We are on course to post a profit for the first five quarters of operation.' Randall had seen the projections just the day before: it was true. 'If your own Member – is that the word you use? – had not put about those rumours in the fall we would have floated the company weeks ago and taken things on to the next stage.' All this was directed at the suddenly not-so-very-Old Carthusian to his right. The next line, however, was delivered straight to the phone in a tone so intimate that Prior – and Jennings, and Randall come to that – might as well not have been in the room. 'You have my word, Prime Minister, every penny owing will have been repaid by this time next year.'

'Your word?' Thatcher, from *her* tone, was somewhat disarmed.

'Absolutely.' His hand as he said this was pressed, hard, against his heart. 'In the short term, though' – the hand that had been on his heart was now flat on the table – 'we are going to need one final cash injection.'

Prior's eyebrows rose, his jaw dropped. Next to him Jennings's face was a frozen mask of horror. Randall had angled himself towards DeLorean, poised to speak, but he was not about to be interrupted or deflected. It was him and the prime minister, to use the old telephone operator's phrase, person to person.

'*Another* one?'

'A final one.'

'And you were thinking of...?'

'What the flotation would have raised: forty-seven million pounds.'

Jennings's eyes closed, Prior's eyebrows practically disappeared into his high hairline. The phone on the table, despite its bulk, actually vibrated.

Randall, meanwhile, had pulled a notebook towards him and scribbled down what he had been trying a moment before to say. He tore off the page and pushed it in front of DeLorean who read what was written there verbatim and as though he had all along intended to say it.

'If you could show the same flexibility that you showed to Lear Fan here last December *thirty-second*.'

Up went Jennings's eyelids. Down came Prior's brows. The phone's vibrating (if Randall had not seen it with his own eyes he would not have believed it) stopped.

'I'll leave it with you then,' DeLorean said, and stood. 'Prime Minister... Secretary of State... Jennings.'

He and Randall were on the steps down to the car before he spoke again. 'Are you going to explain that one to me?'

Only partly was the answer. 'A friend of a friend who I fell into conversation with last week,' Randall said. It was, June assured him, a momentary premarital lapse, occasioned by the cassette tape inlay and the couple of drinks they had had when he called at her place to talk it over. She sat up at one point in bed (hers and her fiancé's, he supposed). 'I never told you Aaron's story,' she said. 'That last time he was back and went for the interview.'

'This friend's friend knows someone pretty senior in the engineering side of things,' Randall told DeLorean. 'According to him it was an open secret among all the managers. The deadline for the first test flight was the end of December, their funding was supposed to be dependent on it, then someone in the Northern Ireland Office came up with the helpful idea of adding a day on to the year, and hey presto, they got a plane up on the thirty-second, they got the money.'

DeLorean was shaking his head as they got into the car. The driver started the engine, which automatically started the cassette player. Drums, drums, clarinet. Randall had forgotten he had given him it. He leaned forward to tell the driver to shut it off after all. 'No,' DeLorean said. 'Leave it.' He listened appreciatively. 'Well, what do you know?'

Liz did have some sympathy for Robert. The last time she had gone to a works Christmas party she had performed oral sex in a stationery cupboard – on Robert, mind you, although the fact that knowing that *he* had submitted to a stationery-cupboard blowjob (to take the passive view of his role in the escapade) *she* had allowed him to go on his own to eighteen more dos since – all those silly wee clerk-typists tipsy on QC-wine punch – was evidently lost on him.

She could sense, throughout the week leading up to it, him struggling not to object. She would nearly rather he had got it out and over with. (She actually wondered for the first time whether she ought to have been more suspicious in the past of those clerk-typists, whether it was not just inconsistency he was battling but hypocrisy.) Instead it was left to her to take a bit of heat out of the situation. (She never pretended to be above a bit of hypocrisy of her own.)

'I doubt I'll stay that long... the place will be so noisy and packed, it'll be worse than the factory when it's going full pelt...' And so on.

Of course she was hoping to see Randall. Not with any stationery-cupboard thoughts in mind, God, no, but they had not left things in a good way. She had to be able to work with him long term without tension or without worrying that he felt she had led him on or let him down.

And there was a bit of her too that hoped maybe, down the line, they could sit somewhere every now and again and... no more than that, really. Just sit.

She bought a blouse from Marks and Spencer and tried it on at home for Robert's approval.

'Is it cut a bit too low at the front, do you think?' she asked.

'Maybe. A fraction. I don't know.'

'No' – she plucked at the neckline – 'definitely, it is. I'll have to return it.'

'But what will you wear?'

'I have that black one.'

'The black one?'

'I got last year. Remember?'

'Oh, yeah.'

So she took the new blouse back and wore the black one, as she had all along intended, not cut so low, but neater fitting in all the places that neater mattered.

'Look at you!' one of the boys said when she walked into the living room. She had been experimenting a bit with her hair, back-combing it to give it volume. A touch too much volume maybe. 'Siouxsie Sioux!'

Robert's brow furrowed. 'Who's Siouxsie Sioux?'

Both boys laughed.

'Who? You mean *what...*'

'She's a dog's dinner.'

'Thank you, and thank you.' Liz nodded to them each in turn. 'Lovely to be appreciated.'

Robert patted her shoulder. 'Never mind them. I think you look all right.'

He dropped her at the security gate in front of the hotel. 'Pick you up again here at ten?'

'Are you sure now? I could always call a taxi, there's bound to be somebody else going the same way.'

'You never know the taxis round here,' he said. 'It's no trouble anyway.'

'I kind of didn't think it would be,' she said under her breath as he drove away. Still: ten – she had more than three hours.

The place was, as she had predicted in her heat-reduction offensive, chock-a-block. The first of her section she found – a full quarter of an hour after arriving – was Amanda, braced in a corner of the bar, holding off all-comers with her elbows.

'Explain white to me,' she said beneath the general clamour.

'As in...?'

'Vodka and white.'

'Oh, you mean lemonade?'

'And a body wouldn't just think to say that?'

'No, because you might get brown.'

'And how would that be different?'

'Well, it would just be, I don't know, *brown*.'

Amanda screwed her face up. 'Right enough. But, here, while I'm getting, what you having yourself?'

'Are you sure? Pernod and...'

'White? Black?'

'Water.'

Amanda smiled. 'I like the hair, by the way. Do I know you well enough yet to tell you it takes years off you?'

'As of this minute, yes.'

They found Anto standing, nursing a pint, on the edge of a group of men reminiscing about their retraining trip to the States – or so Liz deduced from the index fingers of one of the men, held level with his chest and twirling this way and that, like tassels.

'Ladies!' one of them said at their approach and Amanda made a show of looking over her shoulder.

'No, you're all clear. Carry on.'

So of course they didn't.

'No book with you the night?' Liz asked Anto.

'I was afraid it would spoil the line of my jacket.'

His jacket could have taken a couple of dictionaries without noticeable effect. All the same, Liz decided that the very fact of it, like the lack of a book, constituted a Serious Effort. As for the tie, though...

Anto flipped up the broad blade between two fingers. She must have been staring.

'A bit of a horror show, isn't it?'

There was tan in there, there was cream and royal blue, there were two shades of green, either side of something verging on crimson, all apparently alarmed to see one another. She returned his grimace. 'Just a bit.'

A couple of minutes later TC arrived, looking, in his black bomber jacket and jeans, like he had made no effort at all.

'I'm dead sorry, I came here straight from the Tech,' he said before his smile got the better of him. 'And guess what? I got my Level Three. No way they're not going to make me a supervisor now.'

Amanda told him the first thing he had to do was supervise a round of drinks. Liz hugged him. Anto shook his hand. 'Fair play to you, you worked hard for it. There's not many your age would have the dedication.'

TC looked about him, a hundred and eighty degrees in this direction, a hundred and eighty in that. 'I hope I didn't miss the star turn.'

DeLorean had wanted to detour by Warren House, 'get a proper look at those goddamn faucets' – 'what an ass,' was all he could say afterwards – and make a couple calls, the shorter to Cristina and the kids, the longer, by several hundred per cent, to Chapman. From what Randall could not avoid hearing (DeLorean was clicking his fingers looking for something to write on) Chapman ought to have been in Dubai earlier in the month for an exhibition Grand Prix but failed to show in a fit of pique with the Formula 1 authorities who had banned his latest Lotus from two races earlier in the season. Randall had followed that part of the saga at any rate in the papers: technical violations, was the reason the authorities gave. 'What we used to call innovation,' Chapman was quoted as saying.

'I am as frustrated as the next misunderstood engineering genius, but that was an opportunity missed for us,' said DeLorean when he had put the phone down, his tongue as close to his cheek as was compatible with speech. (It was, wasn't it?) 'I had been talking up the Lotus link in my conversations with the sheikh. He's a big, big fan.'

Their car, with the DeLoreland tape still playing, finally made it to the front door of the hotel only eighty minutes behind schedule.

A row of faces on the other side of the glass rearranged themselves into smiles.

'Looks like they have laid on a welcoming committee,' the driver said.

There were a lot of not-at-alls and of-course-of-courses as DeLorean's hand did the rounds. The local society magazine wanted a few photos in the vestibule: the hotel manager and Mr DeLorean; the hotel manager and the hotel manager's wife and Mr DeLorean; the head of the local Chamber of Commerce, the hotel manager and Mr DeLorean; the head of the local Chamber of Commerce, her husband, the hotel manager, the hotel manager's wife... He left a trail of photos such as these wherever he went, a fact he had apparently alluded to in a conversation with Bill Haddad, when Bill – in his version of it, played out in the Grill Room of the Waldorf Astoria this time a year ago – had first raised concerns about some of his business dealings. '"Anyone wants to know where I've been and who I've been talking to any time in the last five years all he has to do is buy the papers, or find a computer that can read the papers for him."' It wasn't a bad impersonation, it had to be said, and not, to Randall's ears then, especially vindictive. 'As though computers have nothing better to do with their brains,' Bill said, himself again, and, yes, maybe Randall should have heard it, with a definite twist.

The hotel manager was extending an invitation to Mrs DeLorean too, next time she was in town. DeLorean by way of reply shook his hand all over again. Randall had *his* hand on the handle of the function room door when a voice called out. 'Mr DeLorean!'

He, and Randall, turned. A young woman in the hotel's livery was standing to one side of the reception desk, blushing at finding herself the object of everyone's attention. 'There's a phone call for you,' she said.

'There's a phone call for you, *sir*,' the manager said, not entirely under his breath.

'*Sir*,' the young woman said and the blush grew fiercer. 'He says it's important.'

DeLorean strode off after her to an office just back of the desk.

There was a bit of half-hearted chanting from the far side of the function room door, audible in the quieter passages of the music and in the silence that had descended on the vestibule. 'Why are we waiting, why-y are we waiting...'

Randall waited, trying to read the blank door that had closed behind DeLorean's back.

Which opened in the end so suddenly it made him jump.

The frown, the set jaw. Oh shit.

Then the most enormous and unaffected smile. He drew Randall aside and spoke into his ear.

'That was Prior. The prime minister has, for reasons that he says escape him, decided not to rule out the new loan. She wants to monitor sales ahead of a final decision in the new year... We'll have Roy wire the dealers, put a little Christmas push on.'

He angled his head back. 'December thirty-second,' he said, and laughed, then followed Randall through the function room door.

The function room – there was only one word for it – erupted.

Liz had never heard or seen anything like it. One of the bar staff must have found him a footstool or something, because from one moment to the next after he had made his way to the middle of the room DeLorean went from head and shoulders above everyone else there to head, shoulders and entire upper body, but no sooner had he achieved this elevation than his expression clouded and in the next moment he had taken a step back, down, to just head and shoulders higher.

'That's better,' he said and from the renewed cheering it was clear that everyone (except maybe the barman who had found the stool) agreed. He held up one finger. Kept it there long after the room had been brought to order. 'Remember this year. Remember where we were at the beginning of it.' Liz would never forget it: the crump of that first car as it hit the assembly shop wall. 'And now look at us. Look at all of you. Look what you have done. Ask yourselves, are there any workers anywhere in the world who could have achieved what you have achieved in the past twelve months in the circumstances you have had to contend with? Seven *thousand* cars? You know what? I don't think there are. And I'll tell you another thing, I don't think I could ever have done this anywhere in the world but here. I sometimes wish poor Preston Tucker could have had the good fortune I had.' ('Preston who?' Liz heard TC asking Anto, a second before she could get the question out herself. 'Tucker: do they teach you nothing at that Tech?') 'There'd be Belfast-built Torpedoes on the roads as well as DeLoreans. But it's not just Tucker, hundreds more over the years weren't able to defy the odds the way we have. You haven't just made cars this year, you've made history.'

Randall had told her DeLorean didn't really drink, but he drank then, deep, from the pint of Guinness that had materialised in his hand: to next year, and the year after that, and the year after that.

When the tumult finally subsided Liz pushed her way through to the bar to get a round in. A woman she had never seen before, a Lotus pin in the lapel of her – jumpsuit, did you call that? Flying suit? – was saying very loudly in an accent Liz could equally not put her finger on (England, west, possibly... or east), 'We're going to be millionaires!'

'I'm happy for you,' Liz said.

The woman smiled sloppily. 'No, no, no.' She was off her face. '*We're* going to be millionaires.' She made a lassoing gesture with her right hand, roping in the entire room. 'You, me... all of us.'

Liz's attention though had already wandered to another part of the bar, another hand – June, she thought the woman it belonged to was called – resting for an instant on a sleeve that she knew, almost without having to see his face, was Randall's. She knew too what his fleeting touch in return signified. There was history there, graphic. She told herself it was no more than was to be expected. No one, man or woman, could go that long without. She couldn't.

She blew out her cheeks and turned to the bar again. The barman was putting the last of her drinks on a tray. Liz took out her purse.

'You only have to give me for three,' the barman said. 'Your Pernod's paid for... The woman that was standing there.'

'The millionaire.'

The barman showed her a piece of paper. 'She gave me this.'

A cheque for fifty pence. 'Told me she'd run out of coins for a tip.'

'Here,' said Liz and handed him an extra pound. 'I'll buy it off you.'

* * *

She was outside by a minute to ten. Robert arrived at two minutes past, which gave her three minutes to top up on smoke-free air.

'I wasn't expecting you to be out so soon.' He sounded almost disappointed.

'Ach, you know the way those things get.'

He gave her hand a squeeze.

She thought they might just be able to survive this. She squeezed back.

Randall had been on his way to talk to her, entirely on impulse, when June stepped in front of him, telling him, fingertips resting lightly on his wrist, that he was not to worry, she had no more desire to draw attention to the two of them than he had. 'Let's pretend we are talking about productivity...'

He was tempted to reply in the same vein, a little light innuendo to tide them both over, then carry swiftly on to where he wanted to be, but he stopped himself, as it dawned on him fully: that story she had told him, sitting in bed, hugging her knees, might turn out to be worth tens of millions of dollars. He slipped his hand under her wrist, felt her pulse quickening.

'I don't think you can possibly know how much I owe you, how much this whole company owes you,' he said.

She withdrew her hand, a quick glance over both shoulders. It was so clearly not what she had been expecting to hear. 'Thank you,' she said, but whatever fire had been threatening to flare a minute before was, he could tell, well and truly doused. 'If I don't get talking to you before' – a weak waist-high wave as she stepped away from the bar – 'have a good Christmas.'

DeLorean had made his customary early exit a few minutes earlier, though with unaccustomed regret. (He had made pretty short work of the pint of Guinness Randall had handed him, and the pint that followed that.) He had a breakfast meeting in Dublin ahead of his flight home otherwise he would assuredly have stayed. He would take the *Sounds of DeLoreland* with him.

'I think you could probably teach me things by now,' he said.

Randall doubted it very much, but a compliment was like a favour, not to be refused.

'I am very glad you think so.'

17

Randall's own flight home, early the following week, had to divert to Pittsburgh: heavy snow in the New York metropolitan area. The first fat flakes were falling too in Pittsburgh as he walked to the terminal building. By the time he walked out the other side he could barely see two feet in front of him. There was a pause overnight then it started coming down in good and earnest.

And coming and coming and coming.

It was still snowing when he left again for Belfast eight days later, by which time perversely, given his problems on the way in, flying was pretty much the only guaranteed way of getting about. Out on the roads nothing much was moving. Out in the car lots even less was selling. And as for innovative gull-wing sports cars... Randall tried his best not to think about it and further spoil an already fraught Christmas. ('Mommy says there's no point you even trying to get across here,' Tamsin told him the one time he got to talk to her. 'She says we're better not leaving the house.')

It was actually something of a comfort to see, as the plane

made its descent through clouds on the final leg of his return journey, the habitual rain-murk enveloping Belfast.

The relief lasted all of ninety-six hours. Then DeLorean called. The mood change, Randall thought afterwards, was palpable before the first word was out.

'We are going to have to put the factory on short time,' he said.

'I don't understand.'

'Prior rang. Thatcher ruled against the loan.'

'But that was just to... I mean, I can appreciate there haven't been many sales this past while...'

'Let me see, in the last week of December? Twenty-five.'

'... but what about contingency... the *whole factory* on short time?'

'I hope after all this time you are not going to start telling me how to run my business, Edmund. I know my margins in ordinarily exceptional circumstances. These are extraordinarily exceptional.'

'That's a new distinction on me.'

'And don't be so asinine as to correct me on my English either. You know damn well what I mean. They are calling this the worst snowfall in a hundred years. You don't legislate for once-in-a-century events, you roll with them as best you can. Ford has shut down its plant altogether. The snow will melt and the sales will pick up and the factory will return to full production and in the meantime maybe Her Majesty's government will realise what's at stake here.'

Randall's head jerked round towards the window.

'I don't believe it,' he said.

'I'm sorry?'

'It's started snowing here too.'

'I'm glad you find it amusing.'

'Amusing? Of course I don't. I just...'

But the phone was already down at the other end of the line and Randall had not the energy or the desire at that moment to try to re-establish contact.

The one stroke of good fortune in that bleak week was an industrial dispute that hit the ferries between Belfast and the other British ports. Vital parts of future DMC-12s were stranded in containers on the Liverpool dockside.

That was the reason they went with when they made the announcement of the three-day week. They were thinking of the press, of course, but they were thinking of the workers too: no point lowering morale any further ('Are things really that bad that the money's run out after a couple of weeks' snow?'). If their luck held, by the time the ferry strike ended the thaw would already have set in, or like DeLorean said, Her Majesty's government would have realised exactly what was at stake.

'Eleven hundred redundancies,' Don said. It was the end of the second three-day week and he had just returned from yet another round of talks in London. (Randall had not been invited to a single one of them.) He still had on his overcoat and scarf when he convened a meeting of the management in the boardroom, or bunker as a few of those present had taken to referring to that windowless box. His face was ashen. 'Eleven hundred redundancies, with immediate effect.'

'How are we going to do that?' Randall asked. Not 'why' any more. Sales back home had appeared briefly to be rallying, despite the whiteout, before nosediving again.

'Lottery,' said Stylianides. 'Section by section. It's the only way. Imagine you are turning down the volume on your record player' – he demonstrated with forefinger and thumb – 'there is less coming out but the balance remains the same.' The man could probably have struck the cheery note in a terminal-illness prognosis. To be honest, he said, the computer could probably make the selection for them, and Randall was guiltily glad not to have to have a hand in it.

Liz was running late: hold-ups on all the main roads, the sort of start-of-the-week, main-road hold-ups that cities the world over were prone to, rather than any more sinister local difficulty. There were jams too on the way in the gates (one of the reasons why she preferred to get in early), though the horns being sounded now were simply the prelude to a wave, or a ribald comment through a side window wound down for that express purpose.

She was still thinking, a little diffusely, as she entered the assembly shop, about how people here could adapt to pretty much anything, when she started to clock individuals passing her, coming from the lockers, with letters in their hands.

'What's the betting this is us back to a full week?' one fella was saying as he worked his finger under the gummed flap, and Liz had barely time to wonder why in that case not everybody was carrying a letter before she turned the corner to her own locker.

'What the fuck?'

It was Amanda. An envelope lay torn on the floor at her feet. The letter, in her right fist, shook.

'They're fucking laying me off.' The fist tightened, the letter shook harder. 'They're fucking laying me off. I moved my whole fucking family here. I took my lasses out of school, away from all their friends. I risked my fucking life, everyone back home told me: "You're risking your fucking life, girl."'

She narrowed her eyes at Liz.

'It's because I'm English, in't it?'

But by then there were shouts, and curses, from all quarters.

'I don't think it's just you,' Liz said, and glancing over her shoulder saw TC holding an envelope in his hand. Poor fella looked as though he was about to throw up.

'Oh, TC,' she said, 'I'm sorry.'

TC blinked. His cheeks bulged and his lips twitched. God, he wasn't really going to be sick, was he? The words came out in a rush. 'It's not mine, Liz, it's yours.'

She had no idea who was leading it, but there was a movement – a swell – in the direction of the administration block (it was becoming traditional with them), those with and those without letters caught up in it alike. The managers (as was traditional with them) had got wind of their approach. They were waiting in a line, Randall one of the middle three with Don Lander and Myron Stylianides. He looked as bad as TC, near, but she thought in his case it was maybe fear. There was no Gardiner from wages, with his inexhaustible supply of pens, to call on this time. He had every right to be scared.

Without warning a hail of objects flew through the air from the front of the crowd. The managers to a man flinched or outright ducked before they realised that they were threatened by nothing more lethal than letters of dismissal, balled up.

There was a sound then, long, drawn-out – *yeeeee-ow* – composed of equal parts contempt and delight at their display of cowardice.

If they hadn't sensed it already her fellow workers knew for certain now who occupied the moral high ground.

'You told us this was different.' Liz recognised Anto's voice, somewhere to her left. 'We're no better off than if we'd been standing on the street corner waiting on the ganger to pick us.'

Don Lander tried several times to speak, but was shouted down. Randall though did manage eventually to make himself heard.

'Give Mr Lander a chance,' he said. 'He did everything he could the past few weeks to make sure this didn't happen. He will do everything he can in the *next* few to make sure these lay-offs are only temporary...'

He stopped. It was a moment before Liz realised the reason was that she had her hand up – *out* in fact, arm rigid, fingers splayed. 'Seriously, how are we expected to trust *anything* you say?'

A round of applause at this.

He held her eye. She held his longer.

'I am – all of us here are – part of this too, you know,' he said, to anyone it seemed but her.

Randall was half expecting someone to shout out and ask if they were all in this together, then which of the managers had got redundancy letters today. No sooner had he finished speaking, though, than the workers seemed to arrive at a collective and unspoken decision to turn their backs on him, on Lander, Stylianides, the lot of them, and walk the other way.

The television cameras were waiting at the gates, reporters jamming microphones under the noses of workers as they walked out, trying to get a comment. Liz dipped her head as she passed, remembering how she had watched John DeLorean those years ago on that knackered TV while serving up the dinner: 'two thousand jobs in eighteen months...'

What she was doing now, she knew, letting hair fall across her face like that, she was hiding from herself.

She caught a bus the whole way into town and for reasons that made no sense even to her killed the time until she normally finished work, the last hour of it in the Bodega on Callender Street, where she ordered, of all things, a schooner of sherry. Speciality of the house, the writing on the board above the bar said. It was special enough that she had another two before fighting with the security turnstile at the bottom of the street to reach the bus stop home. Fucking, fucking, useless thing.

She came into the house by the back door. Robert and the boys were in the living room, waiting on the Dinner Fairy. She must have swayed. Robert went to get up. She set the letter on the arm of his chair. 'Don't say a word, any of you,' she warned and went straight up the stairs to her room, got into bed, shoes and all still on her, and pulled the covers right up over her head.

Only then did she give in and cry.

The week after the redundancies the news crews were back at the factory gates reporting that the remaining workforce had been put on a one-day week.

Liz recognised the hunted look in the eyes of the workers as they passed the cameras. All those carefully calculated HP plans; all those mortgages taken out. Those holidays destined to remain dreams.

DeLorean had not spoken to Randall directly in close on a month. He had not set foot in Belfast since the Christmas party. Roy Nesseth was now working out of 280 Park Avenue, in the office right next door to DeLorean's own. It suggested to Randall a circling of the wagons. (Bill Haddad – if they did not feel embattled enough in there – had filed a suit for slander.) They were concentrating on preparing a portfolio to present to potential investors at the Greater New York

Auto Show in mid February, was the word coming out from behind both doors: the right-hand drive, a sedan – the DMC-24 (twice the car that the sports car was?) – and even a model to compete for part of the four-billion-dollar off-road-vehicle market were all talked up; but the Auto Show came and went and no more investment was forthcoming.

He could have made life a hell of a lot easier for himself, DeLorean was caught on camera saying, if he had chosen to site his car plant anywhere in the world but Belfast. For every pound the British Exchequer had put in he reckoned *he* must have put in a pint of blood. The British Exchequer queried both the Math and the Tact, or want of it.

Cristina went on TV and broke down in tears. It wasn't fair what people were saying about him. It wasn't fair at all.

A couple of days later he was back in London again, with Tom Kimmerly this time, for a meeting with Prior, who brought with him Sir Kenneth Cork, a former Lord Mayor of London, and more pertinently one half of Cork Gully whose meat and drink was companies that had shed half their workforce and left the rest more out of work than in.

Prior came out afterwards and told the press what they had already guessed, DeLorean Motor Cars Limited was from this moment on officially in receivership. 'Constructive receivership,' DeLorean, coming out behind him, was keen to stress, 'which means the receivers will work with us to find the finance we need to get through our present liquidity difficulty.' His take, communicated to Belfast by telex, was that this was preferable to the other option put before him, which was to form a whole new company, entirely under Cork Gully's directorship and taking control of distribution of the cars in the US. 'We bend a little way to keep this guy from breaking us altogether.'

Oh, and, the telex went on to say, he will be in Dunmurry by the end of the day, to take the measure of the factory and its assets.

Sir Kenneth Cork's nickname – the Great Liquidator – went ahead of him, as did his pedigree: father before him a liquidator, son beginning to make his way in the profession. So Randall was pleasantly surprised to see getting out of the chauffeur-driven car a grandfatherly-looking man a little dishevelled in dress, slack of neck, short of sight and almost entirely bereft of hair on top of his high-domed head.

He told Randall that when he got the call from Prior the day before he had been out on his boat: an Anderson 22, if that meant anything to Randall. Randall had to confess it didn't. Sir Kenneth smiled a little vaguely. 'I understood you were with the company when it had offices at Chris-Craft.' The vague smile was a blind: he had done his homework. 'Well, not to worry,' he said, which was good of him.

He counted in that initial inspection five hundred cars, in various states of completion, in the factory and its surrounding lots. 'That's ten million dollars right there,' he said then added wistfully, 'or would be if I only had charge of the American distribution.'

Bend a little to avoid being broken altogether. 'We missed

the Salvage and Repair Crib,' said Randall. 'They might have another one or two cars in there.'

And indeed they had, and gold-plated skins besides from the American Express promotion: enough for one more car, the guys there said. 'Another eighty-five thousand,' Sir Kenneth said, without hesitation.

For the remainder of that week and much of the week that followed not a single tool in the factory was lifted – not a teacup in the canteen – unless it was to have a price tag attached to it. They became literally counters of beans (Crosse & Blackwell, baked, a quarter of a pallet, or four hundred and twenty-five cans, in the kitchen stockroom.) Any or all of this could be sold at a moment's notice if Sir Kenneth so decreed.

About the only thing that could be said was that, for the time being at any rate, there were to be no more lay-offs, although with every one-day-week that passed a few more people quit, like the guy from the door sub-assembly section who told Randall in parting he preferred the certainty of knowing he would be tipping dustbins into the back of a lorry for the rest of his life, on half of what he had been getting here, to sitting waiting on the next piece of bad news. They were actually light a few workers in one or two sections. Eventually Stylianides had to call the supervisors together and ask them to make a pitch for replacements.

It had been six weeks. Liz sat at the dinette table surrounded by the debris of everyone else's breakfast – Shredded Wheat box, lying open, toast crumbs, a handle sticking out of the pineapple jam jar. She was eating a dry Ryvita (no butter in the house, only margarine, which she couldn't take), hating every sawdusty bite when Robert came in dressed for work. He looked, as he had had the sense or self-restraint not to look on the previous twenty-nine weekdays, ever so slightly pleased with himself. He set a newspaper clipping down to the left of the jam jar.

'What's that?'

'Read it and see.'

'Brides Head to Toe... That's a terrible name.'

'Keep reading.'

'"Brides Head to Toe seeks dedicated and discerning part-time sales consultant..." A job ad?'

'Tim at work gave it to me. His wife knows the woman that runs it.'

He had been talking to Tim at work about her? Who even was Tim at work?

'Here he is to me: "People might not always want stainless steel sports cars, but they will always want to get married... Am I right?"' I could swing for you, Tim at work. 'He's told me his wife will put a word in. It would get you out a couple of days, and it would be handy having a wee bit of money coming in again.'

He kissed the top of her head. 'Think about it anyway.'

She listened to the car door shut, the engine catch at the second attempt. She listened to the whine of the reverse gear, the lower register of first as the car reached the end of its arc out on to the street.

She listened to it – first to second, second to third – all the way down to the end and – second again – round the corner and away.

She could not have said how long she sat in the silence it left behind, an hour, hour and a half, longer, before she heard a car coming in the opposite direction, round the corner and up the street, slowing, picking up a little speed and volume, slowing again: looking at the numbers, she decided. It stopped, the engine still turning over; a door opened, but didn't shut. In the next instant the bell on the wall above the dinette door sounded.

She was nearly not going to bother her head. Who could possibly be surprised to get no answer at this time of the day? The bell sounded again, and again.

Ach, to heck with it.

She walked through the living room to the hall. From the outline in the frosted glass she thought it was a pal of one of the boys and was bracing herself for the usual excruciating exchange (oh for them to reach the age of gorm). Even when she had opened the door she was unable for a moment to free herself of the misconception. What did *he* want with the boys?

'TC!'

'You busy?'

'Run off my feet. You?'

'Funny you should ask.'

She tilted her head to the side, narrowing one eye. 'What are you at here, TC?'

'Didn't I tell you they would have to make me a supervisor?' he said and smiled. 'Your overalls clean?'

She couldn't find the notepad that lived, or was supposed to live, in the door below the drainer. She turned over the bridal shop ad on the table and wrote in the margin. 'Away back to work. Home at normal time.'

She had thought she understood it, sitting at home this last lot of weeks, but it was only walking into the assembly shop again now that she was hit by the full knowledge of how much of her was bound up in this factory. She felt in that moment as though she had returned from exile.

And like a returned exile all she could do for the first however many minutes was try to take it all in, looking, touching, adjusting the memory to the reality.

'I honest to God never thought I would see the inside of this place again.'

'Well take a good look,' said Anto, 'because after today it's going to be another week before you see it again.'

He was a union man, Anto, he would not have thanked her for saying it, but it would have been all the same to her, to be honest, if they had her told she was only going to be working a one-day month.

18

The snow was long gone. The sales had not recovered. Barely two hundred coast to coast for the month of March, which, compared to the figures for April, was a veritable bonanza. A deal with Bank of America fell through, a deal with Budget-Rent-A-Car – or Blow-the-Budget-Rent-A-Car as it would have had to be rebranded – fell through. At the end of May, with DeLorean having got no closer than he was at the turn of the year to raising the money needed to restart production, Cork's patience ran out. The gates of the factory were symbolically closed and three-quarters of the remaining employees were let go. To the couple of hundred who were kept on would fall the task of putting together – by hand if necessary – the various parts still about the factory, whose resale value in their unassembled state was virtually nil, and of keeping the larger tools maintained in the event that some rescue plan might, even now, be devised before the new final-final deadline of seven o'clock (it was persuasively precise) on the evening of 19 October.

They were kept company in the canteen by a couple of

hundred of their former workmates who had decided to (symbolically) climb over the closed gates and stage a sit-in.

Cork had informed the management in advance, of course, about the need for a second round of redundancies, and the symbolism of the gates. 'As of tomorrow DeLorean Motor Cars Limited is in a state of cryogenic suspension, a mere flick of a switch away from complete extinction. We cannot illustrate that graphically enough.'

Randall did not know when he had felt so low. His life the previous few weeks had been – to use a phrase he had picked up in the plant – completely up the left. He ate – when he remembered to eat – sitting at his desk. 'Chips' figured prominently, though half the time he could not have told you five minutes after he had finished what he had put in his mouth. That night, before the redundancies were announced, he made a supper for himself in Warren House of the only things he could find in the icebox: a jar of pickle, a pumpernickel loaf he had been astonished to discover in a store in Lisburn (how many weeks ago was that?) and a bottle of duty-free black-label vodka.

He addressed himself to them in unequal proportion.

Some time around ten he collapsed sideways on the sofa. He woke at three in the morning with – Oh, God – barely enough time to reach the kitchen sink before he threw up. He was sick then, off and on, for the next twenty-four hours. In between times he lay under the bedcovers and shivered. At some point he had a something-more-than-dream: he was in an elevator travelling up and up and up – the numbers above the door made no sense – and then suddenly he was out and he knew for certain this was the forty-third floor, knew it even though he all he could see was bare walls, bare floors, glass and empty sky beyond. He ran from room to room: nothing, nothing, nothing, was or ever had been...

His legs went from under him.

He was on the carpet in the sitting room of Warren House, the bed sheet he had tripped himself up with still tangled round his lower right leg. The vodka bottle was on its side under a low table next to his head. He straightened it up and was surprised to discover it was only a little less than two-thirds full. For the first time it occurred to him that whatever was ailing him did not emanate entirely from that source. Only then was he able to rise above his shame and phone a doctor whose first question – he was sorry to have to ask it – was had he been drinking – not *that* much and not for the best part of a day now – and whose second was had he been eating – a bit of stale bread, pickles . . .

The doctor came in person at first light, smelling heavily of pipe smoke, which was to say the least unhelpful. Randall could barely turn his face towards him. He nodded or shook his head weakly to a whole raft of new questions – about work, in the main, but home-life too, who, if anyone, was around to look after him – while the doctor conducted his examination, paying particular attention to the neck, the throat, the underarms and the abdomen.

He put away his stethoscope and took out his pipe, which he began idly to fill. 'The vomiting needless to say will have drained you and the drinking on an empty stomach was, as any teenager could tell you, asking for trouble.' (Randall was going to bring up the pickles and the bread then swallowed hard against the thought of bringing them up.) The doctor returned the pipe to his pocket unlit. 'But I am satisfied there is something else there. Your system, frankly, is in a bit of a mess. You need time away from work.'

Randall found the strength to laugh.

'I mean right away from everything connected to it. I would be happy to write you a line for a week, a fortnight, however long you think you need. You are no earthly use to anyone like this.'

He left time for his words to sink in.

'A week, then,' Randall said at last.

The doctor nodded: that was more like it. He put on a pair of half-moon glasses to write, head tilting back a little more the further he got down the page. 'Here' – tearing off the page – 'I made it for two just in case. If you decide to go back before then they will all think you are a hero.'

In the doorway he turned and looked about the room. 'I hope you don't mind me saying, it's a lovely house and everything, but if you had somewhere else you could be, other people around you, just till you're on your feet again...' His expression as he spoke gradually changed: this was as pointless, he had obviously concluded, as recommending a longer sick-line. He drew in breath. 'I'll see myself out.'

Randall fell asleep again almost at once, and almost at once was back on the empty forty-third floor, returning there at intervals throughout another fretful night. The following morning he felt well enough to make tea in a mug, which he drank, black of necessity, with three spoonfuls of sugar. By midday he was showered and dressed. Three hours later he was at the airport.

The first person he met as he came out of the elevator was Maur Dubin, fur-coated in defiance of the season, and immediately behind Maur a phalanx of uniformly young, uniformly six-foot-plus removal men, toting paintings, pieces of sculpture, sealed cardboard cartons. More cartons lay open on the secretaries' desks, on the floor all around them; the lobby walls were stripped bare.

It was as though he walked into the movie of his life the scene before the one he had been dreaming. He took a step back, but already the elevator was closing behind him.

'Hey, there!' Maur clicked his fingers, to summon the name, it seemed, as much as attract attention. 'Randall! Hold that door!'

No sooner had he called out than DeLorean's own voice roared from inside his office. '*Randall?* Is Edmund here?'

Randall presented himself in the doorway.

DeLorean was standing in the middle of the floor where his desk had used to be, phone in hand. Shirts were strewn about the carpet, some still in their packaging, others unwrapped, arms outstretched, blues and lilacs, plain and striped, white collars and toning. 'But this is crazy,' he said, taking the words out of Randall's mouth. He held the phone at arm's length, earpiece tilted towards Randall. Far, far, away a ring tone sounded. 'I was just this minute trying to call you in Belfast. They told me you were sick.'

'And they told me you weren't giving up yet.'

DeLorean drew back his head, puzzled, then looked about him. Now he got it. 'You mean this?' He laughed. 'Didn't you see the memo? We're not giving up, we're *moving down*, to the thirty-fifth floor.' The thirty-fifth floor – the 'basement' in the DeLorean company parlance – had up to now been home to several of the company's non-executive offices. 'Doing our bit to help the economy drive.'

'Excuse me.' An elderly man slipped into the room through the door behind Randall, suit jacket off to reveal, beneath his vest, a lilac-striped shirt to match one of those spread out on the floor. 'Anything?' he asked DeLorean, and Randall at the second time of asking placed the accent, a variant on Jennings's Scots.

DeLorean glanced apologetically at Randall. 'I wonder if you could give us a couple of minutes. Mr Simpson here has come all the way from Edinburgh, Scotland... not just for me, you understand, but this is his only afternoon in New York.'

Randall felt his brow furrow. At a time like this he was buying shirts? Imported tailor-made shirts?

Of course he was. No matter how parlous the situation he was still the public face of the company, a face, moreover, whose appearance on the cover of a magazine could generate millions of dollars of desperately needed publicity.

What was he to do, go about in a *hair* shirt?

'You don't have to explain anything,' Randall said.

DeLorean walked across the floor and embraced him, fists tightening between Randall's shoulder blades. 'It's good to see you,' he said and Randall could not deny that to be seen by him – to be so warmly welcomed – was good too.

'I'm not going to pretend that I thought it would ever come to this,' DeLorean told Randall when he returned next day, rested, back to his old self, as good as, 'and I am certainly not going to pretend that it is character-forming or any such crap, but we will take what benefit we can from the changes being forced upon us and we will come back stronger than before.'

Later that day, sitting in the new office (Randall thought he looked a little hunched as though the unaccustomed eight floors above him was an actual physical weight), DeLorean told him he had decided, some weeks ago, when it had become inevitable that operations here in Park Lane would have to shrink, to take the opportunity to clear up some of the other... *clutter* that had accumulated over the years. 'I believe I may have given the wrong impression about my father in the past, not just to you, to almost anyone I spoke to about him. I may have suggested that he was from Alsace-Lorraine.' (*I believe I may... I may...* Even decluttering had to be approached with circumspection.) 'He wasn't, he was from a place called Alba, in Romania, Transylvania, to be precise, which, you can imagine, was part of the problem when I was a kid.' He raised his hands, making claws of the fingers. 'Son of Dracula...' His lips settled again over the teeth he had momentarily bared. 'You know how other kids are. It was a problem for the old man too, or he got it into his head that it was. He had ambitions as an inventor, you see, making improvements to the tools they used then on the line – I saw them myself, carved out of wood – but he couldn't get anyone at GM to look at them: no pedigree. I think that's where Alsace-Lorraine came from.'

'Bugatti,' said Randall.

DeLorean nodded, smiled wryly. 'Not that they wanted to know even then, but once he'd made that journey in his head there was no going back. Or maybe I'm not even remembering it correctly, maybe' – circumspect again, testing the hypothesis – 'it was just something he talked about doing, inventing a new back-story, and then later I just ran with it: insecurity.' He stopped. 'Does that seem strange to you?'

'That you were insecure? After what you described? No.'

Another nod, another not-altogether smile. DeLorean opened a drawer and passed across the desk a sheet of heavy writing paper embossed with an eagle that Randall mistook at first for America's own until he noticed the cross held in the beak, the downward sweep of the wings. He looked at the address: Bucureşti.

'I made contact with their Industry and Economic and Financial Activity Commission, who passed me on to the Foreign Policy and International Economic Cooperation Commission, who sent me this.'

Randall read down, *do not anticipate a need for your product... our own excellent Dacia Brasovia... however, on the matter of buses...*

Randall looked up. 'Buses?'

DeLorean shrugged. 'I figured lower individual car ownership, greater need for public transport: we pilot them there then target the whole of the Eastern Bloc.' He had his hand out to take the letter back. 'You'll see it doesn't close the door entirely. I guess it does no harm that I am second-generation Romanian-American ...'

Yes, thought Randall, you are now, aren't you, and might in time be Alsatian again, or Austrian, if that was what it took to protect the brand, stop the void that Dan Stevens had talked of from opening and swallowing all of them, the factory at Dunmurry first.

Liz was on her back contemplating a rotor, the precision of it, as irrefutable in its composition as its own name – and the lustre... like a platinum disc, near, something valuable anyway, awarded then kept out of sight under the stairs. The things you never knew you never knew about. She unhooked the bungee rope holding the calliper clear of the rotor and began to assemble. She greased the guide pins and slid them into place, turning them just enough to hold them for now, then rubbed lubricant on to the faces of the brake pads. Copper. She tried to remember from her schooldays if there had been an actual Copper Age, tried to imagine the circumstances of its first being smelted – wasn't that what you called it? – I mean, for someone to look at a lump of this greeny-browny rock and think, I know, I'll heat it up and chuck in some... What was it you did chuck in? Nah, gone.

She slotted the pads into their allotted calliper cradles – the pad with the wear indicator to the inside – before returning to the pins, tightening each one in turn. Wheel on, hubcap on and that would be it, locked away under the stairs until the fifteen-thousand-mile service.

She worked her way out from underneath the car, using the heels of her hands and the balls of her feet to propel the dolly. There was not a living soul within thirty yards of her. Somebody far distant was whistling 'Tonight' from *West Side Story*, jauntily, with flute-band trills and flourishes.

She had completely lost track of time. Yet if she could have captured one moment and held it out of all the hours she had spent there since her miraculous return – the many hundreds of hours since she first walked through the door – this would be it.

Every bit as miraculous as the return was the fact that she, along with Anto and TC, had survived the end of May cull. They had no way of explaining it to themselves, had been, in truth, more embarrassed than elated the day the announcement was made and had stood at the locked gates with the thirteen hundred of their workmates who would not now be going back in, or who were not expected to be going back in until a portion of them took matters into their own hands and climbed over again to set up camp in the canteen.

The occupiers were cordial and philosophical when, the next morning, they came face to face with Liz and the others in their overalls. Every calamity had its survivors, after all, and it was simply wrongheaded to blame your fate on them. They even – those without work – shared the tea they brought in with them – for they were occupying the canteen, not looting it – with those who still had work to take a break from.

The 'two hundred', meanwhile, were doing what those endless tours around the factory before ever production began had been preparing them for, though it had sounded like just a bit of crack then, the nuclear outcome, in which the very few had to fill in for the great many, carrying out the tasks of the departed as well as their own, hanging doors as well as fitting seats, wiring dashboards and putting on wheels, and before the wheels the brakes.

She replaced the tools in the pouches of her roll then picked up the dolly and moved round to the other side of the car where she worked her way underneath, head and shoulders first, to start work on that rotor.

On his return from the States Randall had made straight for the canteen – past the banners that read *We Want Work* and *DeLorean Workers Demand Their Rights* – to talk to the men and women staging the occupation. It was not what you would call a warm reception.

Where had he been when they were getting their cards? Not a manager to be seen the whole day.

He couldn't speak for the any of the rest, he said, but for his own part – truthfully? – he had been at home with his head down the toilet bowl.

'Oh, good,' said a guy at the front (Randall recognised him from the dive bar in Wilmington), 'wishes sometimes do come true.'

'Well, you must have been wishing pretty damned fervently,' Randall said, 'because I never in my life felt anything to compare with it. If you were able to work the same trick wishing for new finance...' He told them, as truthfully as the head down the toilet bowl, how he saw things, which was hopeless... if it had been up to anyone other than John DeLorean to try to pull it round. There were no lengths he would not go to (in his mind's eye Randall saw that Romanian eagle): literally no lengths. And as he looked around their faces, saw the anger, the anxiety, lose their grip a little, he realised that DeLorean was the one person in all of this they still trusted, because in coming here in the first place he had trusted them.

He repeated this speech half an hour later in the assembly shop, only just managing to keep a rein on his confusion at seeing Liz, looking as though she had never been away, although he had checked the list after the confrontation back in February (the fury in her eyes that day...) and had seen her name plain as day among the laid-off. Some of the workers applauded when he had got to the end of his last line – 'Keep the faith, in the management here, in John Z. DeLorean, and together we will ensure there is life in this plant after October nineteenth.' Liz merely nodded, to herself as it might have been: all right, faith pledged.

DeLorean's calls in the weeks that followed were, more often than not, from international airports: Dubai, Singapore,

Frankfurt on a layover, Zurich, though not in the end Bucharest. There was always a deal just starting to take shape, taking the place of the last deal, which had broken down over some stupid bureaucratic detail or outrageous demand. ('The Romanians basically wanted me to kiss Ceausescu's ass.') He was in the truest sense of the word indefatigable. And as June turned to July, July to August, August to September, Randall thought he detected a note of anxiety creeping in that for all the tens of thousands of miles he was covering – the lengths he was going to – he was getting nowhere.

So when the call came from LA with news of another deal in the making, Randall was relieved as much by the buoyant note he struck as by the prospect of the financing package: buoyant enough to be taken in another, less abstemious person for booze-assisted. The words were coming out faster almost than Randall could take them in. There was a consortium, though – Randall got that: entirely American – he got that too, several times, their Americanness was a big, big part of the attraction – and ready to invest tens of millions of dollars 'within weeks'.

'But, Edmund, none of this yet to Prior or his people, not until I have all my ducks lined up.'

A voice somewhere else in the room said, 'Quack-quack', which was the first that Randall knew, in all the time they had been talking, DeLorean was not alone.

'I'm sorry, I didn't realise you had company.'

'Oh, that was just Jim being funny. You remember Jim Hoffman?'

Randall swallowed a yelp. 'Is he part of the consortium?'

'He sure is,' said DeLorean, 'and a damn fine job he is doing too, aren't you, Jim?'

'If you say so, Captain,' Hoffman said. Whatever about DeLorean, Hoffman had definitely been drinking, and not a little either. What time was it there? Three? No: *two* in the afternoon. Captain, he had called him. Captain.

Randall was unable to settle to anything at all for the next several hours. (*Captain*… No other way to say that but with a smirk.) In the end he did what he ought to have done the first night he had seen him in the lobby of the Sheraton Universal.

Hal Lewis who had sat once upon a time at the desk next to his at the Chicago *Daily News* was working now at another *Daily News*, over in LA, keeping real well, real well, thanks, he said when Randall rang him, enjoying the weather a lot more on the west coast, that was for sure… But what about Randall, had he stuck with DeLorean? Hard times there, Hal heard.

Yes, Randall had stuck with the company, and, yes, things had been kind of tough lately, but that wasn't what he was calling about.

'I need a favour,' he said.

'Shoot,' said Hal.

'I'm trying to find some information on a guy, James Hoffman – Jim. Has a business partner by the name of Morgan Hetrick.'

'What's he done to you?'

'He hasn't done anything. Just someone I met here in Ireland told me he was related and wondered if I had ever come across him, you know the way Irish people are, they think America is a village.'

'That's your official reason?'

'Yes.'

'It's not a very Irish name. Hoffman.'

'He's not a very close relation. Probably how come they lost touch.'

'I'll see what I can do... Not promising anything, you understand.'

'Of course,' Randall said.

Less than twenty-four hours later, Hal rang back.

'That person you met in Ireland will be pleased to know that long-lost cousin Jim has been doing very well for himself indeed: him *and* his partners. Business contacts far and wide, though mostly far, if we take far to mean up and down as opposed to wide's side to side.'

'And by up and down you mean...?'

'Mostly down: south of the border.'

'Mexico way.'

'And beyond, quite a bit beyond.'

'That's certainly interesting.'

'And all perfectly above board, I hasten to add.'

'Should I be detecting a hint of sarcasm?'

'No, that one is straight... Whatever insinuations anyone might try to make.'

'Thanks,' said Randall. 'I hear you better now.'

For two days after that he did little else but write and rewrite the script of the next conversation he needed to have. It rose up in his mind like a mountain that he had to surmount: it would be his triumph if he succeeded, but if he put a foot, or a word, wrong there would be no second chance, that would be him, gone.

So: a question mark next to that word, a line through that… Do not for a single moment allow the thought to form that you have gone behind his back.

He was still tussling with the big reveal ('My pal Hal rang looking for a quote about the October nineteenth deadline…'?) when DeLorean, mistiming his cue, phoned him.

'Edmund, I've got it, the answer to all our problems.'

'You have?'

'I'm just through telling Don, I wanted to let you know myself… a company in London, connected to Lloyd's, they're in for one hundred million – tax-haven money – the Brits know all about it, seems they don't mind havens as long as they are the ones benefiting. We pay them off straight away, we clear our debts and we still have money to upgrade the plant, invest in a *huge* new PR campaign: sedan, right-hand drive, twin-turbo…'

'If I wasn't actually speaking I would say I'm speechless.'

'I know. We have to put up twenty million of our own before it can go ahead, but I'm working on that as well.' There goes the ranch for sure now, Randall thought, the estate in Bedminster too, perhaps. 'I've been talking to some people out in Virginia, I think they will be good for the loan.'

Another loan. 'You *think* they will be?'

'Know. We've as good as shaken on it.'

Randall could have wished they had actually shaken, but at least the government was backing this plan, and at least Hoffman and his consortium had been jettisoned along with all the other fleetingly sure things. Of course DeLorean had to explore every offer that came along, and if that meant carrying on for a few hours like an old drinking buddy of some unsavoury character then so be it. Randall felt guilty for having doubted. He put his script in the garbage and put Hal's call right out of his head.

19

Cork showed up at the plant at the start of the week with Jeanne Farnan, one of those 'people out in Virginia', willing to make the twenty million dollar loan. She did shake Randall's hand, with a surprisingly strong grip. Everything about her, in fact, suggested a reassuring firmness of purpose. Even her hair seemed set.

She and Cork shut themselves away in an office for most of the morning. Peggy, who brought them in coffee and cookies from the canteen, reported that there were papers all over the desk and floor, barely enough clear space for her to set down the chocolate teacakes. When she went in later to lift the leavings, of which there were few, the papers had all been tidied away again and him and her, Peggy said, were sitting laughing and joking, which had to be a good sign, hadn't it?

Lovely teeth she had, said Peggy. All the women 'over there' had but, hadn't they? 'My husband used to say they're made out of different stuff from ours... Joking, like,' she added in case maybe Randall hadn't worked it out himself.

* * *

The American woman and Sir Kenneth Cork stopped in the assembly shop to talk to the workers, who emerged from inside and underneath cars – as though from inside and underneath shelters – at their approach. News of her good humour as she and Cork were winding up business in the office (and of her teeth, of course) had gone before her. What had not – Peggy, the bearer of those titbits not having been privy to any of the actual conversation – was her evident knowledge of the car itself, which she displayed now in a series of questions on everything from tolerance variations in the fibreglass to how the bonnet – hood to her – was bonded to the frame.

'Here, are there stripes across my back?' TC asked when they had moved on to the next interrogation. 'I feel like I've just been grilled.'

'What do you think?' asked Liz, ignoring him. 'Is she the real deal?'

'I don't know,' said Anto. 'Maybe.'

They had been following the various proposed rescue plans as best they could, a combination of what they read about and heard about in the news and what was carried their way in the constant swirl of rumour and speculation that seemed if anything to travel faster now that the factory was nine-tenths empty.

They were officially Not Getting Their Hopes Up over anything, but – human nature – it was hard to keep your thoughts from running away with themselves. 'What if... Just say... Imagine...'

The management in large part left them to their own devices. What was there to be gained after all in urging them on to finish the cars faster? Once these parts were used up, that was it. Better the deadline expire – if expire it must – before the factory.

She remembered from the early days of training, before there was even a shop here to tour, one of the videotapes that was shown in the old carpet factory: DeLorean sitting on the edge of a desk. She was that busy looking at the stuff surrounding him – a bronze bust with the back of its head to the camera, photo frames facing the wrong way too, a telescope in front of the window – that it took her a while to catch up with what he was talking about… duty to the customer. She was looking right into his face when he said there were no shortcuts to quality. (He had a slight tremor in his bottom lip between sentences. For all his fame he was nervous doing this.) Even at Pontiac where they were doing four thousand cars a day he had told his workers that: prepare each new car as though it were your own new car.

She didn't know that she had always managed to live up to that before, but she was doing it now, because each car she worked on was in a very real sense hers alone.

She and Robert were barely speaking. If it wasn't silence it was shouting. 'I don't understand you at all. I could have had a job all lined up for you. Surely to God you can see it, the place is never going to recover.'

'Oh, yes, Fount of all Knowledge?' She gave as good as

she got. 'And how come you're so sure about it when even the government isn't?'

'Because it's Belfast! It's what happens here!'

The boys shouted at the two of them – 'Would yous for God sake quit it?' – and nine nights out of ten stomped out of the house to see their gormless mates.

It was the end of the first week of October before Randall heard that the Virginia loan was only going to be worth half the amount the government was demanding as a condition of the other, bigger loan – the *bail out*. Whether it was Cork's doing, or Prior's, with Thatcher twitching his strings, or whether it was just Jeanne Farnan's inability – for all that firmness of purpose – to sell her colleagues a deal that involved everyone but DeLorean himself risking their money, the simple fact was that they had reached if not the end of the line then the final colon: DeLorean had less than a fortnight to come up with ten million dollars.

All of a sudden Randall's calls were stalling at Carole's desk. She was sorry, John was in a meeting, if he could try again in an hour… She was sorry (one hour to the second later), the meeting had ended five minutes early, John had just walked out the door, she couldn't say when he would be back. Couldn't say or wouldn't say. Couldn't or wouldn't say to Don either, from what Randall gathered.

After another five days of this he wired: *Must talk, prepared to come to you.* The reply arrived within the hour. *Suspect people working to undermine us. Beware of phones.*

Randall read this far and felt something slipping away. *Have important job for you there*, the telex went on. *Await instruction.*

Two days he waited. Late on the third another telex arrived, one word and a clutch of initials: *Chapman GPD.*

By lunchtime the following day he was in a car being driven up the A11 on its way from Heathrow Airport to Ketteringham Hall.

Colin Chapman had agreed, with a pretty poor grace, to take half an hour out from what was – he could not stress this too much – a very heavy schedule. He was only recently returned from an extended spell in the US built around the final race of the Formula 1 season, the Caesars Palace Grand Prix, from which he had watched both Lotuses retire with barely a third of the seventy-five laps gone. Between the early-season rows and the late-season engine problems it had been a wretched bloody year on the track. And even more bloody wretched, frankly, off it. The US market had completely collapsed (because if you thought trying to sell a $25,000 sports car there was hard you ought to try selling one that cost half as much again). American Express International had decided not to renew the loan that had been in place for the past seven years. The auditor's report had had to be delayed, and delayed again, and then, he had been obliged to inform Companies House just the day before, delayed a third time. So, in truth, in answer to the question from Randall that had prompted this litany, no, he was afraid he had not been paying much attention to the trials and tribulations of other motor manufacturers, even ones with whom his own company had in the recent past been intimately connected.

'Is still connected,' Randall said. They were in an upstairs library he remembered from the last time he was there. (He remembered too that there were no keys to open any of the bookcases.) Chapman had not even asked him would he like to take off his coat. 'And we're not just talking about a *bad year* for DMC, we're talking terminal decline.'

'I think John will pull through,' Chapman said complacently. A circle of coloured glass was set in the leaded pane behind his head, *De Tout Mon Coeur* running round the circumference in Gothic script. Randall had no idea what it meant.

'*He* thinks you could help make sure he did.'

Chapman locked his hands together, right thumb-pad tapping out an intricate Morse against the left. For once he seemed to be having to strain for superciliousness. 'Look, I already told John what I just told you. The bank has cut off all further credit. We barely have enough flesh on our bones to sustain *ourselves* through the lean times ahead...'

'I think what he had in mind was the GPD money.'

Chapman's thumb stopped tapping. In the next moment his right hand had uncoupled itself, snatched up the nearest heavy object – a wedge of uncut lapis lazuli doing service as a paperweight – and flung it across the room. It thudded against a wooden panel, well wide of its (Randall) mark, unless the violence of the gesture itself had been the sole aim.

His moustache was twitching but his finger was steady. 'I don't know who you think you are, or more to the point who you think he is. I was not the only one to benefit from GPD. Ask him where his share went. Ask him how he found the money to buy that snowcat outfit.'

Randall walked slowly across the room, doing the calculations in his head: the trips to Geneva and to Utah; he bent to pick the stone up off the floor.

'Don't touch that.' Chapman was on his feet, poised between defence and further attack. 'And don't dare ever come back here.'

Outside again, the hall and its five hundred years of history massed at his back, Randall was struck by a sense of his own powerlessness. He could nearly not be any farther removed from Park Avenue and all that was happening there than in this small corner of the eastern rump of England.

Oh, no... He stopped in his tracks.

He wouldn't have.

Would he?

He would. He did.

DeLorean knew exactly how things stood with Chapman. He never seriously expected to get any money out of him, still less that Randall would be the one to help him get it. He needed to be sure that he did not carry out his threat to come back to New York, was all.

Randall had the car stop at the first pub on the road back to London, gave the landlord twenty pounds for ten pounds' worth of silver from out of his cash register – 'You're cleaning me out here,' the landlord said, struggling to keep his frown in place – and tucked himself into the very corner of the yellowed hood over the pay phone to dial.

Carole, answering, on the far side of the pips, was guarded. 'You don't sound like yourself,' she said.

'I'm in a pub in the middle of the English countryside.' The pips went again. He pumped in another pound in ten pence pieces. 'I have to speak to John.'

'Mr DeLorean is not here.'

Mr DeLorean?

'But he's in New York?'

'I'm not at liberty to say that.'

'Carole...' More damn pips. More coins. 'It's *me*: Randall.'

'I know, and I'm sorry, but I Am Not At Liberty To Say.' He caught her drift finally. It was not him, it was not her, it *was* the phones.

'Hold on.' He shoved in as many coins as the box would take, the ridged rim of the final one visible just beneath the slot. 'Roy, then, can I speak to him?'

A silence. He thought for a moment he had lost the connection.

'Roy's in Wichita,' she said finally, quietly.

'Wichita? What's he thinking of, going to Wichita now?'

She cleared her throat. 'Court,' she said.

So it had finally come to pass. The dispute over the blank lease form and the nine thousand dollar discrepancy in an elderly couple's memory of what had been shaken on and Roy's had gone to trial.

Whatever else he may have misrepresented, Bill Haddad was not wrong in his assessment of Nesseth. He was a bully and a boor and with millions of dollars at stake, the very future of the company, he had allowed himself to be dragged into court over less than ten grand. Very big, Roy, very bad.

While Randall was thinking what to say next his money ran out.

The landlord was still waving as the car pulled out on to the road again. 'Come back any time!'

Arriving back at Heathrow, a sombre couple of hours later, it crossed his mind that he could trade up his return ticket for a flight to New York, to what end though, with nothing in his pockets but his hands?

He submitted himself instead – for the very last time? – to the invasive bag and body searches and police interrogation that Belfast people had been conditioned to accept were part and parcel of flying to that (only slightly offshore) region of the United Kingdom.

20

On the evening before it was all due to end, Liz was cutting
through the parking lot when she saw him a little way off to
her right, head tilted back against the wall blowing smoke
into the frosting air. She thought for a moment of putting her
own head down and hurrying on – he was so lost in thought
she doubted he would even have noticed – but it seemed
somehow churlish, the more so because of the word that had
made its merry way out of the canteen a short time before:
that he had ordered in fish suppers for all the occupiers and
half a dozen cases of Harp to wash them down.

She checked her stride.

'That was a nice thing you did,' she said. He turned –
*re*turned from wherever it was he had just been this October
night to the lot at the back of the DeLorean factory. 'The fish
and chips and the beer.'

He shuffled his feet. 'It was little enough,' he said.

She wasn't about to make more of it than it was. 'I know,
but all the same.' She shrugged. 'I just thought it was nice.'

They stood for an awkward moment looking at the cars

parked about the lot. She couldn't help herself, she sighed. 'It's all a bit heartbreaking, isn't it?'

'There's still time,' he said.

'Don't think bad of me, but I kind of wrote off the cavalry coming over the hill when I heard that your woman...'

'Farnan.'

'... her... when I heard she wasn't stumping up the cash. I mean, I really thought, the day she walked around the factory...' She threw up her hands. 'Ah, well.'

It seemed as though there was nothing else to say. Except...

'Do you know the only thing I regret?' she said. 'I never actually got to drive in one of them.'

He looked at her.

'Don't act so surprised,' she said. 'Not many of us did.'

'No, no, I wasn't... What are you doing now?'

'Going for my bus.'

He gestured to the cars. 'I'll drive you.'

'In one of these?' She laughed. 'You'll not drive me far: eight minutes' worth of petrol, remember, not a second more, not a second less.'

'So I'll drive it round to the service pump and fill it up.'

'You're mad,' she said then gave up arguing. 'Sure, go on ahead.'

He stepped away from the wall into the lot with her. 'You get to choose.'

'Hm.' She walked along, eyeing them up. 'So hard to decide.' She stopped before one, angled her head to the left and the right, shook it finally, 'No.' She turned abruptly and pointed at more or less random. 'This one.'

'A very good choice.' He raised her door before his own. She smiled. Of course she did.

For all the thousands of times she had clambered in and out of them, it was still a surprise on sitting down properly inside a finished car, buckling the seat belt, pulling the door closed behind her, how low the suspension was, and she was reminded, even before the engine started, of the dreams she sometimes had of flying – always close to the ground like this. Then the engine started – a sound of rocket boosters igniting (she was sure that was something that, given time, they would have had to work at) – and the car surged forward.

'Sorry,' he said, 'I haven't driven them very often myself.'

He stopped again, a little untidily, fifty yards further on. The service pump was padlocked, but he had the key for it in his pocket, as it seemed he had a key for everything.

She pressed herself back against the seat, turning her head to one side, into shadow, as they passed the security man – a wave from Randall was all it took – at the gate; passed a banner saying, *Don't Let Our Factory Die.*

'You'll have to direct me,' he said once they were out.

'No,' she said. It was partly the car – she didn't want to have to be getting out so soon after getting in – but there was more to it than that. 'You take me the way you think we should go.'

'You sure?'

She still had her head averted, looking out the window. 'Positive.'

The way he thought they should go was on to the M1 at Dunmurry headed south. The speed – or the concentration of it in her solar plexus – was like nothing she had ever experienced. In every car they overtook, heads turned. Kids put their hands to the windows and frankly gawped. Lisburn passed, Moira, Lurgan, greater or lesser densities of light. They came off finally at the exit for Portadown, went round a roundabout and pulled into a lay-by where they switched over, him in the passenger seat her in the driver's, and – oh! she didn't even want to say what that felt like – drove back on to the motorway again headed in the opposite direction. It was deep dark now, the evening rush hour long since over, few vehicles of any kind driving *into* the city, so that for minutes at a time it was as though they had the entire road system to themselves.

They barely spoke. Even the switchover had been agreed with little more than glances and shrugs. Driver then driven, driven then driver. Two parts of the same thing.

They left the motorway again where they had first joined it then took to the back roads, some of them barely wide enough for the car to pass along, until they had climbed above the housing line in the foothills of Black Mountain or Divis – Liz could never tell the two apart, though as had been explained to her a long time ago there was no real distinction, Divis being the best fist the English could make of *dubh*, the Irish for black.

She cut the engine, letting her head fall back against the headrest.

'That was just unbelievable,' she said.

He peered into the darkness, unrelieved by streetlights, shop signs, the glow even of a screen between badly pulled curtains. 'So is this where you live?'

'Don't be funny. I just needed a bit of time after that before I went back.'

For the moment there was no sound in the car but their breathing.

'Have you lost something?' he asked.

She had, she realised, been feeling around beneath her seat.

'What? No. It's just...' She folded her hands in her lap then thought what difference did it make, really? 'Do you know what it is? They all have messages scratched in them, under the seats sometimes, sometimes behind the dashboard.'

'You're kidding me?' He sounded, as she had hoped he would be, more amused than aghast. 'Don't you know that's a sacking offence?'

She held out her hand. 'Look at me, I'm shaking.'

'So did you...?'

'Once.'

'I don't suppose there's any point me asking...'

'No.' She put a finger on his lips. His lips. On an impulse she took hold of his face with both hands and pulling him to her kissed him long and hard. Drew back eventually. 'Would you mind taking me home now?'

Before he could reply she had pushed up the door, letting the air in, and had stepped out on to the mountain road.

'I am doing the right thing,' she was telling herself. 'I am doing the right thing.'

Randall dropped her, at her request, a couple of hundred yards (she said) from her house on a pleasant-enough-looking housing estate, marked out nevertheless – it was, apparently, inescapable – by flags and painted kerbstones. 'This is probably close enough,' she said. 'It's not as if you're driving a Ford Escort. I usually walk the last bit anyway from the bus stop there.'

The bus stop too had been painted, in three segments, as though to deter the wrong sort of bus from stopping.

She let herself out, but when she had the door halfway down again she stopped and ducked her head underneath.

'Do you really want to know what I wrote in that car? "I made this."'

'I don't think anybody could argue with that,' he said before her head slipped from view again and the door came down the rest of the way.

His last sight of her was illuminated in the sweep of his headlights as he turned the car about. She squinted against the glare, but kept on walking.

He drove back through the quiet suburban streets: gas stations, Chinese carry-out restaurants and bars the only businesses showing signs of life, these last, with their security fences, razor wire, and cameras, having the air of prisons rather than places of public resort.

He drove, without a second glance, past the entrance to the Conway Hotel, before turning right off the main road and a little later right again, and – another wave to security as he passed – through the factory gates. He crawled through the lot, up and down the aisles, until he found the empty bay and reversed the car into it. When he had walked a couple of dozen paces he turned and looked back and already he had trouble picking out the car he had taken. If it hadn't been for the extra miles on the clock and the ache still in his jaw, he could almost have convinced himself the past couple of hours had never happened.

A few of the small upper windows were open in the canteen, to let out the fug of all those bodies in too-close proximity and with it the mingled sound of their voices, like a score of radios playing simultaneously: soaps, comedy, sports chat, songs from the shows and the hit parade, old and new. Randall carried on past, leaving all the factory buildings behind him, until at last he came to the smaller gate opening on to the road up to Warren House. The walk from one end to the other, twice a day, six and a half minutes there, seven minutes back (going against the slope), was what he liked to refer to as his exercise regime.

Tonight he had just become dimly aware that there was no one on the warren when he stopped in his tracks. There *were* lit cigarettes, but not on the other side of the valley: right in front of him.

'Fucking run!' a voice – feet away only – called out.

It was not directed at Randall, but at the other shadows behind the cigarette tips, who at once took to their heels, to the accompaniment of tins jostling, heavily, within the confines of plastic bags. Instinctively Randall shot out a hand and was amazed – horrified almost – to find himself holding a fistful of denim jacket. Palms went up protectively in front of the face.

'Don't hit me! Don't hit me!'

The boy – despite the high pitch of the voice, it was a boy – was no more than fourteen. It occurred to Randall that if this boy and his friends were from the warren then he had been living here through one entire generation of underage drinkers.

'They all said you'd gone.' The boy was snivelling, and almost certainly drunk. 'They were saying we should go in and see if we could get the gold taps off before anyone else did. I never wanted to do it, swear.'

Randall loosened his grip and at once the boy wriggled free and ran off, laughing.

'You fucking dick!' he shouted and there was more laughter from the direction of the stream where his friends had stopped and regrouped.

'I am, though, aren't I?' Randall said under his breath. He stooped to retrieve the bag the boy had dropped, a quart bottle of cider inside, two-thirds empty, and carried it, a finger through one twisted handle, up the drive to the house.

Inside, he set the bag on the floor behind the double-locked door then switched on all the lights, upstairs and down, lest anyone should doubt he was home, and put a call through to the local police station to ask if they had a patrol in the area. 'That,' said the desk sergeant, 'is not the kind of information we give out over the phone, for reasons which I am sure you will understand.'

He had heard and read enough down his years here to understand perfectly.

'But say there was, if you could ask them to check the

perimeter of Warren House.' He looked through the blind. The red glows were restored to their traditional position across the valley. It was on the tip of his tongue to add that the cops might want to do an age check on the crowd drinking up there – Who would be the fucking dick then? – but the answer, he suspected, would still be him, and he let the thought, and the blind slat, drop.

He had already stripped to his shorts and T-shirt when he heard the engines on the road outside. At least two. The patrol that dared not leak its location. A moment later the intercom buzzed. It buzzed again, twice, before he reached it. The instant he flicked the switch the voice barked at him.

'Randall? Open the gates.'

It was Jennings. Randall had only just managed to get his second leg into his pants when the Scot was out of his car (had it even come to a halt?) and thumping on the front door.

'Coming!' Doing up his buttons; the thumping getting louder. Jesus. 'Coming!'

Jennings didn't even bother with his normal potted version of the niceties, but marched past him into the vestibule. 'Pack a bag,' he said (a scowl as he saw the cider bottle, sticking out of its sack). 'Quick.'

'Hold on,' said Randall. 'You can't throw me out of here, and anyway there's still...' He couldn't think where he had set his watch, '... *hours* yet.'

Jennings had walked straight up the stairs. Randall in his astonishment could do nothing for the moment but stare so that by the time he did set off in pursuit Jennings was already on the landing headed for the bedrooms. He was coming out of Randall's own room when Randall caught up, proclaiming violation of civil liberties, international protocols, threatening to phone the American Consul, the papers...

Jennings shoved a shirt into his arms. 'Get dressed.'

'Not until you tell me what is going on.'

Jennings drew a long envelope from his overcoat pocket and held it out towards him.

Randall took a step back. 'What's in it?'

'Bearer bonds.' He held the envelope out further. 'They aren't going to blow up in your face, unless you were to try cashing them yourself, which I don't recommend.'

'But where are they from?'

'People who would rather not see the factory close.'

'Prior? Thatcher?'

Jennings rolled his eyes. 'I am surprised you could even ask.'

'I thought you told me once you only served whoever was in power.'

'Until whoever is in power starts to act in a way that is entirely contrary to logic and justice. There is a difference between neutrality and rank stupidity.'

Randall was feeling suddenly light-headed. That they were standing here on his landing, him only half dressed, discussing matters of state and high finance.

'Your Mr DeLorean is very hard man to defend sometimes,' Jennings said, 'but I am far from alone in thinking that factory down there is its own best argument.'

Long afterwards it was the 'far from alone' that stuck in

Randall's mind, the threat beneath its surface reassurance. Jennings drew from his pocket a second envelope.

'You will find a ticket in there for the six-thirty New York flight from Shannon Airport.'

'But, that's...'

'One hundred and seventy-five miles, although you might as well add on another hundred for the state of the roads on the other side of the border... If you are lucky you will do it in six hours, although the flight, once you are on it, is at least direct.'

Still something in Randall resisted. 'Why like this? Why not just wire it?'

'Because wires inevitably have points of departure as well as arrival that can be traced.'

He looked Randall straight in the eye a moment longer then made to withdraw his hand. 'Or maybe you would rather I just ripped the tickets up.'

Randall reached out and grabbed them and the envelope with the bonds.

'I will put a call through to the police on both sides of the border.' The tail end of the sentence disappeared with Jennings into Randall's room. He returned with two ties, the least worst of which, a tweed-knit (*that* tweed-knit, bought a DeLorean-Motor-Company lifetime ago en route to Detroit), he handed to Randall. 'I'll pass on the registration number and ask them to speed you through the checkpoints.'

Randall was turning round, turning round, scouring the floor.

'Shoes, is it?' asked Jennings. 'You left them on the bathroom floor.'

He got his shirt on, his tweed-knit tie, his jacket, his shoes, finally. He found his watch, his passport and a carry-on into which he threw a couple of things at random. The second envelope, with the tickets, went in there, the first went, uncomfortably to begin with, into his breast pocket.

He had worked his way in the course of this down into the vestibule again. Jennings went ahead of him and opened the front door. He stood aside, holding the handle.

Randall was not quite sure what to. He went to hug Jennings, who stayed him with a raised hand.

'Don't,' he said. 'Just go.'

So Randall did.

At the last moment he detoured into the factory again, lights still on in the canteen from which quarter singing came, not raucous, or confused, a single voice, too far off for him to catch the burden. He wanted to go and tell them not to worry, but there wasn't time for that and for what he had come here to do.

Five minutes, that took. He would make it up between here and Shannon, between here and Portadown. Out the gates he went for the third time that night and that really was him away.

21

Liz heard the rumour as soon as she walked into the assembly shop in the morning that Randall done a runner during the night.

TC said he wasn't the least bit surprised.

Anto cupped a hand to his ear. 'Listen, you can hear the other rats leaving too.'

Liz said nothing at all, not even (an effort of will) to herself, but walked to her locker, where the first thing she saw was a ragged edge of paper protruding from the bottom of the door. She turned the lock and the page – torn from a notebook – floated to the ground, blank side up. She hesitated before crouching and turning it over. *This can all still work out*, it said. *Believe with me.* He had signed it. *E.R.*

Like the Queen, was all she could think. She stayed there a few moments, sitting back on her heels, the page a ball in her fist clasped to her forehead, then she pushed herself forward and up with her toes, locked the metal door and carried on out to the assembly shop again.

They went about their tasks in silence, each keeping to her, or his, own part of the factory floor, choosing not to meet one another's eyes. Liz didn't know about the others but she was torn the whole time between finishing the car (she had been working on the same one for the past eleven days) and putting her spanner through its windscreen.

She made it as far as lunchtime. 'I can't wait around like this,' she said, and started there and then taking off her overalls.

Anto and TC laid down their tools too.

'What'll you do now?' she asked them.

Anto shrugged. 'Go to the canteen, join the sit-in.'

'While there's life...' said TC.

'Yeah,' said Liz, while there's life.

She put her arms around them both.

Back at the house she picked up the first of the day's notes, left by Robert this morning on the dressing table. 'I am still waiting for a proper explanation.'

As to why she had not called last night to say she would be late, as to where she had been all that time.

He had driven up to the factory looking for her an hour before she finally arrived home and of course she was nowhere to be seen.

He came into the kitchen when he heard her at the back door, closing the living room door behind him, letting her trap herself in a lie about a tricky carburettor and no change for the payphone.

'Is it that fella Anto?' he asked.

'Oh, for God sake, Robert.'

'Don't you for God sake me. There's someone, there's something.'

She had allowed herself to be turned around by him, her back to the sink. His face was in the space where hers should have been, her own drawn back so far she thought her neck would snap. His eyes were wild, but it was fear she saw in them, not anger. When it got to the point there was no violence. He reminded her, heartbreakingly, of the boys, all mouth and trousers.

And he was half right. There was something, but though she had kissed another man not half an hour before there was no one. She wasn't even sure she could explain it to herself, not last night, not now.

One day, maybe.

She looked at the figures on the clock radio: 14:59. She slid the button from auto to on as all but the first digit changed and the pips sounded for three o'clock.

She heard the news out then reached under the bed for the suitcase.

It was now or never.

Randall didn't know what set him off – exhaustion, maybe – but all of a sudden, sitting on the lip of that enormous desk on the thirty-fifth floor, he began to shake with silent laughter.

He picked up the envelope with its pink-tinged edge and for a moment he thought he should put it back in his pocket, leave here and go find Tamsin – Pattie too, if that was what it took, and whoever Pattie was sharing her life with now – and just disappear together. How great could the reach of Jennings's associates be, after all? But even as he was asking the question he knew he could not risk his daughter's happiness or safety to find out and knew too that without her he was not disappearing anywhere. He searched in the little dish at the base of the bust of Abraham Lincoln for a thumbtack, turned with it in his hand, looking for a suitable spot.

Carole watched apprehensively from the door. 'I don't think you should do that,' she said, too late, as he made a sudden move across the floor to the photograph of DeLorean and his son in the surf and pushed the tack into it so that the envelope covered the *I recall* that followed *life's illusions*.

'I think thumbtacks in pictures might be the least of his worries now,' he said.

DeLorean was looking down on the clouds from his airplane window, trying to get a sum right in his head. He wrote the answer down on his drinks napkin, next to the other seven- and eight-figure calculations. He had run the numbers dozens – hundreds – of times before, as indeed he had been running them all his working life, but he needed to be absolutely sure. This deal had been months in the making and bar one moment of folly, compounded by noises – to be specific quacks – off, kept from even his closest confidants. (Cristina, much to his regret, was completely in the dark.) There had been other offers on the table at various stages, more or less plausible, more or less attractive, but this was the one he kept coming back to, or rather that had kept coming back to him (for its proposers were the ones who made the running, seeming at times to anticipate events), trustworthy almost in inverse proportion to those involved in it. Morgan Hetrick and Jim Hoffman were not men who you could have brought into a room with Sir Kenneth Cork. They made Roy, frankly, look like a kid stealing apples from his neighbour's yard.

Edmund thought he couldn't see it, but his eyes had been wide open from the start. These men did not have scruples or much in the way of morals. They did though have money to invest and he had a scheme – the trust agreement prospectuses were in his briefcase – to enable them to invest it: a brand new company, DeLorean Motor Cars *Inc.*, which would only come into existence – this was the genius of the thing – at the moment of their investing and which would straight away invest in DeLorean Motor Cars Ltd, or, for the time being at any rate, Cork Gully Receivers.

And, yes, he was aware that they wanted more from him, some reciprocal investment in their own business, but he had concocted a story that he was confident would keep them at arm's length on that. (What was business but telling – and selling – the best story?) He was in hock to the IRA in Belfast was what he had told them, he had zero room for manoeuvre, unless Hoffman and Hetrick wanted to get *them* involved too, which he was pretty sure – if they knew anything of that organisation's methods – they did not.

Still.

Earlier in the week he had written a letter to Tom Kimmerly, sealed inside another envelope, *Only to be opened in the event of my death*, in which he laid out, step by step, the path he had tried to tread in his dealings with these people, from his first casual conversations with Hoffman – in so far as anything Jim Hoffman ever said could be classed as casual – to the legal nicety that was DMC Inc. Emphasis on the legal. He hoped Tom would not mind this once, but he had, as much for Tom's own sake as his own, taken other advice: Hoffman and Hetrick would not be buying John DeLorean, they would be making a donation to the British government.

The trick was to make sure they did not work that out too soon.

The British government's deadline would already have passed by the time the plane touched down, but surely faced with the prospect of all those lay-offs becoming permanent job losses, that factory standing empty, a warning to anyone else tempted to try to set up business there, they would be bound, as soon as he got this deal over the line, to suspend the liquidation proceedings.

Hoffman himself was waiting outside the terminal at the wheel of a white Cadillac, alongside another of the consortium, Benedict, who ran the Eureka Savings and Loan in San Carlos, up beyond San Jose. Vicenza the final member, was joining them at the hotel.

Hoffman shrugged his shoulders inside his jacket, DeLorean assumed for comic effect. 'You ready to do this?'

DeLorean gave it his best drawl. 'Ready if you are.'

It was not much more than five minutes in the car down West Century Boulevard to the Sheraton Plaza. Mainly they talked about the car. He had always had a fondness for Caddies, he told them, though they weren't to whisper that to anyone at General Motors. (Said as though he actually imagined that was a possibility.) In the elevator they did not speak at all. The imminent outlay of double-digit millions he guessed was a sobering prospect for even the most risk-addicted.

Hoffman had forgotten to bring his room key, but explained in the act of knocking at the door of suite 501 that it was nothing to worry about, Vicenza ought to be there by now waiting for them, and, hey presto, there Vicenza was (it had crossed DeLorean's mind in the instant before the door opened that he could not have picked the man out in a line-up), smiling, shaking hands, come on in, come on in, good to see you, good to see you. They were conscious that they were all standing so they all sat on the two sofas at the centre of the room, but that was wrong too so instantly Hoffman and Hetrick stood. DeLorean stayed put, took off his jacket, signalling he was ready to get down to business. He was going to need ten or twelve million straight away (the 'twelve' appeared just like that: long habit, always push for a little more); ten or twelve ought to keep everything together for now.

Hoffman though started to talk about *four and a half* million, which was ludicrous, and tomorrow, not today, which was even more ludicrous, but no, no, he was saying as DeLorean tried to interject, *that* would just be the beginning.

It was kind of hard to follow because someone else had come into the room with a small suitcase and hoisted it on the table between the sofas. Maybe he had picked Hoffman up wrong, maybe he hadn't said tomorrow after all, maybe they had brought the four and a half million with them. Too small a case for actual banknotes: gold bars perhaps – the thud of it on the tabletop just now: there was weight in it that was for sure. Hoffman seemed excited, talking about generating three, four times more money, as the man (who *was* he?) undid the catches of the case and popped open the lid. DeLorean stared. His brain could not quite take in what it was his eyes were looking at: the plump packets of white powder, tight, tight-packed. He knew what they were involved in – knew it as far back as the party the night of the riot at the factory gates, when he had walked in and seen them with a bag on the table. One bag. And here were maybe forty, fifty.

The others were watching him, expecting him to say something. He kept nodding his head, nodding, nodding.

'It's *better* than gold,' was all he could get out.

They laughed. He had one of the packets in his hand. Suddenly there was champagne – he didn't know who had brought that. They were toasting – he was toasting – to a lot of success for everyone. Then the door opened again and *another* guy was coming in. He walked right up to DeLorean.

'Hi, John,' he said.

DeLorean riffled through his memory bank, all the meetings, the handshakes – how many hundreds, *thousands* of meetings and handshakes over the years? – but he couldn't place him. He said hi anyway. His head, tell you the truth, between the champagne and the contents of the suitcase and so many new people was beginning to whirl.

'Jerry West,' the guy said. He was holding something out for him to look at. (DeLorean by that stage would not have been surprised by anything...) A wallet, flipped open, photograph of Jerry pokerfaced one side of the hinge, gold shield the other. (Anything... except that.) 'I'm with the FBI. You are under arrest for narcotics smuggling violations.'

Still more men had entered behind West. They were helping DeLorean up off the sofa and on to his feet, and a long, long way up that felt, turning him about, pulling his hands behind his back, cuffing them.

The door was open all the while. He wondered that Hoffman and Hetrick didn't take the opportunity of everyone looking the other way to make a break for it. And then he saw Hoffman smiling, high-fiving a man with a shield on the hip of his white slacks, and only then did the penny drop, this whole thing – from start to finish – it had all been about him.

Or that was the way he told it in court, and that was the story that a jury of his peers went with in the end.

EPILOGUE

On 22 September 2004 a US federal trademark was filed for DeLorean Automobile Company by Ephesians 6:12, Inc in the category of Vehicles and Products for locomotion by land, air or water. The correspondent of Ephesians 6:12 (also trading as Ecclesiastes 9:10-11-12, Inc) was John Z. DeLorean of the Parsons Village Condominium Complex, Morristown, New Jersey, a twenty-minute drive from Trump National Golf Club, formerly Lamington Farm estate, Bedminster.

John Z. DeLorean died six months later on 19 March 2005 aged eighty, no automobiles, or other vehicles for locomotion by land, air or water, having been built in the interim, or indeed in the twenty-one years since his acquittal in August 1984, on grounds of probable entrapment, for conspiracy to import cocaine.

ACKNOWLEDGEMENT

This novel grew out of a play I wrote for Radio 4, broadcast in July 2011. My thanks to Gemma McMullan and especially to Clare Delargy, who first talked to me about the idea.